THE ULTIMATE TRUTH

Echoes of the Cosmos

RICHARD TAYLOR

ISBN 9798343193756

To my beloved wife Cheri of many years, whose unwavering support and patience carried me through. Your love has been my anchor and my strength.

And to my Lord and Savior, Jesus Christ, who was, is, and is to come—may all glory and honor be His. My thoughts and prayers are focused on the lost and those who are in need. Those who are in prison, homeless or just suffering from one thing or another. I care deeply for all and pray that our Lord will deliver us all from the throngs of the devil himself..

May the Lord of Hosts bless all who read these pages and pick up some of the "between the lines" innuendos to seek and understand a new beginning with our Lord and Savior Jesus.

To my wonderful granddaughter Rylee - just know that I am so very proud of you and for all you stand for! You are a true believer and a one of a kind young woman with awesome potential. You can do anything you set your mind to accomplish. Always trust in our Lord Jesus and you will always be fruitful! Know that I love you beyond measure! Poppie is very proud of his granddaughter!

To my son Nicholas, I am very proud of you as you have turned out to be a great husband to my beautiful daughter-in-law and an even better Father to my awesome granddaughter. I am extremely blessed to have had the experience to try to be a good Father/Dad and I know I failed you many times, but that doesn't change the fact that I love you beyond all measure.

To JS Estep, I am so glad God put us together with the seed planted from my brother Shannon to develop this story and for your talent as a great writer. Your input and writing has been an enormous blessing to getting this story off the ground. You are an inspiration to an aspiring "older" writer and a great mentor with your brilliant ideas and ways of telling a story with conviction and humility.

This has been a very fun time in my life even though it has been a short project in terms of time, it has been a great learning experience and just a blast to be part of such a great story to begin the series.

Richard Taylor

Table of Contents

Foreword

In the tapestry of human history, there are moments that define us, challenge us, and propel us into uncharted territories. This story, which you are about to embark upon, is a testament to one such moment – a cosmic invitation that shook the very foundations of our understanding of the universe and our place within it.

As you turn these pages, you will follow the journey of Dr. Jonathan Avery, a brilliant astrophysicist whose life's work becomes the nexus of humanity's greatest adventure. From the quiet observatories of Earth to the grand stages of global discourse, Jonathan's path intertwines with humanity's collective struggle to stay ahead of events that are beyond our wildest imaginations.

But this narrative transcends the boundaries of science fiction. It is, at its core, a deeply human story. Through Jonathan's experiences, we explore the intricate web of relationships, beliefs, and societal structures that define us. We confront the tension between faith and reason, tradition and progress, unity and individuality. We grapple with questions that have haunted philosophers, scientists, and dreamers for millennia: Are we alone in the universe? Are we ready to take our place among the stars? And at what cost?

I invite you to approach this narrative with an open mind and heart. The questions raised within these pages – about our readiness to join a cosmic community, about the nature of advancement and the price of progress – are not merely fictional constructs. They are reflections of the very real challenges and decisions that may well shape our species' future.

In a world often divided by borders, ideologies, and fear, this story asks us to consider a greater unity, a shared destiny among the stars. Yet it also challenges us to question the cost of such aspirations and the wisdom of our choices.

As you delve into this cosmic odyssey, I hope you will find not just entertainment, but also inspiration to ponder our place in the universe and our responsibilities as a species poised on the brink of a new era.

Welcome to a journey that spans from the smallest atoms to the grandest galaxies, from the depths of human doubt to the heights of cosmic wonder.
The invitation awaits. The choice is ours.

JS Estep
Author

Chapter One: A Celestial Notebook

The old telescope creaked as Jonathan Avery adjusted its position, his eyes fixed on the night sky above Augusta. At seventeen, he was tall for his age, with a mop of unruly dark hair that seemed to defy gravity.

"Come on, come on," he muttered, fiddling with the focus. The Perseid meteor shower was supposed to peak tonight, and he wasn't about to miss it.

Now in high school, Jonathan had to think about the important things, like that stack of college brochures on the shelf.

But on this night, for Jonathan, this humble old shed with a homemade retractable roof was more than just a shack—it was an observatory, a gateway to the universe, a portal through which he could explore the cosmos that had captivated him since childhood.

As Jonathan peered through the eyepiece, his worn notebook lay open beside him, its pages filled with meticulous sketches, notes, and hypotheses.

The first streak of light blazed across the sky, and Jonathan's breath caught in his throat. More followed, creating a stunning display as it entered Earth's atmosphere. He furiously scribbled notes, recording times, directions, and intensities. Jonathan was determined to document every detail.

As the shower reached its peak, Jonathan witnessed something extraordinary. A meteor, brighter than any he'd ever seen, streaked across the sky. The fireball left a glowing trail in the atmosphere in its wake.

"Incredible," Jonathan whispered, his pen hovering above the page. His heart raced with excitement. This was no ordinary meteor—it was a bolide, a rare and spectacular event that few were privileged to witness.

Jonathan's hand shook as he sketched the bolide's path and noted its characteristics on a free page.

"What secrets are you hiding?" he whispered to the stars, a smile playing on his lips. As the night wore on, the meteor shower gradually subsided, leaving behind a profound silence and a sky full of twinkling stars. Jonathan stood motionless, his eyes fixed on the spot where the bolide had disappeared. His mind whirled with questions, theories, and possibilities.

As the town of Augusta, Kentucky began to stir, unaware of the celestial spectacle that had unfolded above them, Jonathan clutched his notebook tighter, feeling the weight of its pages as he walked slowly down the hill towards home.

Exhausted but exhilarated, he pushed open the front door, the scent of freshly brewed coffee and bacon greeting him.

"There you are!" his mother called from the kitchen. "I was beginning to worry. Come on, breakfast is ready."

Jonathan tossed his notebook onto the dining room table with a satisfying thud. "Sorry, Mom. The meteor shower was incredible. You wouldn't believe what I saw!"

He slid into his usual seat at the table, immediately flipping open his notebook. His eyes danced over the hastily scribbled notes and diagrams, reliving the extraordinary moments of the night.

His mother set a plate of steaming eggs and bacon in front of him. "Eat up, sweetie. You can tell us all about it once you've had some food."

Jonathan had just taken his first bite when the door to the garage swung open. The familiar scent of motor oil enveloped the room.

"Morning, son," he said, his voice gruff but not unkind. "Another late night with the stars, I see."

Jonathan nodded, swallowing his mouthful of eggs. "Dad, it was amazing. There was this bolide—a rcally bright mctcor—and I think I might bc onc of thc few people who saw it!"

His father's brow furrowed as he poured himself a cup of coffee. "That's... nice, Jonathan. But don't you think it's time you started focusing on more practical matters? You'll be applying to colleges soon, and—"

"Robert," Jonathan's mother interjected, her tone warning.

But his father pressed on. "I'm just saying, Margaret. There's nothing wrong with having a hobby, but Jonathan needs to think about his future. A solid business degree could set him up for life."

Jonathan felt his excitement deflate, replaced by a familiar tension. He pushed his eggs around his plate, no longer hungry.

"Why can't you be like the other kids, Jon?" his father sighed, wiping the grease off his hands with a shop towel.

"Astronomy isn't just a hobby, Dad," he said quietly. "It's what I want to do with my life. There's so much we don't know about the universe, and I want to be part of discovering it."

His mother placed a gentle hand on his shoulder. "And you will be, honey. Your father just wants to make sure you have a stable future."

"There's nothing stable about staring at stars all night," his father muttered.

"That's enough, Robert," Margaret said firmly. "Jonathan has a gift. You've seen his grades, his dedication. If this is what he wants to pursue, we should support him."

A tense silence fell over the kitchen. Jonathan stared at his notebook, at the pages filled with his observations and dreams. He thought about the bolide, about the way the entire sky had lit up for that brief, magical moment. How could he possibly give that up?

His father sighed, "Look, son, I just want what's best for you. This astronomy thing... It's a tough field. I don't want to see you struggle."

Jonathan met his father's eyes, seeing the concern there. "I know, Dad. But this is what I'm meant to do. I can feel it. Last night... It was like the universe was speaking to me. I have to follow this path, wherever it leads."

Another moment of silence passed before his father nodded slowly. "Alright, Jonathan. If this is really what you want... we'll figure it out. But promise me you'll at least consider some backup options?"

"I promise, Dad," Jonathan said, relief washing over him.

"Eat up, sweetie." His mother said, with a knowing smile.

As his parents began to discuss the day ahead, Jonathan turned back to his notebook. His fingers traced the outline of the bolide's path, a smile tugging at his lips. The road ahead might be challenging, but he was ready to face it. After all, he had the entire universe on his side.

The school day passed in a blur of lectures and assignments. Jonathan found himself doodling constellations in the margins of his notes, his mind still up among the stars despite the mundane surroundings of

Augusta High School. In physics class, he perked up, eagerly participating in discussions about gravitational forces and the laws of motion. His enthusiasm earned him a few eye rolls from classmates, but he hardly noticed.

As the final bell rang, Jonathan's thoughts were on those brochures waiting for him at home. The excitement of the previous night's celestial display had momentarily pushed aside the looming decision about his future, but now it came rushing back with full force.

Arriving home, Jonathan dropped his backpack by the door and made his way to the living room. Opening his laptop, he pulled up the bookmarked pages for various universities, each one a potential stepping stone to his future. But as he scrolled through the program offerings, the familiar doubt crept in.

Astrophysics. The word both thrilled and terrified him. It was everything he'd ever dreamed of studying, a direct path to unraveling the mysteries of the cosmos. But then there was Business Administration, practical and safe, the path his father believed would secure his future.

Jonathan was so engrossed in his thoughts that he didn't hear his mother enter the room.

"How's the college search going, honey?" Margaret asked, setting a glass of iced tea next to the computer.

Jonathan startled slightly, then sighed. "I don't know, Mom. I'm looking at all these programs, and I just... I'm not sure what to do."

Margaret pulled up a chair next to her son, her eyes soft with understanding. "Talk to me. What are you thinking?"

"Well," Jonathan began, gesturing at the screen, "there's this amazing astrophysics program at Columbia. The research they're doing there is groundbreaking. But then..." He clicked to another tab. "There's the business school at Maysville Community right here in Kentucky. It's got great job placement rates, and it's what Dad wants."

His mother was quiet for a moment, studying Jonathan's face. "And what do you want, Jonathan?"

The question hung in the air, heavy with implications. Jonathan ran a hand through his hair, a habit he'd picked up when wrestling with difficult problems.

"I want to study the stars, Mom. I want to unlock the secrets of the universe. When I think about spending my life doing that, it feels right. But..." He trailed off, his eyes dropping to his hands.

"But you're worried about disappointing your father," Margaret finished gently.

Jonathan nodded, unable to meet his mother's gaze.

Margaret reached out, placing her hand over her son's. "Jonathan, look at me." He raised his eyes to meet hers. "Your father and I, we want you to be happy and successful. But happiness and success can mean different things to different people."

She glanced at the screen, a small smile playing on her lips. "I remember when you were five years old, and you insisted on having glow-in-the-dark stars on your ceiling. You would lie there for hours, just staring up at them, asking questions about the real stars beyond our atmosphere. That passion, that curiosity – it's always been a part of you."

And she was right. From the moment he drew his first breath, it seemed the universe had woven a celestial thread into him.

He felt a lump forming in his throat. "But what if... what if I can't make a career out of it? What if Dad's right, and I end up struggling?"

His mother squeezed his hand. "Life is full of uncertainties, sweetie. Your father will come around. He just needs time to see that your passion can lead to a fulfilling career."

She stood up, resting her hand on Jonathan's shoulder. "Apply to the programs that excite you, that challenge you. And who knows? Maybe you'll end up combining your love for astronomy with business someday. The universe works in mysterious ways."

As his mother left the room, Jonathan turned back to the computer screen. He took a deep breath and clicked on the Columbia application. The path ahead was still uncertain, but for the first time in weeks, he felt a sense of clarity.

The next three weeks were the longest of Jonathan's life. Each day, he rushed home from school, his heart pounding as he checked for that all-important email. The waiting was excruciating. He tried to distract himself with schoolwork and stargazing, but his thoughts always circle back to the astrophysics program that represented all his dreams.

His parents noticed his anxiety. His mother offered words of encouragement, while his father maintained a cautious silence, as if afraid to influence the outcome one way or another.

Then, on a Tuesday afternoon, it happened. Jonathan was absently scrolling through his inbox when he saw it: an email from Columbia Admissions. His breath caught in his throat. This was it. With trembling fingers, he clicked to open the message.

"Congratulations, Jonathan Avery. Your application to Columbia University has been accepted."

As he read through the email, the details began to sink in. Not only had he been accepted, but Columbia was offering him a full ride - tuition, room and board, even a stipend for living expenses.

"Mom! Dad!" he shouted, his voice cracking with emotion. "I got in! I got in!"

The sound of running footsteps filled the hall as his parents rushed to his room. His mother reached him first, enveloping him in a tight hug. "Oh, Jonathan! I'm so proud of you!"

His father appeared in the doorway, his expression a mix of surprise and pride. "You did it, son," he said softly, a smile finally breaking across his face.

As the reality of his acceptance sank in, his heart pounded with excitement and vindication. All those nights of stargazing, all the skeptical looks and well-meaning but misguided advice to "be practical"—none of it mattered now.

The summer passed in a blur of preparation and anticipation. Jonathan's acceptance to Columbia University's astrophysics program had set his world spinning on a new axis. Each day brought him closer to the realization of his dreams, and yet, as the departure date loomed, a bittersweet ache settled in his chest.

On the morning of his departure, Jonathan woke before dawn. He lay in bed for a moment, staring at the glow-in-the-dark stars on his ceiling—the same stars that had watched over him since childhood. Soon, he'd be looking at a different ceiling, in a city where the real stars were often obscured by light pollution and towering skyscrapers.

He dressed quickly and made his way downstairs. The house was quiet, but he could smell coffee brewing in the kitchen. His mother stood at the counter, packing something into a small pouch.

"Morning, sweetie," she said, her voice soft. "I made your favorite breakfast."

Jonathan sat at the table, where a plate of blueberry pancakes waited. As he ate, his father joined them, clutching his own mug of coffee.

"Big day, son," he said, his gruff voice tinged with an emotion Jonathan couldn't quite place. Was it pride? Worry? Perhaps a bit of both.

After breakfast, they began the task of loading the car. The old station wagon sat in the driveway, its back ready to swallow up this chapter of Jonathan's life.

As Jonathan made one last trip to his room, he paused at the garage door. He hesitated for a moment before pushing it open. The smell of motor oil and metal greeted him—familiar and now suddenly precious.

The garage had once been a place of wonder, where he and his father had spent countless hours building model rockets. Now, it held the remnants of those dreams: half-finished rockets, spare parts, and tools lay scattered about. These were the physical manifestations of a shared passion that had, over time, diverged into different paths.

Jonathan ran his hand along the workbench, memories flooding back. The countless launches, the failures and successes, the quiet conversations with his father as they worked side by side. He picked up a small rocket fin, turning it over in his hand before slipping it into his pocket. A piece of home to take with him.

Back outside, his parents were waiting by the car. His father was doing a final check of the tires, while his mother stood clutching a small, hand-stitched pouch.

"Almost ready?" his father asked, straightening up.

Jonathan nodded, not trusting himself to speak.

His mother stepped forward, her eyes glistening with unshed tears. "I made you something for the trip," she said, holding out the pouch. "Your favorite chocolate chip cookies. Just in case you get homesick."

Jonathan took the pouch, the familiar scent of home-baked cookies wafting up to him. "Thanks, Mom," he managed, his voice thick with emotion.

They stood there for a moment, the three of them, on the precipice of change. Then, without a word, his father pulled him into a tight hug. "I'm proud of you, son," he whispered, his voice rough. "You're going to do great things."

As they broke apart, Jonathan saw the tears his father was trying to hide. His mother was next, holding him as if she never wanted to let go. "Remember, you can always come home," she said. "But don't be afraid to spread your wings."

Finally, it was time. Jonathan climbed into the driver's seat, his father checked the tires one last time for the long drive to New York City. As he pulled out of the driveway, Jonathan looked back at his childhood home.

His parents stood in the doorway, waving, until he turned the corner and they disappeared from view.

The familiar streets of Augusta gave way to the highway. Jonathan looked at the pouch of cookies in the passenger seat, a tangible link to the life he was leaving behind. Ahead lay New York, Columbia University, and the unexplored territories of his future.

As the miles rolled by, Jonathan's mind drifted to the challenges that awaited him. The rigorous classes, the competitive atmosphere, and the bustling city were so different from his quiet hometown. But underneath the nervousness, a thrill of excitement pulsed through him. He was on his way to studying the stars, to unraveling the mysteries of the universe.

The car hummed along the highway, carrying Jonathan towards his destiny. Augusta and his childhood were falling away behind him, but the lessons learned there—the wonder instilled by his mother, the practical skills taught by his father, the unwavering passion for the cosmos—these would always be with him.

The lecture hall buzzed with excited chatter as students filed in, their faces a mix of anticipation and nervousness typical of the first day of classes. Jonathan Avery, now a freshman at Columbia University, slipped into a seat near the front, his trusty notebook already open on the desk before him. As the professor began to speak, introducing the fundamentals of astrophysics, Jonathan felt a thrill of excitement. This was it—the beginning of his journey to unravel the mysteries of the universe.

Dr. Larry Wilcox, a renowned astrophysicist known for his work on dark matter, commanded the room with his presence. His eyes sparkled with enthusiasm as he outlined the course syllabus, peppered with tantalizing hints of the cosmic wonders they would explore over the semester.

"In this class," Dr. Wilcox announced, his voice carrying to the back of the hall, "we will journey from the birth of stars to the death of galaxies. We will grapple with the fundamental forces that shape our universe and peer into the very fabric of space-time itself."

Jonathan's pen flew across the page, capturing every word. He glanced around, noticing the mix of excitement and intimidation on his classmates' faces. For him, each concept introduced was like a piece of a grand cosmic puzzle he'd been trying to solve since that night in Augusta when he'd witnessed the spectacular meteor shower.

As the lecture progressed, Dr. Wilcox posed a question to the class. "Can anyone tell me about the life cycle of a star?"

Jonathan's hand shot up almost of its own accord. When Dr. Wilcox nodded in his direction, he took a deep breath and began to speak, his voice steady despite the nervous flutter in his stomach.

"Stars begin their lives in nebulae, clouds of gas and dust," he started, his mind racing back to all the books he'd devoured over the years. "Gravity causes these clouds to collapse, forming protostars. If the protostar has enough mass, it will eventually reach a temperature that allows for nuclear fusion, marking the birth of a true star..."

As he continued, explaining the main sequence, red giant phase, and the various possible end states of stars, Jonathan noticed Dr. Wilcox watching him with growing interest. When he finished, he smiled approvingly.

"Excellent explanation, Mr...?"

"Jonathan Avery."

"Well, Mr. Avery, it seems you've come to us with a solid foundation. I look forward to seeing how you apply that knowledge in this course."

The rest of the lecture passed in a blur of equations and cosmic concepts. When class ended, Jonathan felt as if he'd been transported across the universe and back. As he packed up his things, he overheard snippets of conversation from his classmates.

"Did you hear that guy's answer? It was like he swallowed a textbook..."

"I can't believe how much we're expected to know already..."

Jonathan's cheeks flushed, suddenly self-conscious. He'd been so caught up in the excitement of finally being in a real astrophysics class that he hadn't considered how his enthusiasm might come across to others.

As he made his way out of the lecture hall, a voice called out to him. "Hey, star boy! Wait up!"

He turned to see a girl with curly red hair and a mischievous smile hurrying to catch up with him.

"That was some answer you gave in there," she said, falling into step beside him. "I'm Sherry, by the way."

"Jonathan," he replied, adjusting his backpack nervously. "And thanks, I guess. I hope I didn't come off as a know-it-all or anything."

Sherry laughed, a warm, genuine sound that immediately put Jonathan at ease. "Are you kidding? It was impressive! Besides, we're all here because we're passionate about this stuff, right? No need to dim your light."

As they walked across the campus quad, Sherry peppered Jonathan with questions about his background and what had drawn him to astrophysics. He found himself opening up, sharing stories about stargazing in Augusta and his dreams of unraveling the universe's mysteries.

"Sounds like you've got your work cut out for you," Sherry said with a grin. "But hey, that's why we're here, right? To take on the big questions."

Jonathan nodded, feeling a sense of camaraderie with this vibrant, curious girl. "What about you?" he asked. "What made you choose astrophysics?"

Sherry's eyes lit up. "Oh, I'm actually pre-law," Sherry replied with a smile. "But I've always been fascinated by science. The way it helps us understand the world around us, you know? I figured an intro to astrophysics would be an interesting elective."

Jonathan was impressed by her diverse interests. As they continued to chat, he found himself drawn to Sherry's intelligence and warmth. The conversation flowed easily, touching on topics from the ethics of space exploration to their favorite sci-fi movies.

Their conversation was interrupted by the chiming of the campus clock tower. "Oh shoot," Sherry exclaimed, checking her watch. "I've got another class in five minutes. But hey, a bunch of us from the department are getting together at the student union later. You should join us!"

Jonathan hesitated for a moment, his natural introversion warring with his desire to connect with fellow star enthusiasts.

"Yeah," he said finally, a smile spreading across his face. "Yeah, I'd like that."

As Sherry dashed off with a wave, Jonathan found himself standing in the middle of the quad, taking in the bustling activity around the imposing buildings of Columbia University.

He pulled out his phone, thumb hovering over his mom's number. He wanted to share everything with her – the exhilaration of his first class, the kindness of Dr. Wilcox, the unexpected friendship with Sherry. But he hesitated, realizing that this was just the first step to his future. Jonathan tucked his phone away and began walking towards his next class, his steps light and purposeful. As he navigated the pathways of Columbia, he felt as if he was charting a course through the cosmos itself, each step bringing him closer to the stars that had captivated him for so long.

It was as if the universe had aligned in ways he couldn't have predicted, opening up new possibilities he had never considered.

Sherry's ambitious drive to pursue law perfectly balanced Jonathan's passionate focus on the cosmos. She grounded him when he got lost in the stars, and he reminded her to look up and wonder at the vastness of the universe.

Their late nights in the library turned into coffee dates, and coffee dates blossomed into something more. Their relationship deepened through their college years, surviving the stress of finals, the joy of academic achievements, and the occasional argument over whose turn it was to do the dishes in their shared apartment. By the time graduation rolled around, they had become not just partners in life, but in their shared vision of the future.

On a crisp autumn evening, under a sky full of stars that had brought them together, Jonathan proposed. Sherry's eyes shimmered with happy tears as she said yes, the diamond on the ring catching the starlight just as he'd hoped it would.

The drive to Sherry's father's house the next morning was tense. They had to convince her father, a stubborn and traditional man, that this was the right move.

They sat in the living room, the silence heavy as they broke the news. Sherry's father, a man of few words, studied them both, his eyes betraying his concern.

"So much life for you to see, and you want to throw caution to the wind?"

Jonathan spoke calmly, explaining the situation—their need to be together, the protection that marriage could offer. He didn't mention his long hours at work, but the urgency in his voice spoke for itself.

After what felt like an eternity, Sherry's father sighed heavily. "Alright. But you better take care of my little girl, you hear me?"

The car was filled to the brim with her possessions—reminders of a life that was now forever changed. As they drove away, the courthouse grew smaller in the rear view mirror, a symbol of the past they were leaving behind.

The years that followed were a whirlwind of change and growth. Jonathan threw himself into his doctoral studies, his research on exotic stellar phenomena drawing attention in the academic community. Sherry excelled in law school, her sharp mind and dedication marking her as a rising star in her own right.

Their wedding was an intimate affair, held in the university's observatory. The vows were quick and to the point, the words echoing in the empty chamber. They exchanged rings, and kissed. The sweetness of their union, very different to the bitter reality that awaited them in the world outside.

After completing his Ph.D., Jonathan secured a position as an assistant professor at his Alma mater. His classes quickly became some of the most popular on campus, his passion for the subject infectious. Students would leave his lectures with their minds buzzing, eyes turned skyward, newly awakened to the wonders of the universe.

Sherry, now a successful corporate lawyer, watched with pride as Jonathan's reputation grew. His research papers on gravitational waves and dark matter detection methods were making waves in the scientific community. Invitations to speak at conferences started pouring in, and soon Jonathan found himself traveling the world, sharing his insights and discoveries.

One particularly memorable night, as they sat on the porch of their new home, Jonathan turned to Sherry, his eyes alight with excitement. "I've been invited to give a Cosmic Talk," he said, his voice a mix of disbelief and joy. "They want me to speak about the search for extraterrestrial intelligence."

Sherry squeezed his hand, her smile radiant. "I always knew you'd reach the stars, one way or another," she said softly.

The interview was a resounding success. Jonathan's eloquence and enthusiasm captivated the audience, his ideas sparking discussions that extended far beyond the confines of the auditorium. As he stepped off the stage to thunderous applause, he felt a sense of fulfillment. He was doing what he had always dreamed of—pushing the boundaries of human knowledge, inspiring others to look up and wonder.

Yet, even as accolades poured in and his career soared to new heights, Jonathan never forgot the night in Augusta that had set him on this path. The memory of those mysterious lights dancing in the sky still sent a shiver down his spine. He knew, deep in his bones, that there was still so much more to discover.

As he stood in his university office, surrounded by star charts, academic awards, and treasured photos of his life with Sherry, Jonathan's gaze drifted to the window. The first stars of the evening were just beginning to appear in the darkening sky. A familiar sense of wonder washed over him, mingled now with the determination of a seasoned scientist.

Chapter Two: Unspoken Debate

Standing at the front of the lecture hall, Dr. Jonathan Avery's eyes scanned the sea of faces before him. The years since his time as a wide-eyed freshman at Columbia had flown by, and now he found himself on the other side of the podium, a respected educator of astrophysics at his alma mater.

"Today," he began, his voice carrying easily across the room, "we'll be discussing the formation of galactic superclusters and their role in the large-scale structure of the universe."

He clicked to the first slide of his presentation, a vivid image of the Laniakea Supercluster filling the screen behind him.

As Jonathan delved into the complexities of cosmic web theory, he noticed a hand shoot up near the back of the hall. He paused, gesturing for the student to speak.

The young man, usually attentive and engaged, seemed distracted.

"I'm sorry, Dr. Avery, but have you seen the news? Israel has just been declared a sovereign state. The President just announced that the U.S. is recognizing Jerusalem as its capital."

A murmur rippled through the class. Jonathan blinked, momentarily thrown by the sudden shift from celestial matters to Earthly politics. He glanced at his watch, realizing that the announcement must have come during their class time.

"I... I wasn't aware," Jonathan said, his mind racing to process this information and its potential implications. "That's certainly a significant development in international relations."

Another student chimed in, her voice tinged with concern. "Dr. Avery, how do you think this will affect the ongoing conflicts in the Middle East?"

Jonathan took a deep breath, acutely aware of the diverse backgrounds of his students and the sensitivity of the topic. "As an astrophysicist, geopolitics isn't my area of expertise," he began carefully. "However, it's important to recognize that this decision will likely have far-reaching consequences, both in the region and globally."

He paused, looking out at the sea of expectant faces. Many of his students were clearly hungry for discussion on this breaking news. Jonathan made a quick decision.

"Tell you what," he said, closing his prcscntation. "Given the significance of this announcement, let's take a few minutes to discuss it. But I want us to approach this the way we approach our scientific studies – with objectivity, critical thinking, and respect for differing viewpoints."

For the next twenty minutes, Jonathan moderated a thoughtful discussion. Students from various backgrounds shared their perspectives, asking questions and expressing both hopes and concerns about the implications of this decision.

As the conversation wound down, Jonathan brought the focus back to their course material. "What we've just experienced," he said, "is a reminder that we don't study science in isolation. The universe we explore is huge and ancient, yet we observe it from a planet filled with complex, ever-changing human dynamics."

He clicked his presentation back on, returning to the image of the Laniakea Supercluster.

"As we continue our discussion on cosmic structures, I want you to keep this in mind: Just as these superclusters connect regions of space, events on Earth are interconnected in ways we're still trying to understand."

The rest of the lecture proceeded as planned, but there was a new energy in the room. Students drew parallels between the complex interactions of galactic structures and the intricate web of international relations.

As the class ended and students filed out, many lingered to continue the discussion. Jonathan overheard snippets of conversation, noting how seamlessly his students were connecting their astrophysics lesson with the day's breaking news.

Packing up his materials, Jonathan couldn't help but reflect on his own journey. From the boy who stared at glow-in-the-dark stars on his ceiling in Augusta to a doctor guiding students through both cosmic wonders and worldly events, he felt a profound sense of responsibility.

He thought of Sherry, now his wife and a successful corporate lawyer. She would undoubtedly have insights into the legal and diplomatic ramifications of the day's news. He made a mental note to discuss it with her over dinner.

As Jonathan left the lecture hall, he felt a renewed appreciation for his role as an educator. In a world where celestial horizons and Earthly matters often seemed disconnected, he had the privilege of helping young minds see the interconnectedness of it all.

The universe, in all its wonder, and the world, in all its complexity, were both classrooms. And Dr. Jonathan Avery was committed to being a lifelong student in both.

As Jonathan made his way across the Columbia campus, the buzz of conversations about the day's news followed him. Students huddled in groups, their animated discussions a mix of excitement, concern, and confusion. The weight of the world's events seemed to hang in the air of the serene autumn day.

Reaching his office, Jonathan closed the door behind him and sank into his chair. He took a moment to gather his thoughts, his eyes wandering to the framed photo on his desk – a snapshot of him and Sherry at an observatory in Chile, both grinning widely under a sky full of stars. The memory of that trip, a perfect blend of his professional passion and personal joy, brought a smile to his face.

Turning to his computer, Jonathan began to type out an email to his department head, Dr. Elaine Foster. He felt it necessary to inform her about the impromptu discussion in class, aware that such deviations from the curriculum could be a sensitive matter.

As he crafted the email, Jonathan reflected on the session. The engagement of his students, their eagerness to connect cosmic concepts with Earthly events, had been inspiring. It reinforced his belief in the importance of a holistic approach to education, one that didn't shy away from real-world implications.

Just as he was about to hit send, a knock on his door interrupted his thoughts.

"Come in," he called out.

The door opened to reveal Zara Patel, one of his graduate students. Her expression was a mix of excitement and nervousness.

"Dr. Avery, do you have a moment?" she asked, stepping into the office.

Jonathan gestured for her to take a seat. "Of course, Zara. What's on your mind?"

Zara sat down, her hands fidgeting slightly. "It's about the discussion in class today," she began. "I was wondering if... well, if we could incorporate more of these real-world connections into our research."

Jonathan leaned forward, intrigued. "Go on," he encouraged.

"I've been thinking about your work on dark matter distribution in galaxy clusters," Zara continued, her confidence growing. "What if we could use similar modeling techniques to analyze complex geopolitical situations? Like how different factors interact to influence global events?"

Jonathan's mind raced with the possibilities. It was an unconventional idea, to say the least, but not without merit. The principles of systems thinking that they applied to cosmic structures could potentially offer new insights into terrestrial affairs.

"That's quite an innovative proposal, Zara," he said, a note of pride in his voice. "It would require interdisciplinary collaboration, perhaps with the political science department. But it could lead to some fascinating results."

They spent the next hour brainstorming, sketching out potential research methodologies on Jonathan's whiteboard. As Zara left, her eyes shining with enthusiasm, Jonathan felt a renewed sense of purpose. This was why he had become an educator – to inspire and be inspired, to push the boundaries of knowledge and understanding.

The rest of the afternoon flew by in a flurry of emails, research proposals, and preparation for the next day's lectures. As evening approached, Jonathan packed up his things, his mind still buzzing with ideas.

On the drive home, he called Sherry, eager to share the day's events with her.

"Hey, star man," Sherry's warm voice came through the car speakers. "How was your day?"

Jonathan recounted the class discussion, Zara's proposal, and his thoughts on bridging the gap between astrophysics and global affairs. Sherry listened intently, offering her legal perspective on the potential implications of such research.

"It sounds exciting, Jonathan," she said. "But be careful. Venturing into politically charged territories can be tricky, especially in academia."

"I know," Jonathan sighed. "But I can't help feeling that we have a responsibility to use our knowledge and skills to address real-world issues, even if it means stepping out of our comfort zones."

“On a different note, could you grab dinner? I’m pretty busy with these briefs for tomorrow.”

As he approached the café, the air was thick with anticipation. The streets were quieter than usual, as if the city itself was holding its breath.

He pushed open the door, the bell chiming a welcome that seemed almost too cheerful.

He ordered their usual - a Greek salad for her and a chicken sandwich for him - and waited.

He was sitting at the bar watching a silenced sitcom on the TV that hung above the register when a waitress spoke.

“You know, it's like we're all just actors in some twisted reality show,” she said, while adjusting a chair, the plastic creaking as she shoved it up to a table.

“Everything's a lie. The news, the internet, even our conversations.” She said as she stuck a piece of bubble gum in her mouth.

“Don't be so dramatic,” he mumbled, trying to keep his voice quiet.

“Did you hear that we have had four shootings this week?” she said. “Four…”

But he wasn’t paying attention to her, his eyes were glued to the TV screen and the image of the American flag flying over a gleaming new building in Jerusalem. He was reading the words that scrolled the bottom.

‘The United States of America recognizes the truth of the ages. Jerusalem is the capital of Israel.’

“Yep,” she said, smacking on her gum. “The President made a declaration to stand with Israel today…”

He didn't respond, instead, he was staring at the corner of the screen at a map of the Middle East. And the red dot representing Israel that was surrounded by a large area of unfriendly blue.

"They moved the U.S. Embassy to Israel's Capital." she said, nonchalantly as she popped her bubble gum.

The newscaster appeared again, and the reports of war and disaster returned.

When his meal was ready, he reached for his wallet, pulled out a twenty dollar bill and handed it to the waitress.

"Where's the tip jar?" he asked, his eyes looking over the counter where it once was.

"It's been stolen twice so we keep it behind the counter now." the waitress replied.

Jonathan handed her a few dollars, "Thank you." he said. The chimes on the door echoed with his departure.

It can't be that bad... he thought.

But it was. And people were starting to feel it.

The doubt clung to the very fabric of society. Trust had become a commodity. Even the cafe, once a haven of community and comfort, now felt like a battleground of suspicion and silence.

......As he drove out of the parking lot, a car honked angrily, jolting him back to reality. And then he saw it—a car spinning out of control, slamming into another. The sound of crunching steel and shattering glass filled the air.

Jonathan slowed down in an attempt to see if anyone needed help. When the driver stepped out of the car, he was relieved.

He took one last look at the wreckage, feeling the inexplicable pull to stay, but he had promised Sherry to come straight home, and he was already late.

The sight of the carnage on the side of the road was only the beginning of the chaos that seemed to be spreading through the town.

As he pulled into their driveway, Sherry's words echoed in his mind. He knew she was right – this new direction would come with its own set of challenges. But as he looked up at the darkening sky, the first stars of evening just beginning to appear, Jonathan felt a sense of resolve.

The universe had always been his passion, his guiding light. But perhaps now was the time to turn some of that cosmic perspective back towards Earth, to use the lessons learned from the stars to illuminate the path forward on his home planet.

Stepping out of the car, Jonathan took a deep breath of the cool evening air. Tomorrow would bring new challenges, new opportunities to explore the connection between the cosmic and the Earthly. And he was ready to face them, armed with the wonder of the stars and the grounding force of his experiences here on Earth.

As he walked towards the house, where the warm light of home and the promise of an evening with Sherry awaited, Jonathan Avery felt like he was on the brink of a new discovery – not just about the universe, but about his place within it.

When he opened the door, Sherry looked up from the pile of legal briefs for the trial she was preparing for the following day. The justice system had been straining under the weight of a city in chaos.

Her eyes were weary but brightening at the sight of him.

"That was... intense," Jonathan said, taking off his coat. "I can't recall the last time I saw so many road rage drivers."

"I'm sorry, Jon," she said, not looking up from her papers. "I've got to finish going over these for tomorrow."

He sat down on the couch next to her, glancing over her shoulder at the complex legal jargon.

"We had a partners' meeting today. Now they're talking about taking on some of the looting cases from last week."

Jonathan nodded with understanding. He knew her career was just as demanding as his.

"We've been in constant motion since the crime wave hit. Every lawyer was pulling double shifts."

“Are you hungry?” he asked.

“I guess.”

They ate in silence, the only sounds being the scrape of forks on plates and the occasional rustle of paper as Sherry turned a page.

The TV in the background played a constant stream of news about Israel.

He glanced over at Sherry, her face etched in concentration as she worked.

“Remember when they actually had good news to talk about?” Jonathan asked.

Sherry looked up and gave him a weak smile, "I miss those days," she said. “And now it's like everyone's out to get someone."

The silence stretched out between them, filled with the weight of the world's problems, and their own unspoken fears.

“Did you know about them moving the US embassy in Israel?” Jonathan asked.

“I did… It's like everyone's out to get them.” Sherry said, never taking her eyes off her paper. “Maybe, just maybe, the world hasn't forgotten how to stand for something good.” Sherry said.

The words hung in the air, unanswered for a brief moment.

As they were finishing their meal, Sherry's expression grew more serious. "Jonathan," she began, setting down her fork, "I've been thinking about something all day, and I want to run it by you."

Jonathan nodded, encouraging her to continue.

"I want to go to Jerusalem," Sherry said, her eyes meeting him with determination.

Jonathan blinked, caught off guard by the sudden change in topic.

"Jerusalem? Now? But with everything that's happening..."

"That's exactly why I want to go," Sherry interrupted.

Jonathan frowned, concern etching lines across his forehead.

"Sherry, I understand the professional interest, but it could be dangerous. The situation there is volatile, unpredictable."

Sherry reached across the table, taking his hand in hers. "I know you're worried, and I appreciate that. But this is important to me, both professionally and personally."

"Personally?" Jonathan questioned, his brow furrowed.

Sherry nodded, a soft smile playing on her lips.

"Yes. You have your stars, Jonathan. For me, Jerusalem represents a different kind of celestial connection. It's a place of profound spiritual significance."

Jonathan shifted uncomfortably in his seat. While he respected Sherry's faith, as a scientist, he sometimes struggled to reconcile it with his own worldview.

"I understand that," he said carefully, "but faith won't stop bullets or bombs if conflict breaks out."

"Jonathan," Sherry said, her voice gentle but firm, "we have God on our side. I believe this is something I'm meant to do."

The phrase hung in the air between them, highlighting the fundamental difference in their perspectives. Jonathan, the astrophysicist who sought to understand the universe through equations and observable phenomena, and Sherry, the lawyer whose faith informed her worldview as much as her legal training.

"Sherry," Jonathan began, trying to find the right words, "I respect your faith, you know that. But as someone who deals with measurable, verifiable facts every day, I can't in good conscience encourage you to put yourself in harm's way based on... on a feeling."

Sherry withdrew her hand, a flicker of hurt crossing her face. "It's more than just a feeling, Jonathan. It's a calling. I thought you of all people would understand the pull of something greater than ourselves."

Jonathan sighed, running a hand through his hair. "The universe I study is big and often dangerous, but it's predictable in its own way. What's happening in

Jerusalem right now... it's chaotic, driven by human emotions and centuries-old conflicts. It's not the same."

They sat in silence for a moment, the weight of their disagreement between them. Finally, Sherry spoke, her voice quiet but resolute.

"I hear your concerns, Jonathan, and I love you for them. But this is something I need to do. I'm not asking for your permission, just your understanding."

Jonathan looked at his wife, seeing the determination in her eyes. He recognized that look – it was the same one he got when pursuing a particularly challenging research problem. He realized that, just as his pursuit of cosmic truths was integral to who he was, this was a fundamental part of Sherry's identity.

"I may not fully understand it," he said at last, "but I understand that it's important to you. Just... promise me you'll be careful. Take every precaution. The universe may be infinite, but my world wouldn't be the same without you in it."

Sherry's eyes softened, and she reached for his hand again. "I promise. And who knows? Maybe seeing Jerusalem will help you understand my perspective a bit better. There's a different kind of infinity there, Jonathan. One that can't be measured with telescopes, but can be felt in the soul."

As they began to clear the table, Jonathan's mind was awash with conflicting thoughts. He worried for Sherry's safety, yet he admired her conviction. He struggled to reconcile her faith-driven decision with his scientific worldview, yet he recognized the parallel between her spiritual calling and his cosmic one.

That night, as they lay in bed, Jonathan stared at the ceiling, his mind too full for sleep. He glanced at Sherry, peaceful in slumber beside him, and then turned his gaze to the window, where stars twinkled in the night sky.

In that moment, caught between the woman he loved and the cosmos he studied, Dr. Jonathan Avery realized that some of life's most profound mysteries weren't found in distant galaxies, but right here on Earth, in the complexities of human hearts and minds.

The months that followed were a blur of late nights and early mornings, of hypotheses and experiments, of triumphs and setbacks. But the thought of visiting Jerusalem never left their minds or conversations.

Sherry threw herself into her work, her legal mind sharper than ever. But the stress of her cases began to weigh on her. She found solace in the quiet moments they had together, planning their journey to the Holy Land.

Meanwhile, Jonathan spent most evenings after work going through the archives in the library learning everything he could about Jerusalem. Stuck within a book he stumbled upon a set of ancient star charts that seemed to indicate something extraordinary happening , there would be a total eclipse in the skies above the holy city.

The days grew longer, the nights shorter, as the excitement of the trip approached. Jonathan's desire to witness the eclipse grew more intense.

One night, as Jonathan and Sherry sat watching TV, a reporter was doing a segment on the eclipse that would cover Jerusalem the following September. He really wanted to see it but he knew that with Sherry's interest in the history and architecture of the ancient city, she would not want to see the eclipse through any type of telescope.

His mind drifted to his deep longing to see that in person, he tried to ignore it, focusing instead on the warmth of Sherry's hand in his. But the shiver grew stronger, turning his skin to gooseflesh.

Sherry noticed and turned to him. "You okay?" she asked.

He nodded, but his gaze remained fixed on the screen. "Just a bit... cold," he managed, his voice distant.

Her eyes searched his, looking for something, anything that might explain his sudden shift in demeanor.

"Jon, what is it?" she pressed, setting her fork down.

He took a deep breath, his heart racing. "I... really want to see that." he whispered, the words barely escaping his lips.

Sherry leaned in closer. "The eclipse?"

"Yeah…" he said, his eyes not leaving the TV, "It's just... I know you would want to see the city," Jonathan mused, his voice trailing off.

“We can try,” she said, touching the top of his hand.

They talked about the sights they would see, and the history they would walk through. But the shadow of the world's current troubles loomed, casting doubt on their plans.

That night, as they were getting ready for bed, Sherry looked at him with a serious expression. "What if we can't go?" she whispered, the words barely audible.

Jonathan pulled her into a tight embrace. "We will," he assured her. "We'll find a way."

The following day, they decided to visit a travel agent to get a better idea of the logistics involved in such a trip. The office was small and cluttered, the walls covered in posters of exotic locations and a large map of the world with pins scattered across it.

The travel agent, an elderly woman with a kind smile, listened to their story with a mix of curiosity and concern. She tapped away at her computer, her fingers moving with surprising speed.

"It's doable," she said finally, looking up at them over her glasses. "But it's not going to be cheap."

They nodded in unison, willing to pay almost any price to escape the turmoil that was closing in around them.

Having settled for spending two weeks in Jerusalem and coinciding the trip with the eclipse, their flight was booked.

As they left the office with a stack of brochures and a tentative itinerary, the sound of sirens pierced the air. They stepped out onto the sidewalk to see a line of police cars racing down the street, their lights flashing.

The tension grew thick with a sense of foreboding. They quickened their pace, eager to get home.

Once inside their apartment, they turned on the news again. The same images of chaos and destruction filled the screen, but now it had hit closer to home. The local university was on lockdown after a series of threats.

Jonathan's heart sank. His beloved stargazing spot, the One World Observatory in New York City, was now a crime scene. He couldn't shake the feeling that the world was unraveling around them.

The night before they were set to leave, Jonathan couldn't sleep. He lay beside Sherry, his mind racing with the implications of his findings.

"You okay?" she whispered, her hand tracing patterns on his chest.

“Yeah, I’m just... thinking about Jerusalem,” he said, his voice filled with wonder.

Sherry chuckled softly. We’re quite the team, aren’t we?”

“We are,” he said, his eyes shining in the moonlight.

The next morning, they packed their bags and said their goodbyes. As the aircraft ascended into the heavens, Jonathan turned to Sherry, her eyes sparkling with excitement, and squeezed her hand.

Chapter Three: A Prophet In The Streets

The flight to Jerusalem was long, but the anticipation kept them both wide awake. They landed in the early morning, the air thick with the history of the city.

The taxi wound its way through the narrow streets, navigating between ancient stone walls and sleek, modern buildings. Jonathan pressed his face against the window, taking in the surreal juxtaposition of old and new that defined modern Jerusalem.

"It's like stepping into a time machine," Sherry breathed, her eyes wide as she tried to absorb every detail.

Their driver, an older man named Moshe, chuckled. "First time in Jerusalem?" he asked, his accent thick but warm.

"Is it that obvious?" Jonathan replied with a sheepish grin.

Moshe's eyes crinkled in the rearview mirror. "Everyone has that same look of wonder. But don't worry, you'll get used to it. Just don't expect to understand it all – even those of us who've lived here our whole lives are still in awe of its beauty."

As they approached the Old City, the landscape shifted. Modern high-rises gave way to weathered limestone structures, their golden hue glowing in the late afternoon sun. The walls of the Old City loomed before them, a testament to thousands of years of history.

"We can't drive inside," Moshe explained, pulling up to a stop. "The streets are too narrow. But the Shalom Inn is just a short walk from here. I'll help with your bags."

Stepping out of the air-conditioned taxi was like stepping into another world. The air was thick with the scent of spices and incense, mingling with the unmistakable aroma of street food.

The sounds of multiple languages – Hebrew, Arabic, English, and others Jonathan couldn't identify – created a cacophony that was somehow both chaotic and harmonious.

As they walked towards Jaffa Gate, pulling their suitcases behind them, Jonathan and Sherry were struck by the seamless blend of ancient and modern. A group of Orthodox Jews in traditional black garb walked past a teenager in jeans and a t-shirt, his eyes glued to a sleek smartphone.

They passed through Jaffa Gate, the massive stone archway transporting them fully into the Old City.

"Look," Sherry said, pointing to a street vendor selling vibrant spices arranged in perfect pyramids.

Jonathan nodded, still trying to process the sensory overload. "It's incredible. It's like the whole history of civilization compressed into a few square miles."

Here, the modernity of the outer city fell away almost entirely. The streets narrowed into a labyrinth of cobblestone alleys, lined with shops selling everything from handmade jewelry to ancient artifacts.

"The inn should be down this way," Jonathan said, consulting the map on his phone.

Their destination was a small, unassuming inn located in the old city, the kind that blended into the ancient stone like a secret waiting to be uncovered.

The innkeeper was a weathered old woman with eyes that had seen too much, took them in without question, the gold coins they offered for lodging a small price to pay for the safety they sought.

“Welcome.” the owner said. Her name was Martha and she had an accent that was thick and comforting. “You’ve come a long way. Lunch will be served in one hour.”

They nodded, their hands clasped tightly together.

The room was on the inn's top floor, with a small private balcony overlooking the Old City. Ancient wooden beams crossed the ceiling, and a worn Persian carpet covered most of the stone floor. The furniture was a charming mix of antique pieces: a heavy wooden armoire, two overstuffed chairs that had seen better days but remained surprisingly comfortable, and a massive bed that the innkeeper proudly claimed was over a hundred years old. The scent of lavender and beeswax candles filled the air.

The afternoon sun warmed the stone walls of the inn as Jonathan and Sherry made their way down to the small dining room. The aroma of freshly baked bread and aromatic spices filled the air, making their stomachs rumble in anticipation.

“Are you ready to see Jerusalem?” Martha beamed with pride. "Let me bring you some lunch. You must be famished after your journey."

As Martha bustled off to the kitchen, Jonathan and Sherry took in the cozy atmosphere of the dining room. Colorful tapestries adorned the walls, and potted herbs on the windowsills filled the space with a fresh, green scent.

Martha soon returned, her arms laden with plates of steaming food. "Here we are," she said, setting down a spread that made their eyes widen. "Homemade hummus, fresh pita, shakshuka, and a variety of meze. Please, enjoy!"

As they savored the delicious meal, Martha pulled out a well-worn map and spread it on thcir table. "Now, I'm sure you're eager to explore our beautiful city. This map will help you find your way around."

Jonathan leaned in, studying the intricate network of streets and alleys. "This is great, Martha. Thank you."

"My pleasure," she replied. "Oh, and you're in luck. There's a wonderful marketplace just a short walk from here. It's where many locals do their shopping, and you'll find all sorts of interesting things there."

Sherry's eyes lit up. "That sounds perfect! What do you think, Jonathan? Should we check it out this afternoon?"

Jonathan nodded, still poring over the map. "Definitely. It looks like it's not far at all. We could easily spend a few hours there and still have time to see some other sights before dinner."

As they finished their meal, Martha provided them with more details about the marketplace. "You'll find everything there from fresh produce to handmade crafts. Be sure to try the street food – the falafel stand near the eastern entrance is particularly good."

"Any other recommendations?" Sherry asked, pulling out a small notebook to jot down ideas.

Martha thought for a moment. "Well, there's a lovely artifact shop about halfway through the market. The owner, Eli, is a bit of a local historian. If you're interested in the city's past, he always has fascinating stories to share."

Jonathan made a mental note of the location on the map. "Sounds interesting. We'll be sure to stop by."

As they prepared to set out, Martha handed them each a bottle of water. "Remember to stay hydrated. The city can get quite warm this time of year."

Thanking Martha for her hospitality and advice, Jonathan and Sherry stepped out into the Jerusalem afternoon. The streets were alive with a mix of locals going about their day and tourists excitedly exploring.

"Ready for an adventure?" Sherry asked, linking her arm through Jonathan's.

He smiled, folding the map and tucking it into his pocket. "Absolutely. Let's go see what treasures we can find in this marketplace."

As they walked around the market, the sounds of vendors calling out their wares grew stronger. The smell of spices and baking bread filled their noses when the sound cut through the low murmur of ten thousand voices. A child's wail, sharp and distinct. The sea of people parted around a young mother cradling a thrashing boy, his small body contorted in a seizure.

“Let me through." A voice rolled across the crowd like thunder.

The man moving towards the child looked to be a prophet. The people in the marketplace swayed their bodies from his path. They stopped to watch, Jonathan’s eyes focusing on his face.

The man was younger than most prophets – maybe forty years old, with sharp fcaturcs and eyes so dark they seemed to swallow light.

The prophet reached the seizing child. The boy's mother looked up at him with desperate hope, tears cutting tracks through the make up she had applied on her cheeks. She wore the simple brown dress, likely one hand stitched by her own mother.

"Please," she whispered. "Help him."

The man knelt beside them. The crowd pressed closer, holding their breath.

“I am the prophet,” he said, placing his hand on the boy's forehead.

He looked at the mother with a long pause before the words flowed from his mouth, "Be at peace, child."

The seizure stopped instantly.

The boy's eyes fluttered open, clear and aware. There was no post-seizure confusion, nor gradual recovery. One moment he was convulsing, the next he was sitting up and looking around with perfect lucidity.

“Impossible.” Jonathan mumbled.

He ran a quick diagnostic through his scientific knowledge, checking for anything that could explain what they'd just witnessed. But nothing registered on any spectrum.

The crowd erupted in gasps and cries of wonder. The mother clutched her son, sobbing thank-yous as the man smiled benevolently.

He raised his hands and the crowd fell silent. Sherry’s eyes never left the prophet as he spoke.

"My children," he said, his voice carrying to every corner without visible amplification. "You have witnessed but a small demonstration of the power that flows through me!”

The boy stood up, steady on his feet. He had no weakness, or disorientation. The mother bowed to the prophet, pressing her forehead to his feet. He raised her up with gentle hands.

"No!" he said, loud enough for everyone to hear. "We are all vessels of the same power. Some of us have simply learned to channel it more effectively."

Sherry watched in awe. “Can you believe we witnessed a miracle?”

Jonathan nodded, hesitantly in agreement.

The prophet turned to look at the crowd again. Jonathan's eyes met his across the crowd. For a moment, the prophets' serene expression slipped. Confusion flickered in his dark eyes, and he turned away.

He felt Sherry's hand on his shoulder.

"We should follow him," she said, her voice filled with excitement.

And despite his doubts, Jonathan found himself nodding again.

They kept their distance, watching the prophet move through the crowd touching people at random. Where his hands passed, chronic pains vanished. Old injuries healed. Even cosmetic blemishes faded away. Crowds swarmed the man, all eager to touch the hem of the prophet's garment.

Jonathan and Sherry paused at a stand selling fresh vegetables. The vendor, a man with a knowing smile, nodded.

“You follow the prophet? yes?” he said, as he began to tell stories about the miracles he has seen since the man’s arrival in the old city.

By the time the man stopped talking, the prophet and his inner circle had vanished into the complex.

They made their way down to the pathway, where the crowd was starting to disperse. The healed boy and his mother were already gone.

“I can’t believe we witnessed a miracle on the first day,” Sherry said as she took Joanthan’s hand in hers.

Jonathan couldn’t shake the feeling that he’d witnessed something else.

A hoax, he thought. But watching Sherry he wasn’t going to tell her anything different.

They stopped at a small café, the smell of coffee and shisha mingling with the scent of blooming jasmine.

They sat outside, watching the people go by, feeling both insignificant and incredibly alive amidst the timeless beauty of the city.

“It's like nothing I've ever seen before,” Sherry murmured, her eyes wide with wonder.

“Yeah,” Jonathan said, his voice low.

The sun was starting to set as they walked the cobblestone streets back to the inn.

Martha was waiting for them with a tray of mint tea and a knowing smile.

"You've had quite the day," she said as they sat at the small table in the courtyard.

They nodded, recounting the events of the day, their words spilling out like a dam had broken.

Martha listened, her eyes never leaving them as they spoke.

"He is a true prophet," she said, her voice filled with reverence. "You're blessed to have seen his power."

Sherry nodded eagerly, but Jonathan was silent, his eyes on the horizon where the sun was sinking below the ancient walls.

The air grew cooler as they finished their tea in contemplative silence, the weight of the day taking hold of them.

"Tomorrow, you should go to the Wall," she suggested. "It's beautiful."

They thanked her, and climbed the stairs to their room.

As they reached the door, Sherry turned to him with an astonished look.

"And we saw a prophet," she said, "a real prophet."

Jonathan nodded, feeling the weight of his doubt settle on him once again.

The next day, they ventured to the heart of the city, the Western Wall. The ancient stones seemed to hum with the prayers of those who had come before them, a testament to the unyielding spirit of humanity.

They approached the wall, the heat of the sun beating down on their heads. Sherry reached into her bag and pulled out a scrap of paper, her hand trembling slightly.

"What's that?" he asked.

"A prayer," she said, her voice soft. "For peace. For us, for everyone. I want to leave it here, in this sacred place."

He watched as she placed the paper into a crack in the wall, her eyes closed in silent supplication. The moment was so intimate, so powerful, that he felt like he was intruding just by being there.

When she turned to him, her eyes were wet with tears. He pulled her into a hug, holding her tightly as she sobbed.

"It's okay," he whispered. "We're okay."

As they walked away, Jonathan noticed a figure in the distance. It was the prophet, his arms folded over his chest, talking to a man in a soldier's uniform.

"Let's go see him," Sherry said, putting her hand in his.

But as they approached, the crowd grew denser, and the prophet disappeared into the sea of faces.

The rest of the day, they walked around taking in the layers of history. The streets told stories of crusaders and kings, of conquerors and the conquered. The sun painted shadows on ancient stones, casting a warm glow over the buildings that had stood for centuries.

As the sun began to set, painting the sky in shades of pink and gold, their steps were weary but their hearts were full. The evening call to prayer echoed through the streets, a haunting melody that told them it was time to go.

They climbed the stairs to their room, the worn wood creaking under their weight. Inside, the candles they had left lit flickered in the gentle breeze, casting dancing shadows on the walls.

They collapsed onto the bed, their bodies heavy with the weight of the day's experiences. Sherry curled into him, her head on his chest, as he wrapped his arms around her.

"I'm so happy you're here with me," she murmured, her voice muffled by his shirt.

"Me too," he said, kissing the top of her head. "We're going to find something amazing here. I can feel it."

The city outside grew quiet, the sounds of the day giving way to the night. Sherry closed her eyes as they lay there, holding each other tightly, listening to the rhythm of their hearts beating in unison with the pulse of the universe.

Unable to sleep Jonathan reached over and turned the TV on. The news blared to life.

"And in the news today…" the sound of a newscaster's voice filled the room. "As anticipated, the prophet has performed another miracle.

The screen switched to a prerecorded feed of the marketplace, showing the prophet's gleaming white robe with the child in his mother's arms behind it.

Jonathan muted the TV and watched the broadcast. He couldn't help but think his healing was too smooth, the timing was too perfect. He thought the prophet must have known where the sick child would be, and when the crowd would be heaviest.

Scrolling across the bottom were the words, 'The prophet plans to preach to the people of the city, calling for peace and unity.'

Jonathan felt his stomach tighten. Something was off about this whole situation.

The decision to follow the prophet had been Sherry's, driven by her belief and her hope. But now, as he stared at the image of the man on the TV screen, Jonathan couldn't shake the feeling that the prophet was something much more than meets the eye.

He lay there, wide-eyed in the darkness, listening to Sherry's gentle breathing, his mind racing with questions and suspicions.

The weight of the prophet grew heavier with every passing minute.

He knew he had to tell Sherry about his doubts, but how could he when her faith was so strong?

He decided to sleep on it, hoping that clarity would come with the morning light.

The next day over breakfast Jonathan sat listening to Sherry as she went over the plans for the day.

“The prophet is preaching in the park today,” Jonathan hesitantly told her.

Excitement lit up on her face as she grabbed his hand, "We have to go, we have to see him."

The anticipation was thick as they walked to the park, weaving through the throngs of people, everyone eager to hear the prophets' words of wisdom and hope.

The park was a sea of faces, some there in hopes of witnessing another miracle, others looking for salvation. A few there for the show and nothing more.

As the prophet's motorcade approached, the crowd grew silent. The doors of the black car opened, and out stepped the prophet, his gaze sweeping over the people.

He climbed the steps to the makeshift podium, his eyes scanned the crowds briefly before he began to speak. His words were soothing, a balm to the wounds of the world.

“My brothers and sisters," he began, his voice resonating through the speakers, clear and commanding.

Jonathan felt his skepticism rise as the prophet spoke, his words flowing like a river of sweet honey over the eager crowd.

But for Jonathan, the magic was missing. There was something about the way he talked, something that didn’t quite sit right.

He glanced at Sherry, her eyes shining with belief. He didn't want to shatter her hope, but he couldn't ignore the nagging doubt in his gut.

Back in the room, they sat on the edge of the bed. The silence stretched out between them as they watched the TV. It was playing the same images of the prophet in the park on a loop.

Martha, the inn owner, knocked gently on their door, a tray of steaming tea and warm bread balanced in her arms.

"Did you get to see the prophet in the park?" she asked, her curiosity piqued by their tired expressions.

They nodded, and Sherry's eyes lit up as she recounted the experience, her voice filled with a reverence that made Jonathan feel a twinge of jealousy.

"It was incredible," she said, her eyes shining. "His words... they just... it's like he was speaking directly to my soul."

Martha listened intently as she set the tray down on the small table by the window.

As the woman left the room, she looked to the couple sitting on the bed, "You two should come to the dining room to eat in the morning."

They exchanged a look, the excitement of the day's events still fresh in their minds.

The next morning as the sun was rising, they heard Martha's voice calling from the hallway. "Breakfast is ready."

They followed the scent of warm bread and spices downstairs, into the communal dining area.

They sat at a wooden table that had seen more than its share of meals, the surface scarred with the history of countless conversations.

Martha, a round-faced woman with a warm smile, laid out a feast for them. There were olives, cheeses, pita bread, and a steaming pot of shakshuka.

As they sat down, Martha joined them, her eyes sparkling with curiosity.

"So, what are your plans for today?" she asked, pouring them each a cup of strong, dark coffee.

She had insisted on them drinking Israeli coffee while sharing stories about her grandmother's secret pastry recipes.

Jonathan took a sip, the bitter taste ground him into reality.

"We're going to the Old City," he said, choosing his words carefully.

Martha nodded, seemingly satisfied with his answer.

The conversation flowed easily, thc warmth of Martha's personality putting them both at ease.

On this day they visited the Old City's Jewish Quarter, where the morning light streamed through narrow alleyways. At a small café, they discovered chocolate rugelach that made Sherry close her eyes in bliss.

They decided that it was also a good day to visit the Church of the Holy Sepulchre, drawn by the conversations of something profound occurring there. The church was a maze of chapels and altars, each one telling a story of faith and devotion. The air was thick with incense and candle smoke, the walls adorned with gold and marble, yet there was a humility to the space that seemed to resonate with their own search for meaning.

As they moved through the church, their eyes drawn to the light that streamed through the stained glass windows, casting a kaleidoscope of colors on the stone floor, they felt a strange pull towards the back of the building.

They followed the sensation, navigating through the throngs of worshippers and tourists until they reached a small, unassuming chapel. The room was empty, save for a solitary figure kneeling before the altar. They approached cautiously, not wanting to disturb the individual lost in prayer.

As they looked at the art that hung on the walls of the sacred place, Sherry stopped to look at a sculpture.

"What's this?" she whispered, pointing to the base of the sculpture. Jonathan leaned in, squinting in the dim light. Etched into the metal were the same symbols of the binary star system that he had spent years studying as a student at the university.

Looking up, his breath hitched. Suspended from the ceiling was an exact replica of a binary star system.

Jonathan stood in awe as he watched the sculpture twirling slowly. The sculpture was a masterpiece, the two stars orbiting each other in a silent ballet of gravity and light.

Chapter Four: Dancing with Disillusion

The afternoon sun beat down mercilessly on the ancient stones of Jerusalem's Old City as Jonathan and Sherry pushed through the growing crowd. The narrow streets were packed with people, all straining to catch a glimpse of the man they called the Prophet.

"There he is!" Sherry grabbed Jonathan's arm, pulling him toward the edge of the crowd. Her eyes sparkled with an intensity that made him uncomfortable. "Look at how he moves, Jon. There's something different about him."

Jonathan watched as the ethereal figure in a flowing white robe glided through the parting crowd. The Prophet's feet seemed to barely touch the ground, and the air around him shimmered on the summer pavement. But Jonathan picked up something else – microscopic distortions in the light around the man's body, patterns that shouldn't be there.

“Different isn't always divine," he muttered, but Sherry wasn't listening.

The Prophet stopped before a weeping man cradling a sick woman. The prophet’s hand, adorned with strange, silvery markings, reached out to touch the woman's forehead. A pulse of blue-white light emanated from his fingertips, and the woman's labored breathing suddenly eased. The crowd gasped in unison.

"Did you see that?" Sherry whispered, her voice trembling with awe. "He just healed that woman. No medicine, no hospital, nothing but his touch."

Jonathan's eyes zoomed in, analyzing the scene. There was something oddly familiar about those silver markings, something he thought he had seen before.

"Sherry, we need to talk about—"

"Blessed are the children of Earth," the Prophet's voice rang out, somehow both gentle and commanding. "For they shall inherit the stars." His eyes swept across the crowd, and for a brief moment, they locked with Jonathan's.

"He's the one," Sherry breathed. "He has to be." She turned to Jonathan, her face flushed with excitement.

"Blessed are the skeptics," the Prophet said, his voice carrying clearly to Jonathan despite the distance between them.

Sherry tugged at Jonathan's sleeve. "Please, Jon. Just open your mind to the possibility. What if he really is the chosen one?"

Jonathan placed his hand over hers, feeling the trembling excitement in her fingers. How could he explain what his augmented senses were telling him? How could he make her understand that the Prophet's miracles just were not adding up?

"Sometimes," he said carefully, "the most dangerous lies are the ones we desperately want to believe."

Sherry's eyes were fixed on the Prophet, tears streaming down her face.

The sun began to set over Jerusalem's ancient walls, casting long shadows that seemed to reach for them like grasping fingers. In the gathering darkness, the Prophet's form began to glow with an inner light that made the crowd gasp in wonder. But to Jonathan, it looked less like divine radiance and more like a carefully crafted performance.

He squeezed Sherry's hand tighter, knowing that the hardest part wouldn't be exposing the truth – it would be getting her to accept it.

Jonathan couldn't sleep that night. Through the window of their rented room, the Dome of the Rock glowed against the night sky, its golden surface reflecting the strange auroras that had become increasingly common as the eclipse date approached. Beside him, Sherry tossed fitfully in her sleep, mumbling fragments of the Prophet's sermon.

His tablet displayed the latest atmospheric readings he'd been gathering. As one of Columbia's leading astrophysicists, he'd planned this trip to Jerusalem around the eclipse. He wanted an opportunity to study its unusual characteristics – its extended duration and the unprecedented corona patterns his models had predicted. But now his instruments were picking up something else entirely: highly organized quantum fluctuations and artificial gravitational lensing that had nothing to do with natural celestial mechanics.

He glanced at Sherry, remembering how she'd spent hours after the sermon writing down every word the Prophet had spoken, especially his predictions about the eclipse being a divine sign.

"You're analyzing data again," Sherry murmured, her eyes still closed. "I can hear your tablet's cooling fan."

“Sorry.” Jonathan said as he slipped the tablet on the table beside him.

"Do you remember that little inn in Scotland?" Sherry asked, not opening her eyes. "The one where we got snowed in for three days?"

Jonathan smiled, adjusting the pillow behind his back. "The owner kept apologizing while secretly being delighted to have someone to play chess with." He glanced at their cramped but charming room, with its arched ceiling and worn stone floor. "Though I have to admit, this place has a bit more character."

Sherry opened her and stretched. "Martha said this building was once a monastery. Can't you feel all the history in these walls?"

"I can feel something in these walls," Jonathan replied, patting the rough limestone. "Probably several centuries of other people's stories."

The night's light slanted through their balcony doors, carrying with it the distant sounds of the city: church bells, and the muezzin's call to prayer.

They woke the next morning to the warm breeze stirring the gauzy curtains, bringing with it the scent of za'atar and baking bread from the kitchen below.

"I saved some of that breakfast pastry for you," Sherry said, reaching for a small wrapped package on the nightstand. "Martha said it's called buttrema. Family recipe."

"Is that why you were chatting with her so long yesterday?" Jonathan took a bite of the sweet pastry. "I thought you were getting the inside scoop on the city."

Sherry threw a pillow at him. "Can't a girl just enjoy a conversation about cooking? Though..." She hesitated. "She did say something interesting about the old tunnels under the inn."

"Sherry..."

"Not everything is about the Prophet! Apparently, they connect to a whole network of ancient passages under the Old City. Martha uses part of them as a wine cellar. She offered to show us later."

Jonathan brushed pastry crumbs from the bed. "As long as you're not expecting to find any divine revelations down there."

"The only revelation I'm expecting is whether her wine collection lives up to her cooking." Sherry got up and walked to the balcony, leaving the doors open as she stepped out. "Though I wouldn't mind a small miracle right now – like that breeze getting stronger."

Jonathan watched her lean against the railing, her hair lifting slightly in the warm air. The dome of the Rock glinted in the distance, and for a moment, he saw their room and the city beyond through her eyes – not as a collection of data points and phenomena to be studied, but as something magical in its own right.

He joined her on the balcony, wrapping his arms around her from behind. "We could go down to the garden courtyard," he suggested. "It's cooler there, and Martha mentioned something about afternoon tea."

"In a minute," Sherry said, leaning back against him. "Right now, this is perfect."

They stayed that way for a while, watching shadows lengthen across the Old City's maze of rooftops and domes. A pair of doves had made a nest in one of the ancient olive trees that grew in the inn's courtyard, and their soft cooing drifted up to the balcony.

When they finally went down to the garden, they found Martha had set up tea in the shade of a grape arbor. The small courtyard was a hidden gem: flowering vines climbed the old walls, and a tiny fountain burbled quietly in one corner. Clay pots of herbs lined the edges, their fragrance mixing with the jasmine that tumbled over an ancient arch.

"My grandmother planted those roses," Martha told them as she poured the tea. "And her grandmother before her. We've been keeping this inn for five generations now." She gave them a knowing look. "You see many things, running an inn in Jerusalem. Many strange and wonderful things."

As the afternoon mellowed into evening, they stayed in the courtyard, talking with Martha and her husband about the city's history. The old couple had stories about everything – from wars and pilgrimages to small, everyday miracles like the time all the roses bloomed in December.

“Do you have your plans for the eclipse ironed out?” Martha asked.

They exchanged a look before Jonathan spoke up. "Not yet, Do you suggest anything?”

Martha’s eyes lit up. "Ah!" she exclaimed. "You will find your own place to watch. The city is your guide."

Jonathan smiled, though his mind was preoccupied.

“You're right. As an astrophysicist, I relish in the science of the eclipse itself, but Sherry is more interested in history and culture. We need to go somewhere that has both. But it’s going to be incredible,” he said, “I can’t wait to see the sun’s corona. It reminds us of how small we really are.”

"But tell me," she said, leaning closer. "Did you get to see the prophet Bennett yesterday?"

The question hung in the air like an unspoken secret. They exchanged a look before Sherry spoke up. "We did. It was... moving."

Martha's eyes searched theirs, a knowing look in them. "Good," she said, her voice low. The old woman's smile was enigmatic. "I have not seen him in person yet. He's promised great things, but so far, I haven't heard about much more than a few healings in the city. But I remain hopeful. Having him here, so close, it feels like maybe, just maybe, he'll remember the people who need him most."

Martha's words echoed in Jonathan's mind. His thoughts raced. *What could Bennett possibly show them that could be that amazing?*

When the stars began to appear, they retreated to their room, carrying a bottle from Matha's promised wine cellar. The night air had cooled, and they left the balcony doors open to the sound of the city settling into darkness.

The old limestone walls of the inn kept the summer heat at bay, their room was a sanctuary of cool shadows and Jerusalem light. Sherry sat cross-legged on their bed, surrounded by the loose papers of her travel journal, while Jonathan tinkered with his eclipse-viewing equipment by the window.

"It's strange," Sherry said, taking a sip of the wine, "I came to Jerusalem looking for something extraordinary, but today..." She gestured at their room, the city beyond, the comfortable silence between them. "Maybe the extraordinary is in moments like this."

Jonathan looked up from where he'd been making adjustments to his telescope. The moonlight caught the silver in Sherry's hair, and for a moment, he saw all their possible futures in her smile.

"You know what's really extraordinary?" he said. "The statistical probability of us both choosing to be at Columbia University, in that exact city, at that exact moment in time."

Sherry laughed. "Only you would make probability sound romantic."

As they drifted off to sleep that night, the sound of distant singing floated up from somewhere in the city. Tomorrow would bring its own plans, but for now, they had this: an ancient room in an ancient city, the history in the walls, and the simple miracle of being together.

Just before sleep took him, Jonathan realized he hadn't checked his telescope once since sunset. Sometimes, he thought, the most important measurements were the ones you felt rather than calculated.

Morning came with the smell of fresh bread and cardamom from the inn's kitchen. They lingered over breakfast in the courtyard, where Martha insisted they try her homemade labneh with olive oil and za'atar. The eclipse was still two days away, and despite Jonathan's anxiety about his preparations, Sherry convinced him to explore the morning market.

"Your instruments will survive without you for a few hours," she teased, pulling him through the inn's ancient doorway into the already bustling street.

The market filled the narrow lanes of the Muslim Quarter, awnings creating a patchwork of shade above the crowds. Vendors called out their wares in a melodic mix of Arabic, Hebrew, and English.

Using the map, they located Eli's shop tucked away in a quiet corner of the market. It was cluttered with artifacts and curios from every era of Jerusalem's long history. An elderly man with a long white beard sat behind a counter. He had his magnifying glass poised over a small figurine. He looked up as they entered, his rheumy eyes twinkling with interest.

"Ah, welcome, welcome!" The vendor greeted them, his accent a melodious blend of cultures. "What can Eli show you today? Perhaps a piece of the True Cross? Or a fragment of the Tablets of Moses?"

Sherry couldn't help but smile at the obvious tourist traps. She started to tell him about staying in the Shalom Inn when she was interrupted by a man with a weather-beaten face framed by a wild mane of graying hair. His eyes glowed with an inner fire as he hollered Eli. "The prophet is coming!" His voice boomed.

Eli's head snapped up, "Crazy old man," Eli whispered with a grin. Then with an emphasis on the word prophet, Eli said, “The ‘prophet’ is always coming…”

Before Eli could go back to selling them anything, a commotion in the middle of the marketplace caught their attention. A crowd was gathering near one of the larger intersections, their voices a mix of excitement and concern. Without discussing it, they both moved toward the sound.

In the center of the growing circle stood a young boy, perhaps seven or eight years old, his clothes dusty from the street. He was crying, speaking rapidly in Arabic to his mother, who knelt beside him. Jonathan caught enough words to understand – the boy had lost something precious.

Then the Prophet appeared.

He moved through the crowd like silk through water, his white robe somehow unsullied by the dusty street. This close, Jonathan could see details he'd missed before – the strange iridescence of his eyes, the way light seemed to bend slightly around his hands.

The Prophet knelt before the boy, and the crowd fell silent. Even the persistent calls of vendors died away. Sherry's hand found Jonathan's and squeezed.

"What troubles you, little one?" the Prophet asked in perfect Arabic, though his voice seemed to reach everyone in their own language.

The boy, hiccupping through his tears, explained that he had lost his father's ring – an heirloom passed down through generations. He'd been carrying it to the craftsman for repair when he tripped. In the chaos of the market, it had vanished.

The Prophet smiled, and the air around him seemed to shimmer. He reached out, passing his hand through empty air as if drawing aside an invisible curtain. Light gathered around his fingers, coalescing into something solid.

There, spinning slowly in the air above his palm, was a golden ring.

The boy's cry of joy broke the spell of silence. The crowd erupted in exclamations and prayers as the Prophet gently placed the ring in the boy's trembling hands. The mother began weeping, reaching to kiss the Prophet's robes, but he stepped back, raising his hands in humble denial of praise.

"The universe holds all things in its memory," he said, his voice carrying easily despite its softness.

"Come on," he said, gently tugging her arm.

As they walked away from the dispersing crowd, the boy's laughter echoed through the market. The narrow streets of Jerusalem's marketplace bustled with activity, a vibrant tapestry of colors, sounds, and scents. Jonathan and Sherry meandered through the crowd, still buzzing from the unexpected event they had just witnessed.

"Did you see the look on that child's face?" Sherry exclaimed, her eyes wide with excitement.

"When the prophet found his ring, it was like... like magic!"

Jonathan nodded, a bemused smile playing on his lips. "It was certainly something. Though I'm sure there's a logical explanation."

"Logical explanation or not," Sherry continued, "it was beautiful. The way his whole face lit up... it's moments like that that make traveling so special, don't you think?"

Jonathan squeezed her hand affectionately. "You're right. It's the unexpected moments that often become the best memories."

As they continued down the street, the aroma of freshly baked bread wafted from a nearby stall. Jonathan's stomach growled, reminding him that it had been hours since Martha's delicious lunch.

"Hungry?" Sherry asked with a laugh. "Come on, let's try some of that bread. And look, there's a cheese vendor right next to it. Perfect combination!"

They spent the next hour sampling various local delicacies. The bread was still warm from the oven, its crust crackling pleasantly as they tore into it. The cheese vendor, an older woman with a kind smile and calloused hands, insisted they try her specialty – a tangy, crumbly cheese that paired perfectly with the bread.

"This is incredible," Jonathan mumbled around a mouthful. "We should buy some to take back to the inn."

As they continued to walk they found themselves drawn to a stall selling handcrafted jewelry. Sherry's eyes sparkled as she examined the intricate designs.

"These are beautiful," she breathed, holding up a delicate silver bracelet etched with what looked like ancient symbols.

The vendor, noticing her interest, stepped forward. "Ah, you have a good eye, miss. That bracelet is inspired by designs found in some of Jerusalem's oldest ruins. It's said to bring good fortune to the wearer."

Jonathan raised an eyebrow at the claim but said nothing, seeing the joy on Sherry's face as she tried on the bracelet.

"We'll take it," he said, reaching for his wallet.

As the afternoon wore on, they found themselves loaded with bags containing their various purchases – the bread and cheese, a beautifully illustrated book of local legends that had caught Jonathan's eye, and a small ceramic pomegranate that the vendor had assured them was a traditional symbol of prosperity.

"Oh!" Sherry exclaimed suddenly, coming to a stop. "We didn't get to look around Eli's shop. Should we go back?"

Jonathan glanced at his watch, then at their full hands. "It's getting late, and we're pretty loaded down. Why don't we head back to the inn and rest up? We can always come back tomorrow. Besides," he added with a grin, "we wouldn't want to miss Martha's dinner."

Sherry nodded, looking a bit disappointed but also visibly tired from their day. "You're right. And we do have the eclipse to look forward to tomorrow."

As they made their way back through the winding streets, the setting sun painted the ancient stones in warm hues.

"You know," he said, putting his arm around Sherry as they walked, "I'm glad we got sidetracked today. Sometimes the best experiences are the ones you don't plan for."

Sherry leaned into him, smiling. "Absolutely. Though I still want to check out Eli's shop tomorrow. I have a feeling there are still plenty of souvenirs waiting for us to buy in this city."

As they turned the corner towards their inn, the last rays of sunlight glinting off Sherry's new bracelet, they were stopped by an old woman huddled in a doorway. Her weathered face crinkled into a smile as she spoke.

"Did you hear?" she asked, her voice quivering with excitement. "They say he healed a blind man yesterday. Just like that!" She snapped her fingers for emphasis, the sound sharp in the quieting street.

Jonathan reached into his pocket and pressed some money into the woman's hand. As she mumbled her thanks, he turned to Sherry with a raised eyebrow. "Looks like your prophet's been busy."

Sherry's eyes widened, a mix of wonder and skepticism crossing her face. "A blind man? Really?" She looked back at the old woman, who was now clutching the money to her chest with a toothless grin. "How... how did he do it?"

The woman shrugged, her smile never faltering. "Miracle. They say. Touched his eyes and spoke some words. The blind man cried out that he could see the sun for the first time in years!"

Jonathan gently tugged at Sherry's arm. "Come on, we should get back. Thank you," he nodded to the old woman, who waved as they continued down the street.

As they walked the last few steps to the inn, Jonathan was uncharacteristically quiet, her brow furrowed in thought.

"What's on your mind?" Sherry asked, juggling a bag to open the inn's door.

He hesitated before responding. "It's just... first the sick boy, then the ring, now this story about healing blindness. Don't you think it's a bit... strange?"

Sherry shrugged as they entered the cozy warmth of the inn. "People love a good story, especially tourists. I'm sure there's a reasonable explanation for both."

The scent of Martha's cooking wafted up from the kitchen, reminding them of the simple pleasures that had filled their day. Yet as they settled in for the evening, the anticipation of the eclipse the following day would require them to be well rested.

Chapter Five: The Unveiled Sky

The day of the eclipse dawned with an electric atmosphere. Jonathan awoke to find Sherry already up, gazing out the window at the bustling streets below.

"You're up early," he yawned, stretching as he joined her.

Sherry turned, her eyes bright with excitement. "How could I sleep? Today's the big day! And look," she gestured to the street, "everyone's already out and about."

Indeed, the normally busy streets of Jerusalem seemed even more alive than usual. Tourists and locals alike filled the walkways, many carrying eclipse viewing glasses or homemade pinhole cameras.

"We should get going," Jonathan said, glancing at his watch. "We still want to check out Eli's shop before the eclipse starts."

As they made their way down to breakfast, they found Martha in a flurry of activity, preparing meals for the inn's many guests.

"Good morning!" she called cheerfully. "Isn't it exciting? I've set out an early lunch for everyone. Make sure you eat well before the eclipse!"

Over a hearty meal of shakshuka and fresh bread, Jonathan and Sherry discussed their plans for the day.

"So, Eli's shop first," Jonathan said, tracing a path on their map. "Then we should probably find a good spot to view the eclipse. Any preferences?"

Sherry hesitated for a moment. "Actually... I was thinking we could try to find that prophet again. You know, the one who found the ring? I'd love to hear what he has to say about the eclipse."

Jonathan raised an eyebrow. "You're really intrigued by him, aren't you?"

"Aren't you?" Sherry countered. "After what we saw yesterday, and then that story about healing the blind man... don't you want to know more?"

Before Jonathan could respond, Martha approached their table, a knowing smile on her face. "If you're looking for the prophet, word is he'll be somewhere in the square this morning. Quite a few people are looking for him. They want to hear from him before the eclipse."

Sherry's eyes lit up. "See? It's perfect. We can stop by Eli's shop on the way."

Jonathan nodded, unable to resist Sherry's enthusiasm. "Alright, let's do it."

Street vendors had set up stalls selling eclipse-themed souvenirs, and impromptu astronomy lessons were taking place on street corners.

As they arrived at Eli's shop, they found the narrow street unusually crowded. A group of people had gathered, murmuring excitedly.

"What's going on?" Sherry asked a nearby woman.

The woman turned, her eyes wide. "The prophet said he will be here. We are hoping to see him before today's event."

Jonathan and Sherry exchanged glances when they saw the crowds of people walking towards Eli's shop. "Should we leave?" Jonathan asked.

Sherry checked the time seeing that it was still several hours before the eclipse. "We will miss the prophet if we do."

They managed to work their way through the crowd and into the dimly lit interior of Eli's shop. The space was crammed with shelves full of curiosities, artifacts, and ancient-looking texts. Behind a cluttered counter stood an elderly man with bright, inquisitive eyes.

"Ah, you are back!" he said, his voice surprisingly strong for his apparent age. "What brings you back to my humble shop on this auspicious day?"

"We didn't get a chance to see your beautiful stones before," Sherry said eagerly.

Eli's eyes twinkled. "Ah, yes. Let us see what we have."

"What is your most precious stone?" Jonathan asked.

Eli leaned in conspiratorially. "Let me tell you a story," he began, his voice dropping to a near whisper.

"Years ago, an artifact was discovered in the caves near the Dead Sea. It was unlike anything ever seen before - a small, intricately carved stone that seemed to glow from within."

Sherry and Jonathan leaned in, captivated by Eli's words.

"But this was no ordinary artifact," Eli continued. "Those who studied it reported strange experiences. They claimed the stone could speak directly into their minds, sharing knowledge of things long past and yet to come."

"That's impossible," Jonathan said, but his voice lacked conviction.

Eli smiled enigmatically. "Many things seem impossible until they are experienced, young man. The artifact chose who it would communicate with, and its words were said to be profound and life-changing."

"What happened to it?" Sherry asked, her eyes wide.

"Ah, therein lies the mystery," Eli said with a sigh. "The artifact vanished years ago. Some say it was stolen, others believe it chose to disappear until the right time came for it to be found again."

"And when would that be?" Jonathan couldn't help asking.

Eli's gaze seemed to pierce right through them. "Who can say? Perhaps during a moment when the veils between worlds grow thin. A moment like, say... a total eclipse."

A shiver ran down Sherry's spine, and even Jonathan felt a strange sense of foreboding.

"Now then," Eli said, his tone suddenly lighter, "Perhaps you'd be interested in some eclipse viewing glasses? Guaranteed to provide the safest viewing experience!"

As they purchased the glasses from Eli, Sherry had a feeling that there was more to his story than he had let on. Jonathan, too, found his skepticism wavering in the face of Eli's tale.

And then there he was– the prophet, standing there, his neatly trimmed hair and beard framing an intense gaze that seemed to pierce through the crowd.

Sherry gripped Jonathan's arm. "It's him."

"The heavens themselves shall darken," the voice proclaimed, "but fear not, for in darkness, truth is revealed!"

He spoke of the eclipse not as a mere astronomical event, but as a moment of great spiritual significance. His language was a mix of biblical allusions and scientific terminology that Jonathan found both impressive and slightly unsettling.

"And when the shadow passes," the prophet intoned, his voice rising, "we shall all be changed. For what is hidden shall be revealed, and what is dark shall be brought to light!"

The prophet's words washed over them. A murmur ran through the crowd. Jonathan felt Sherry's grip on his arm tighten.

"What do you think he means?" she whispered.

Before Jonathan could answer, a commotion near the front of the crowd caught their attention. A man was pushing his way forward, his face contorted with anger.

"Charlatan!" he shouted, pointing at the prophet. "You're nothing but a fraud, preying on people's fears!"

The prophet's gaze settled on the man, his expression serene despite the accusation. "My friend," he said, his voice gentle but carrying clearly over the now-hushed crowd, "why do you fear the truth?"

"Truth?" the man scoffed. "Your miracles and revelations, where's your proof?"

A tense silence fell over the square. Jonathan held his breath, wondering how the prophet would respond.

Slowly, deliberately, the prophet approached the angry man. "You seek proof?" he asked softly. "Very well. What troubles you, my son?"

The man's anger seemed to falter in the face of the prophet's calm demeanor. "I... my wife," he stammered. "She's ill. The doctors say there's nothing more they can do."

The prophet nodded solemnly. "Take me to her," he said. "Let all who doubt come and see."

As the crowd began to follow the prophet and the troubled man, Sherry's expression shifted from excitement to disappointment. She turned to Jonathan, her eyes pleading.

"Jonathan, can't we go with them? This could be incredible," she said, her voice tinged with frustration.

Jonathan shook his head, his gaze fixed on the sky. "Sherry, we came all this way for the eclipse. It's a once-in-a-lifetime opportunity. We need to find a good spot soon."

Sherry's shoulders slumped, her enthusiasm deflating. She glanced longingly at the departing crowd, then back at Jonathan. "I understand, but... what if we're missing something important?"

Jonathan gently took her hand, trying to soften the blow. "I know you're interested, but we have to stick to our plan. The eclipse won't wait for us."

With visible reluctance, Sherry allowed Jonathan to lead her away from the prophet's procession. As they joined the crowd moving towards the eclipse viewing areas, she couldn't help but cast frequent glances over her shoulder.

"I hope we're making the right choice," she murmured, her voice barely audible over the excited chatter of the eclipse-watchers around them.

Jonathan squeezed her hand reassuringly, but Sherry's steps were hesitant, her mind clearly torn between the celestial event they had traveled so far to see and the mysterious prophet whose actions might prove equally momentous.

As they joined the procession moving through the ancient streets of Jerusalem, the sun climbed higher in the sky, the moment of the eclipse drawing ever nearer, and with it, perhaps, the revelation the prophet had promised.

The anticipation in Jerusalem had reached a fever pitch as the moment of the eclipse drew near. After the commotion with the prophet and the angry man, Jonathan and Sherry had decided to focus on finding the perfect spot to view the celestial event.

"Over there," Jonathan pointed, guiding Sherry through the bustling crowd. He'd spotted a small hill just outside the Old City walls, offering an unobstructed view of the sky and the ancient cityscape below.

As they climbed, Sherry clutched the eclipse glasses Eli had sold them. "I can't believe it's finally happening," she said, her voice tinged with excitement

They reached the top of the hill, finding a small gathering of other eclipse-watchers already there. The atmosphere was electric, a mix of scientific curiosity and almost spiritual reverence.

"Look," an elderly man nearby said, pointing to the sun. "It's starting."

Jonathan and Sherry quickly donned their protective glasses. Sure enough, a small dark curve had appeared on the edge of the sun's disk.

"I've waited so long for this moment." he said, his voice trembling with emotion.

The city below them had grown quiet, as if holding its breath. The usual sounds of traffic and bustle had faded away, replaced by an almost reverent hush broken only by occasional gasps of awe.

As the eclipse neared totality, Sherry reached for Jonathan's hand. He squeezed it, feeling a connection that went beyond the shared experience.

"Ten seconds to totality," someone in the crowd called out.

"Five... four... three... two... one..."

In that moment, the world transformed. The last sliver of sun disappeared behind the moon, and a collective gasp rose from the watchers. They removed their glasses, and there, hanging in the sky, was a sight that defied description.

The sun's corona blazed around the black disk of the moon, ethereal tendrils of light stretching out into the darkened sky. Stars and planets, usually invisible in the daytime, winked into view.

"It's beautiful," Sherry whispered, her voice choking with emotion.

Jonathan could only nod, too awestruck for words.

As they put their protective glasses back on to watch the sun reemerge, Jonathan had the feeling that the world had shifted in some fundamental way.

For those brief minutes of totality, time seemed to stand still. All the worries and doubts of the modern world faded away, replaced by a sense of connection to something greater, something eternal.

As quickly as it had come, the moment passed. A bright bead of sunlight appeared on the edge of the moon's disk – the famous "diamond ring" effect – signaling the end of totality.

"Glasses on," Jonathan reminded Sherry, his voice hoarse.

They watched as the moon continued its journey across the sun's face, gradually returning the world to its normal state. As sunlight returned, Jonathan heard sighs of both disappointment and lingering awe from the crowd around them.

Sherry turned to him, her eyes shining. "That was... I don't even have words for it."

Jonathan nodded, still processing the experience. "It was incredible. Like nothing I've ever seen."

As they began their descent back into the city, the streets of Jerusalem were coming back to life, the spell of the eclipse was slowly fading. The streets, which had been eerily quiet during the eclipse, now buzzed with excited conversations and laughter. Everywhere they looked, people were sharing their eclipse experiences, showing each other photos on their phones, and discussing what they had witnessed.

"I still can't believe how beautiful it was," Sherry said, her voice filled with wonder. "It's like... like the whole world changed for those few minutes."

Jonathan nodded, still processing the experience himself. "It was certainly something," he agreed, giving her hand a gentle squeeze.

As they turned a corner, they found themselves back in the marketplace. The vendors were out in full force, many now selling eclipse-themed souvenirs alongside their usual wares.

"Oh, look!" Sherry exclaimed, pointing to a nearby stall. "That vendor is selling pendants with the eclipse design. Should we get one as a memento?"

The streets of Jerusalem buzzed with excitement as Jonathan and Sherry made their way back to the inn. The afterglow of the eclipse seemed to linger in the air, with people animatedly discussing their experiences on every corner.

"I still can't believe how beautiful it was," Sherry said, her eyes bright with wonder. "The corona, the stars coming out in the middle of the day... it was like nothing I've ever seen before."

Jonathan nodded, a thoughtful expression on his face. "It was truly spectacular. A once-in-a-lifetime experience."

As they walked, Sherry's excitement slowly gave way to a furrowed brow. "You know, it's strange," she mused. "For all the prophet's talk about revelations and truths being unveiled, I didn't see anything... well, prophetic. Did you?"

Jonathan shook his head. "No, I didn't. It was an incredible natural phenomenon, but nothing supernatural that I could see."

"I wonder what he meant then," Sherry pondered. "All that talk about the heavens darkening and truths being revealed. It seemed so certain, so specific."

They reached the inn, the familiar facade a welcome sight after the long, eventful day. As they stepped inside, they were greeted by the warm aroma of cooking food and the sound of excited chatter from other guests.

Martha bustled out from the kitchen, her face alight with enthusiasm. "There you are!" she exclaimed. "Wasn't it wonderful? I hope you found a good spot to watch from."

"We did," Sherry replied with a smile. "We were on a hill just outside the Old City walls. The view was perfect."

"Marvelous, simply marvelous," Martha said. "Now, you must be hungry. I've prepared a special post-eclipse dinner for all my guests. Why don't you go sit, and it'll be ready in about twenty minutes?"

They made their way down to the dining room, which was abuzz with excited conversation.

Martha emerged from the kitchen, carrying a large pot. "Everyone, please, take your seats," she called out cheerfully. "I've prepared a traditional Jerusalem artichoke soup to start, followed by a feast of local specialties. I hope you'll all enjoy it!"

As Jonathan and Sherry settled at a table, bowls of steaming soup placed before them, they couldn't help but overhear snippets of conversation from nearby tables.

As they began to eat, savoring the rich, Earthy flavor of the soup, the day's events had left Jonathan with more questions than answers.

But for now, surrounded by the warm glow of the inn and the excited chatter of fellow travelers, he decided to simply enjoy the moment. Whatever revelations or adventures awaited them could wait until tomorrow.

Jonathan and Sherry headed up to their room, both glad for a moment to relax and process the day's events. As Sherry washed her face, she caught Jonathan's reflection in the mirror, noticing again the thoughtful, almost preoccupied look on his face.

"Penny for your thoughts?" she asked.

Jonathan seemed to snap out of his reverie. "Oh, just thinking about the eclipse, and that prophet's words, all of it. It's been quite a day, hasn't it?"

Sherry nodded, her own mind full of the day's experiences. They spent the evening discussing their observations, both of the eclipse and the mysterious prophet. The next few days were a whirlwind of sightseeing and exploring Jerusalem, their conversations often returning to the events surrounding the eclipse.

Life in Jerusalem had settled back into its familiar rhythms. The excitement of the celestial event had faded, replaced by the usual bustle of daily life in the ancient city.

Jonathan and Sherry sat at their favorite cafe near the Old City walls, enjoying a late breakfast and watching the people go by. The morning air was crisp, carrying the scent of freshly baked bread from a nearby bakery.

"You know," Sherry said, stirring her coffee thoughtfully, "I haven't seen the prophet since the eclipse. Have you?"

Jonathan shook his head. "No, now that you mention it, I haven't. It's been pretty quiet on that front."

As if on cue, they overheard a conversation from the table next to theirs. Two local men were chatting over their meals.

"Did you hear? No one's seen that prophet for days," one man said.

His companion nodded. "I heard he left the city right after the eclipse. Probably moved on to the next big event, you know how these types are."

Sherry and Jonathan exchanged glances. "Seems like we're not the only ones who've noticed," Jonathan murmured.

They finished their breakfast and decided to take a stroll through the marketplace. The streets were lively but lacked the charged atmosphere of the days leading up to the eclipse.

Vendors called out their wares, tourists haggled over souvenirs, and locals went about their shopping – all perfectly normal.

As they strolled through the marketplace, they noticed a subtle change in the atmosphere. While life continued as normal, there was an undercurrent of wistfulness among some of the locals.

Passing a fruit stand, they overheard the vendor talking to a customer. "The prophet's gone, and with him, a bit of the magic. His words made even an ordinary day feel special."

In the small square where children played, an elderly woman sat on a bench, looking thoughtful. As Jonathan and Sherry passed, they heard her say to her companion, "I miss seeing the prophet in the mornings. His miracles brought a sense of purpose to the day."

Near the Western Wall, they noticed a group of people engaged in quiet conversation. As they drew closer, they caught fragments of what was being said.

"It's not just about his predictions," one man was saying. "His presence reminded us to look beyond our daily concerns, to think about bigger questions."

A woman nodded in agreement. "The city feels a little less vibrant without him. I hope he returns someday."

As they passed the spot where they had last seen the prophet preaching, Sherry paused. "It's strange, isn't it? How quickly things go back to normal."

Jonathan nodded. "I suppose that's just how it goes. Big events come and go, but life continues."

They continued their walk, taking in the sights and sounds of the city. Children played in a small square, the laughter echoing off ancient stones. An old man sat on a bench, feeding pigeons and enjoying the sunshine.

Later in the afternoon, they found themselves near the Western Wall. The plaza was filled with its usual mix of worshippers and tourists, but there was no sign of the fervent crowds that had gathered to hear the prophet's predictions.

"You know," Jonathan said as they observed the scene, "part of me wondered if something dramatic would happen after the eclipse, given all the prophet's talk. But it's almost reassuring to see everything so... normal."

Sherry agreed. "It is. Though I have to admit, a small part of me is a little disappointed. All that build-up, and then... just an ordinary eclipse. Beautiful, but ordinary."

As the day wore on, they heard more snippets of conversation about the prophet's disappearance. Some speculated that he had been disappointed when his predictions didn't come true. Others suggested he had simply moved on to the next city, as traveling preachers often do. Not many of the townspeople seemed particularly concerned or upset by his absence.

Jonathan and Sherry found themselves in a small, out-of-the-way cafe, seeking refuge from the warm sun. The place was nearly empty, save for an elderly couple at a corner table and a middle-aged man reading a newspaper at the counter.

While they sipped their cool drinks, they overheard the man at the counter strike up a conversation with the barista.

"You know," he said, leaning in conspiratorially, "everyone's saying the prophet disappeared right after the eclipse, but that's not quite true."

The barista raised an eyebrow, intrigued. "Oh? What do you mean?"

The man folded his newspaper, clearly relishing the attention. "My cousin – he's a security guard up at the Temple Mount – he swears he saw the prophet the very next day."

Jonathan and Sherry exchanged glances, and tried to look nonchalant as they listened in.

"Go on," the barista urged, voicing their unspoken curiosity.

"Well," the man continued, "it was early morning, just after sunrise. My cousin was doing his rounds near the ruins, you know, where they're always doing those archaeological digs. And there he was – that prophet, standing among the old stones, looking out over the city."

"Did your cousin speak to him?" the barista asked.

The man shook his head. "No, that's the strange thing. He said he blinked, and in that instant, that guy was gone. Like he'd vanished into thin air."

The barista whistled low. "That's quite a story. But if it's true, why didn't your cousin tell anyone?"

"Oh, he did," the man chuckled. "But who's going to believe a sleepy security guard who claims he saw a vanishing prophet at dawn? Most people just assumed he was tired and seeing things."

As the conversation drifted to other topics, Jonathan turned to Sherry. "What do you make of that?" he asked quietly.

Sherry shrugged, a thoughtful expression on her face. "It's an interesting story. Could be true, could be someone's imagination running wild. Either way, it adds to the mystery, doesn't it?"

Jonathan nodded, a slight smile playing on his lips. "That it does. Jerusalem does seem to have a way of blending the ordinary with the mysterious."

They finished their drinks and stepped back out into the warm afternoon sun. As they walked, they noticed people going about their daily lives – shopping, chatting, hurrying to appointments. Yet now, after overhearing the story in the cafe, they couldn't help but wonder how many other untold encounters might be hidden behind the city's ancient stones and winding alleys.

The tale of the prophet's possible appearance at the ruins added a touch of intrigue to the day, a reminder that even in the quiet aftermath of the eclipse, Jerusalem remained a city where the line between the mundane and the miraculous was often blurred.

That evening, as they sat on the rooftop terrace of their inn, watching the sunset paint the city in golden hues, Jonathan reflected on the past few days.

"You know, Sherry, I think there's something beautiful about how life just goes on. The eclipse was amazing, the prophet was intriguing, but in the end, Jerusalem is still Jerusalem. Timeless, unchanging in some ways, yet always moving forward."

Sherry leaned her head on his shoulder, taking in the panoramic view of the city. "You're right. It's comforting, in a way. All the excitement and predictions, and here we are, just enjoying another beautiful evening in an incredible city."

As the stars began to appear in the darkening sky, Jonathan and Sherry sat in comfortable silence, appreciating the peace of the moment. The prophet may have disappeared, his predictions unfulfilled, but the enduring beauty and spirit of Jerusalem remained, a constant in an ever-changing world.

The day ended as it began – quietly, peacefully, with the gentle rhythms of city life continuing uninterrupted. Whatever mysteries or excitements the future might hold, for now, all was calm in the holy city.

Jonathan and Sherry woke early, acutely aware that this was their last day in the ancient city before flying home.

"I can't believe it's already time to leave," Sherry said, stretching as she got out of bed. "It feels like we just got here."

Jonathan nodded, a hint of something unreadable in his eyes. "It's been quite a trip, hasn't it? The eclipse, the prophet, all of it."

They headed down to breakfast, where Martha greeted them with her usual warmth. "So, it's your last day with us," she said, a touch of sadness in her voice. "Any special plans before you go?"

Sherry looked at Jonathan questioningly. They hadn't really discussed how to spend their final day.

"I thought we might revisit some of our favorite spots," Jonathan suggested. "Maybe do a bit of last-minute shopping for souvenirs. What do you think, Sherry?"

"Sounds perfect," Sherry agreed. "I'd love to take one more walk through the Old City."

After a leisurely breakfast, they wandered through the pathways of the Old City, retracing their steps from the past week. The market was as lively as ever, filled with the sounds of haggling.

As the day wore on, they visited the Western Wall one last time, its ancient stones seeming to pulse with centuries of prayers and hopes. They walked the Via Dolorosa, reflecting on the layers of history beneath their feet.

As the sun began to set, casting a golden glow over the city, they made their way back to the inn to pack and prepare for their early morning flight.

"So, you're off early tomorrow," Martha said, a hint of sadness in her warm smile. "How has your stay been? Did you see everything you wanted to see?"

Sherry nodded enthusiastically. "It's been wonderful, Martha. This city is just... magical."

"We've seen so much," Jonathan added. "The Old City, the Western Wall, the Church of the Holy Sepulchre. And of course, the eclipse. That was truly spectacular."

Martha's eyes twinkled. "Ah yes, the eclipse. Quite an event, wasn't it? I've lived here all my life and never seen anything quite like it. Did you enjoy the prophet's speech beforehand?"

Sherry and Jonathan exchanged glances. "It was... interesting," Sherry said diplomatically. "Very passionate."

Martha chuckled. "Oh, he's always like that. Adds a bit of color to the city, don't you think? But tell me, what was your favorite part of the trip?"

As they recounted their experiences, from the bustle of the marketplace to the solemnity of the holy sites, Martha listened attentively, occasionally adding her own insights about the city's history and culture.

"You know," she said as their conversation wound down, "Jerusalem has a way of staying with people. Even after they leave, a part of it remains in their hearts."

Jonathan nodded, a thoughtful expression on his face. "I can believe that. There's something... timeless about this place."

"Don't stay up too late, now. You have an early flight to catch."

After Martha left, Jonathan turned to Sherry. "I was thinking of setting up the telescope one last time. Care to join me for some stargazing?"

Sherry smiled. "I'd love to."

They made their way up to the inn's rooftop terrace. The night was clear, the stars twinkling brightly above the Jerusalem skyline. Jonathan carefully set up his telescope, adjusting it with practiced ease.

"You know," he said as he peered through the eyepiece, "seeing the stars from here, above this ancient city... it really puts things in perspective, doesn't it?"

Sherry nodded, gazing up at the night sky. "It's beautiful. And to think, just yesterday we saw those stars in the middle of the day during the eclipse."

They spent the next hour stargazing, with Jonathan pointing out constellations and Sherry marveling at the clarity of the planets through the telescope.

As the night grew cooler, they reluctantly packed up the telescope and headed back to their room. It was time to prepare for their departure.

"I can't believe we're leaving already," Sherry said as she began to fold clothes into her suitcase.

Jonathan nodded, carefully wrapping his telescope.

They packed in comfortable silence, each lost in their own thoughts and memories of their time in Jerusalem. Once their bags were ready for the morning, they settled into bed, the distant sounds of the city providing a soothing backdrop.

"We'll come back someday, won't we?" Sherry asked sleepily.

Jonathan smiled in the darkness. "I'm sure we will. Jerusalem isn't a place you visit just once."

As they drifted off to sleep, their minds were filled with memories of their journey and the simple anticipation of returning home. The eclipse had been a wonder, the prophet's words intriguing, but in the end, it was the timeless beauty of Jerusalem itself that had left the deepest impression.

Their alarm was set for an early hour, their bags packed and waiting. Tomorrow would bring the familiar routines of travel and the comfort of home. But for now, they slept peacefully, their dreams filled with the golden light of Jerusalem's sunset and the starry skies above its ancient walls.

The next morning came early. As their taxi wound through the awakening streets of Jerusalem towards the airport, Sherry looked back at the ancient walls receding in the distance.

Their flight home was a blur, their minds racing with thoughts of what they had seen and experienced.

Chapter Six: Echoes of Urgency

The screech of sirens pierced the evening air as Jonathan and Sherry Avery trudged up the steps to their house, arms laden with grocery bags. Three police cars raced past, their lights painting the street in flashes of red and blue.

"That's the second time this week," Sherry muttered, her voice tight with concern.

Jonathan nodded grimly, fumbling for his keys. "Yeah, I noticed that too."

While Sherry unpacked their groceries, she watched the news. Jonathan disappeared into the bathroom. The sound of running water filled the house as he stepped into the shower.

The warm water washed over him, cleansing him of the dust of the stress and the tension of the day.

He let out a deep sigh, feeling the warmth seep into his bones.

The news was ablaze with the events of the last week. A reporter was standing in front of a burning building.

"Things are crazy here," she said, her voice carrying the distant sounds of sirens. "People are burning down the old warehouses, and the petty crime rate is through the roof."

The station showed images of shop owners boarding up their windows, "And with the increase in robberies, stores are closing early." The reporter added, her voice tight with worry.

The news report ended with a plea for vigilance, the reporter's smile forced and brittle. The image of the burning building lingered on the screen long after it had returned to the regularly scheduled programming.

The gentle clink of silverware against plates filled the dining room of Jonathan and Sherry Avery's dining room. Outside, the city hummed with its usual evening energy, while a thoughtful silence settled between the couple.

Jonathan glanced up from his meal to study his wife's face. Sherry seemed preoccupied, her fork pushing a piece of grilled chicken around her plate without ever lifting it to her mouth.

"Everything okay?" Jonathan asked, breaking the silence.

Sherry looked up, as if suddenly remembering where she was. "Oh, yes. Sorry, I was just thinking."

"About?"

Sherry set down her fork and met Jonathan's gaze. "Our cases are showing a trend. There was another report today about the crime rate in the city. It's gone up another 15% since last year."

Jonathan nodded slowly. This wasn't a new topic of conversation, but something in Sherry's tone suggested she had more on her mind than just sharing statistics.

"I know we've talked about this before," Sherry continued, "but I think it might be time to seriously consider moving."

The words hung in the air between them. They had indeed discussed the possibility of leaving New York before, but it had always been in abstract terms, a 'someday' kind of conversation.

"You really think it's come to that?" Jonathan asked, setting down his own utensils.

Sherry nodded, her expression a mix of determination and apprehension.

"I do. It's not just the crime rate, Jonathan. It's the overall quality of life. The constant noise, the crowding, the stress. Don't get me wrong, I love the energy of New York, but..."

"But it's wearing on you," Jonathan finished for her.

He understood. While his work at the university still energized him, he too had felt the weight of city life growing heavier over the years.

"Where were you thinking?" he asked, though he had a feeling he knew the answer.

"Well," Sherry began, "We could consider Oklahoma City. It's where I grew up, and my dad is still there. The cost of living is lower, and the pace of life is... calmer."

Jonathan nodded, considering. Oklahoma City was a far cry from the bustling metropolis they'd called home for so long. He thought about the observatory at Columbia, the cutting-edge research he was involved in, the graduate students he mentored.

"What about my work?" he asked softly.

Sherry reached across the table, taking his hand. "I've considered that too. The University of Oklahoma has a respected astrophysics department. It's not Columbia, I know, but it could be an opportunity for a fresh start, maybe even to lead your own research team."

Jonathan squeezed her hand, appreciating the thought she'd clearly put into this.

"It's definitely worth considering," he said. Then, after a moment's hesitation, he added, "What about Augusta? It's where I grew up, and the University of Kentucky isn't far. They have a solid physics department."

A small smile played on Sherry's lips. "I knew you might suggest that. I did some research on Augusta too. It could be a good option."

They fell into a comfortable silence, both lost in thought. Jonathan's mind wandered to the small town where he'd first fallen in love with the stars. He pondered about the quieter pace of life, the clear night skies unobstructed by skyscrapers and light pollution. There was an appeal there, a chance to reconnect with what had first inspired his cosmic journey.

As they continued their meal, they discussed the pros and cons of each location. Oklahoma City offered familiarity for Sherry and the support of her family. Augusta promised a return to Jonathan's roots and perhaps a purer connection to the night sky that had first captured his imagination.

"We don't have to decide tonight," Sherry said. "But I think we should start seriously looking into our options."

Jonathan nodded, then paused, a thought occurred to him. "You know, before we make any big decisions, maybe we should take some time off. Get away for a while, clear our heads."

Sherry looked up from the dishes she was rinsing, a spark of interest in her eyes. "A vacation? That does sound nice. Where were you thinking?"

"Somewhere far away," Jonathan mused, drying a plate. "Somewhere completely different from New York. Maybe... I don't know, Bali? Or New Zealand?"

A small smile played on Sherry's lips. "New Zealand could be interesting. You could show me the southern constellations you're always talking about."

Jonathan grinned, warming to the idea. "Exactly! And we could visit Aoraki Mackenzie International Dark Sky Reserve. It's supposed to be one of the best places in the world for stargazing."

"Of course you'd know that," Sherry teased, but her tone was affectionate. "It does sound wonderful. A chance to relax, recharge, and maybe gain some perspective on this whole moving situation."

They continued discussing potential vacation ideas as they finished cleaning up, the tension from earlier in the evening gradually easing. The prospect of a trip, of escaping the pressures of the city even temporarily, seemed to lighten both their moods.

As Jonathan wiped down the counter, he found himself saying, "You know, it's been a while since we've taken a big trip together. Not since..."

He trailed off, suddenly realizing what he was about to say. Sherry had stilled beside him, her hand pausing on the dish she was putting away.

Neither had mentioned the trip to Jerusalem in five years. That journey, once so pivotal, had faded into an unspoken memory. Its aftereffects had rippled through their lives in subtle ways, changing their perspectives and priorities in ways they were only now beginning to fully understand.

The silence stretched, filled with the echoes of their time in Jerusalem. Jonathan remembered vividly the day they had visited the Western Wall. Sherry had been moved to tears, pressing her forehead against the ancient stones in prayer. He had stood back, observing with the detached curiosity of a scientist, feeling a disconnect he couldn't quite bridge.

"Sherry," he began hesitantly, "I never told you this, but... I didn't feel Jerusalem the way you did."

Sherry's eyes widened slightly, a mix of surprise and curiosity crossing her face. "What do you mean?" she asked, her voice soft but intent. "How can you not have felt it?"

Their discussion had turned into a heated debate.

"I felt the history," he replied, struggling to find the right words. "But spiritual energy? There's no scientific basis for that. It's just... emotion and belief."

Seeing the hurt in Sherry's eyes, Jonathan feared he'd damaged something irreparable between them.

But then there was the night in the Judean Desert. Away from the city lights, the stars had been breathtaking. Jonathan had set up his portable telescope, eager to show Sherry the wonders of the night sky from this unique vantage point.

Jonathan ran a hand through his hair, searching for the right words. "When we were there, at all those holy sites, I saw how moved you were. The Western Wall, the Church of the Holy Sepulchre... you seemed to be experiencing something profound. But for me..." he paused, then continued, "I felt like an observer. I appreciated the history, the architecture, but that spiritual connection you described? I just didn't feel it."

He watched Sherry carefully, half-expecting to see hurt or disappointment in her eyes. Instead, he saw a spark of interest, an intensity he hadn't anticipated.

"Why didn't you tell me this before?" Sherry asked, leaning forward slightly.

Jonathan shrugged, a bit uncomfortable. "I didn't want to diminish your experience. It clearly meant so much to you, and I... I guess I felt like admitting this would somehow let you down."

Sherry was quiet for a moment, processing his words. Then, to Jonathan's surprise, a small smile played on her lips. "You know, I always suspected you might have felt that way. But hearing you say it now... it actually makes me appreciate our trip even more."

"It does?" Jonathan asked, puzzled.

Jonathan had been about to launch into further explanation, but something in Sherry's expression had stopped him. He was rambling now, grasping at facts and trivia to fill the void, to soften the impact of his admission.

"And the view from the Mount of Olives at sunset, remember that? The way the light hit the Dome of the Rock... it was like something out of a painting. I might not have felt the spiritual connection, but I could certainly appreciate the aesthetics."

Jonathan's words tumbled out, each sentence an attempt to build a bridge across the chasm he feared he'd just opened between them. He talked about the food they'd tried, the markets they'd visited, anything to keep the conversation going, to prevent the silence from settling back in.*

Finally, he ran out of steam, his litany of memories and facts trailing off into another uncomfortable pause. He looked at Sherry, his eyes pleading for some kind of response, any kind of reaction to break this unbearable silence.

"Sherry?" he said softly, his voice barely above a whisper. "Please say something."

"I won't lie, there's a part of me that's a little sad you didn't share my experience in Jerusalem," Sherry admitted. "What if we planned a trip to somewhere that speaks to your scientific side? Somewhere you might feel that deep connection?"

"You know," he said softly, breaking the silence, "I think Jerusalem taught us how to disagree productively."

Jonathan nodded. "Your faith challenges my rigid scientific thinking sometimes, makes me consider perspectives I might otherwise dismiss. And I like to think my skepticism helps you question and ultimately strengthen your beliefs."

"It did?" Sherry asked, the look of worry in her eyes.

"Maybe," Sherry said hesitantly, "maybe we need something like that again. Not nccessarily Jerusalem, but..."

"Something transformative," Jonathan finished for her. "Something that challenges us, makes us grow. Together."

Sherry nodded, her eyes bright with anticipation. "Exactly. Whether it's New Zealand or somewhere else, maybe this could be an opportunity for us to reconnect - with each other and with what's really important to us."

As they stood there, the New York skyline glittering beyond their windows, Jonathan felt a sense of anticipation he hadn't experienced in years. Jonathan was staring out the window at the few stars visible through the city's light pollution.

That night had been a turning point. They had talked until dawn, not trying to convince each other, but truly listening, truly trying to understand. They had realized that their differences weren't weaknesses, but rather complementary strengths. Sherry's faith gave her a sense of purpose and connection that Jonathan admired, while his scientific rigor and quest for knowledge inspired her.

Jonathan's fingers drummed nervously on the steering wheel as he inched through the morning traffic. The radio droned on, a grim backdrop to the sea of brake lights ahead.

"...in the wake of the rising crime rate New York City officials have announced increased security measures. Citizens are advised to allow extra time for--"

He switched it off with a frustrated jab. He was going to be late. Again.

The day had unfolded in a series of tense moments and unexpected challenges. At Columbia, Jonathan found himself mediating a heated argument between students in his afternoon seminar.

What had started as a discussion on historical parallels to the current crisis had quickly devolved into a shouting match about government overreach and public safety.

"Alright, alright," Jonathan called out, raising his hands for quiet. "Let's take a step back here. Remember, in times like these, it's more important than ever to listen to each other. To really hear different perspectives."

As the students settled, a hesitant hand rose from the back of the room. "Dr. Avery," a young woman asked, her voice quivering slightly, "do you think... do you think things will ever go back to normal?"

Jonathan paused, weighing his words carefully. "I think," he said slowly, "that we're living through a transformative moment in history. What comes next might not look like the 'normal' we're used to. But that doesn't mean it can't be something we work together to shape."

The room fell silent, each person lost in their own feelings about an uncertain future.

Across town, Sherry was facing her own set of challenges. The courthouse was a madhouse, packed with a backlog of cases and frayed nerves. As she argued a motion before a visibly exhausted judge, a commotion erupted in the hallway outside.

The judge's gavel came down hard. "This court is in recess until order is restored," he announced, as bailiffs rushed to investigate the disturbance.

Sherry gathered her papers quickly, her heart racing. Through the open door, she could hear angry voices and what sounded like a scuffle. She debated whether to stay put or try to make it back to her office.

Before she could decide, a familiar face appeared in the doorway. It was Mark, one of the firm's junior associates, his usually immaculate suit disheveled and his eyes wide

"Sherry," he panted, "you need to see this. They're saying there's been another attack."

As evening fell, Jonathan and Sherry once again found themselves in their house, this time huddled around Sherry's laptop. The images on the screen were chaotic: smoke rising from a building in midtown, crowds of people running, police lights flashing.

"...while authorities have not yet confirmed the nature of the explosion, sources close to the investigation suggest it may be linked to the ongoing unrest following the UN President's assassination," the news anchor was saying, her voice steady despite the gravity of her words.

Jonathan ran a hand through his hair, his face pale. "This is getting out of control," he murmured.

Sherry nodded, her legal mind already racing. "If this is connected, we're looking at a coordinated attack on a scale we haven't seen before. The implications for national security, for international relations..."

She trailed off as her phone buzzed with an incoming call. It was the senior partner. Sherry answered, listening intently for a moment before her eyes widened.

"You're sure?" she asked, her voice tight. "Yes, of course. I'll be right there."

As she hung up, Jonathan was already reaching for his coat. "What is it?" he asked.

Sherry took a deep breath, her world shifting once again. "That was David. The firm... we've been asked to take on a high-profile case."

Jonathan stared at her, the implications sinking in.

Sherry nodded, her mind racing with possibilities and dangers. "Yeah," she said softly. "I think this is going to be a long one."

The sirens outside seemed to grow louder, a constant reminder of the tenuous thread by which normality now hung.

Hours later, after Jonathan and Sherry reunited in their house, they moved around each other, a well-rehearsed dance of exhaustion.

"There's a neighborhood watch meeting tomorrow night," Jonathan said, breaking the silence. "Maybe we should go."

Sherry paused, a fork of reheated pasta halfway to her mouth. "I don't know, Jon. I've got depositions until 8, and I really need to prepare for court on Friday."

"I know, I know. It's just... don't you think we should be doing something? Anything?"

The weariness in his voice made Sherry set down her fork. She reached across the table, taking his hand.

"We are doing something. Every day. You're educating the next generation, I'm fighting to uphold the law. That matters."

Jonathan squeezed her hand, managing a small smile. "You're right. Of course, you're right. It's just... everything feels so uncertain."

As if on cue, a siren wailed in the distance. They both tensed, eyes darting to the window.

"Another one," Sherry murmured.

Their moment of connection was suddenly interrupted by the wail of sirens. Another police car sped by their house, its lights painting the kitchen walls in flashes of red and blue. Hot on its heels came the deeper rumble of a fire truck, its siren adding to the cacophony.

Jonathan and Sherry rushed to the window, their previous conversation momentarily forgotten. They watched as the emergency vehicles disappeared around a corner, leaving behind an unsettling quiet.

"That's the second time tonight," Sherry murmured, her brow furrowed with concern.

Jonathan nodded grimly. "Yeah, and what, the fifth time this week? I wonder what's happening now."

Sherry pulled out her phone, quickly scrolling through local news alerts. "Nothing specific yet, but there's been an uptick in reports of break-ins in the area.

And that fire last week in the apartment building on 86th street? They're saying it might have been arson."

Jonathan ran a hand through his hair, a gesture of frustration. "This neighborhood used to be so quiet. Remember when we first moved in? We barely heard a siren once a month."

"I know," Sherry sighed, moving away from the window. "It's changing so fast. Mrs. Goldstein from 4B told me she doesn't feel safe going to the corner store after dark anymore."

"So," Jonathan said, a smile spreading across his face, "where should we go? CERN in Switzerland? Mauna Kea Observatory in Hawaii?"

Sherry laughed, the sound full of warmth and anticipation. "Why not both?"

The hours slipped by unnoticed as they pored over websites, comparing crime statistics, job markets, and quality of life indices for various cities. They even considered completely new options – cities they'd never visited but that promised a fresh start.

As the darkness began to creep through their windows, Jonathan and Sherry finally closed their laptops, their minds swimming with information and possibilities.

"We don't have to decide everything tonight," Sherry said, stifling a yawn.

Jonathan nodded, stretching in his chair. "You're right. But I think we've made a good start."

They stood up, both feeling the weight of a sleepless night but also a sense of excitement about the future. As they moved towards their bedroom, another siren wailed in the distance – a final reminder of why they'd begun this conversation in the first place.

Chapter Seven: Awakening of Defiance

The morning arrived with an unwelcome jolt. Jonathan's hand slammed down on the alarm clock, silencing its insistent beeping. Beside him, Sherry stirred, her eyes flickering open reluctantly.

"What time is it?" she mumbled, reaching for her phone.

Jonathan squinted at the clock. "6:30. We should probably get moving if we want to beat the checkpoint lines."

As they went through their morning routine, the TV hummed softly in the background, a constant stream of updates and warnings. Jonathan paused as he poured his coffee, his attention caught by a familiar face on the screen.

"Sher," he called out. "Come look at this!"

Sherry emerged from the bathroom, toothbrush in hand, to see an intense debate unfolding on the morning news. One of the professors from the college was gesticulating wildly as he argued with a stern-faced government official.

"...cannot simply suspend civil liberties in the name of security!" The man was saying, his voice tight with barely contained fury. "The very foundations of our democracy--"

The official cut him off. "In times of crisis, extraordinary measures--"

Jonathan switched off the TV, a knot forming in his stomach. "This isn't going to go over well on campus," he muttered.

Sherry nodded, her expression grim. "Be careful today, okay? Things are getting heated out there."

They shared a quick kiss before heading out, the weight of the world seeming to press down on their shoulders as they stepped into the bustling, anxious energy of the city.

The early morning fog hovered just above the treetops, obscuring the horizon as if the sky had kissed the Earth and decided to linger. Jonathan Avery's breath condensed in the cold air as he stepped out of his house, the dampness seeping into his bones. He had a peculiar feeling, as if the world was humming a tune only he could hear.

"*Damn*," he murmured, buttoning his tweed jacket, the smell of the musty fabric bringing a hint of comfort. "*It's going to be one of those days*."

Jonathan gripped the steering wheel of his Volvo, the leather worn smooth from years of use. The car's engine rumbled to life, a comforting sound that echoed to the steady beat of his heart. The headlights pierced the thick fog, casting two yellow cones of light that danced over the wet, cracked asphalt. Each revolution of the tires sent a fine spray of mist into the air, leaving a temporary trail behind him as he drove.

Fumbling with the radio dial, the latest song came to life, but the static was a reminder of the isolation the fog brought. When the song ended the voice crackled. So only a few words got through. And. Joe. Now. President. Today.

Jonathan's eyes shot to the radio, his hand over the dial as he frantically searched for a clearer frequency.

"...UN vice president steps in after the assassination of the UN's President earlier this morning. The news has left the nation in shock and mourning. The tragic event occurred during a public appearance in Iraq. Details are still emerging, but sources confirm the assailant has been taken into custody. The nation is on high alert as the implications of this heinous act unfold. More information to come as the story develops..."

Jonathan's heart hammered in his chest as the words sank in. The fog outside the car suddenly felt denser, suffocating. The usually bustling streets were eerily quiet, as if mourning the loss of a universal truth.

The wipers swiped back and forth in a hypnotic rhythm, a metronome keeping time with his thoughts as they raced from the peculiar feeling of the morning.

At the traffic light, he picked up his cell phone and noticed a text message from Sherry. A slight grin came to his lips as he read the words.

Jonathan's eyes flicked to his phone, the screen illuminating the foggy interior of the car. Sherry's message glowed back at him:

"You got this. You are the best one on your team."

Sherry's unwavering support warmed him, even as the gravity of the situation pressed down on his shoulders.

For a brief moment, Jonathan considered texting her back. His thumb hovered over the reply button, ready to type out a response, but he hesitated, then let his hand fall away from the phone. He knew Sherry was buried in her own crucial work at the law office, tackling the rising tide of cases that came with the increasing crime rate. She had her own battles to fight, her own responsibilities weighing heavily on her.

"She's probably busy," Jonathan murmured to himself, his voice barely audible over the rhythmic swish of the windshield wipers.

He tucked the phone away, his mind racing with the possible legal issues involved with the assassination of the UN President throwing everything into chaos.

As he navigated through the fog-shrouded streets, Jonathan knew that his skills—the very ones Sherry had just praised—would be put to the ultimate test. Whatever lay ahead, he was certain of one thing: nothing would be the same after today.

The traffic light ahead turned green, barely visible through the mist. Jonathan eased the car forward. The fog grew denser as he approached the Columbia campus, he could see the new security checkpoint looming ahead. A line of cars snaked around the block, each driver submitting to scrutiny before being allowed into university grounds. Jonathan's mind wandered to the astrology club meeting scheduled for later that day.

As Jonathan pulled into the faculty parking lot, the usual bustle of university life was noticeably subdued. The fog seemed to have followed him, hanging low over the campus grounds and muffling the few sounds that broke the eerie silence.

He stepped out of his car, briefcase in hand, and made his way towards the main building. The weight of the morning's news pressed down on him, made heavier by the somber atmosphere that enveloped the campus.

Students moved slowly along the pathways, their faces drawn and conversations hushed. Many clutched their phones, undoubtedly refreshing news feeds for the latest updates. The grief of a shared sorrow that transcended borders for a leader who, despite being from another country, had clearly touched many lives.

As Jonathan approached the entrance, he overheard snippets of conversation:

"I can't believe it happened..."

"He was changing things..."

"What's going to happen now?"

The shock and uncertainty in their voices mirrored his own. Yet, as an educator Jonathan knew he had a responsibility to maintain a sense of stability for his students.

Entering the building, he noticed small groups of faculty members huddled together, their discussions intense but quiet. A few colleagues nodded in his direction, their expressions a mix of disbelief and concern.

Jonathan made his way through the misty corridors to the astronomy department. As he reached for the door handle, he paused, taking a deep breath. Whatever lay on the other side of that door - be it a room full of distraught students or an empty classroom - he knew that today's lesson would be unlike any other he had taught before.

With a sense of resolve, Jonathan opened the door, ready to face whatever challenges this unprecedented day might bring.

The moment he entered the classroom, an unexpected hush fell over the room. The students were seated with rapt attention, their eyes fixed on him. He had prepared a lecture on the recent discoveries in exoplanetology, eager to share the latest revelations about the potential for life beyond Earth. But today, something felt different. The universe was whispering to him, hinting at secrets that lay just beyond his grasp.

He set his bag down and pulled out his notebook, his hand shaking slightly. The pages were filled with his meticulous notes, each line a testament to his unyielding dedication. Yet, as he gazed upon the faces before him, he knew that although the UN President's death was important, he still had a class to teach. He looked up, his eyes scanning the room.

"Today, class," he began, his voice steady and filled with passion, "we're not just going to talk about exoplanets. We're going to embark on a journey, together, into the mysterious expanse that is our universe."

The students leaned in, their curiosity piqued. They could feel the shift in the room, a tangible energy that seemed to pulse with each word he spoke.

"We're going to explore the possibility of life beyond our solar system, and in doing so, we're going to challenge ourselves to think beyond what we know," he continued, his voice growing stronger. "We're going to confront the unknown, the uncharted territories of our cosmic neighborhood, and we're going to do it with open minds."

As the students searched their text, he could hear the chatter about the morning news.

The hand of a young student shot up in the air, breaking the silence.

"Is it true, Dr. Avery?" The voice was tentative, hopeful. "What we're hearing about the UN President?"

Jonathan took a deep breath and nodded solemnly.

"Yes, it's true," he confirmed. “The vice president has already taken office. They should be alright.”

The room was still, the only sound the occasional drop of condensation falling from the windows. He paused, allowing the gravity of the moment to sink in before he spoke again.

"Now, let’s please get back to the lesson. Turn your gaze to the stars and see what secrets they hold for us today."

With that, he flipped open his notebook and began to write on the board, the chalk scraping against the surface like the call of a distant planet yearning to be heard. The class watched, eager to learn, to escape, if only for a brief moment, into the infinite.

The chalk dust floated in the beam of light from the single window, a silent reminder of the tumultuous world outside, and the boundless universe they sought to understand.

For the remainder of the hour, the lecture hall was silent, the only sound was the occasional rustle of pages turning.

As the class drew to a close, the room remained still. The students sat, absorbing the magnitude of what they had just been told. Jonathan could see the confusion in their eyes.

He knew that the news touched something within them, something primal and profound.

As the students filed out, their heads lowered in somber silence.

Jonathan took a moment to reflect before he gathered his belongings and stepped into the corridor, the sound of his footsteps echoing off the walls. The universe was vast and mysterious, but in that moment, it felt just a little bit smaller, a little bit more knowable. And as he walked towards his 3:00 meeting. The day was dragging on, each second feeling like an eternity.

His thoughts drifted to the first time he met with the astrology club. The memory was as vivid as the stars he studied—the nervous excitement of a young man stepping into a new world of knowledge and camaraderie.

The door to the conference room was open, and he stepped inside, his heart racing with anticipation. The room was a hodgepodge of star charts, telescopes, and textbooks, each item speaking to a shared yearning to understand the cosmos.

His eyes scanned the sea of familiar faces already there, huddled around a large table, their eyes glued to a laptop screen that displayed a series of complex equations.

The room grew quiet as he approached, the weight of their collective gaze heavy upon him.

"Did you hear about the UN President?" one of the students asked, her voice barely a whisper.

Jonathan nodded solemnly. "It's a tragic loss," he said.

The group nodded in unison, a shared acknowledgment of the gravity of the situation.

Then, almost as if on cue, the discussion shifted. They began to talk about their latest project, their voices growing in excitement.

He cleared his throat, ready to dive into their world of stars and equations.

But as he opened his mouth to speak, his phone buzzed with an incoming message from Sherry.

"Are you okay?" it read.

He took a deep breath and typed back, "I'm here. I'm okay. I'll come straight home after work."

It was a few minutes before she responded. "And Jon, be safe. It's been crazy out there today."

With a promise to be cautious, he returned to his duties. But the weight of the day's events lingered, pressing down on him like gravity from an invisible black hole.

The group's chatter of ideas and hypotheses grew around him. They were discussing a recent breakthrough in their research on binary star systems, a topic that had been the focus of his scholarly passion for years.

With a renewed sense of purpose, he sat down at the table and joined the fray, eager to contribute to the quest for truth that had brought them all together.

Jonathan listened intently, his mind racing with thoughts of the universe and its infinite mysteries. He knew that in the grand scheme of things, their research was but a drop in the cosmic ocean, but it was their drop, their contribution to the tapestry of human understanding.

And as they spoke, he realized that the death of the UN President was not just a political event but a human one, a reminder of the fragility of existence, even amidst the cosmos.

Their conversation grew more fervent, the fog outside forgotten. Ideas were thrown around the room, each one more intriguing than the last.

He watched as the students debated and collaborated, their passion for knowledge a beacon in the murky haze of the world's troubles.

By the time he pulled away from the University, the fog outside had lifted, revealing a crisp, clear sky.

Jonathan glanced at his watch and sighed.

By the time he arrived home, the world seemed to hold its breath as the news of the UN President's assassination spread like wildfire, dominating every headline, every conversation, every thought. It was as if the globe itself had stumbled, unsure of its next rotation.

The usual cacophony of New York traffic seemed muted, as if the city itself was in shock. He paused at the door, taking a deep breath before entering, unsure of what atmosphere he'd find inside.

The sound of furious typing greeted him as he stepped into the house. Sherry sat at the kitchen table, her laptop open, papers strewn around her, a half-empty cup of coffee forgotten at her elbow. She barely looked up as Jonathan entered, her fingers flying over the keyboard with intense focus.

"Hey," Jonathan said softly, not wanting to startle her.

Sherry glanced up, offering a tight smile before returning to her work.

Sherry sighed, finally pausing in her typing. "You have no idea. The assassination... it's causing ripples through every aspect of international law. We're scrambling to understand the implications, to advise our clients on how this might affect their global operations."

Jonathan brought his warmed dinner to the table, sitting across from Sherry. "I can imagine. The university was in an uproar too. Classes were practically useless today – everyone was too distracted, trying to get updates on their phones."

They sat in silence for a moment, the gravity of the day's events hanging heavy between them.

"Have they released any more information about the assassin?" Jonathan asked.

Sherry shook her head. "Nothing concrete. There are rumors, theories, but nothing official yet. The uncertainty is just making everything more chaotic."

Jonathan watched as Sherry's eyes drifted back to her laptop screen, her fingers twitching as if eager to return to work. He recognized the look – it was the same one he got when deep in a research problem. But he also saw the exhaustion lurking behind her professional facade.

"Sherry," he said gently, "maybe it's time for a break?"

She looked up, ready to protest, but Jonathan continued before she could speak.

"I know this is important, and I know you have responsibilities. But you've been at this all day. Taking a short break will help you come back to it with fresh eyes."

Sherry hesitated, glancing between Jonathan and her laptop. "I don't know, Jonathan. There's still so much to do..."

"Just thirty minutes," Jonathan pressed. "That's all I'm asking. Let's watch somcthing mindless on TV, get your mind off work for a bit. The world will still be here in half an hour."

For a moment, Jonathan was sure that she might refuse. But then Sherry's shoulders sagged, and she nodded. "Okay. Thirty minutes."

Relief washed over Jonathan as Sherry closed her laptop. He stood, offering his hand to help her up from the table.

"Come on, I think there's a game show marathon on channel 7. Nothing like watching other people make fools of themselves to take your mind off a global crisis."

Sherry let out a small laugh – the first Jonathan had heard from her all evening. "That sounds perfect, actually."

They settled onto the couch, Jonathan's arm around Sherry's shoulders as she curled into his side. As the colorful game show set filled the screen and the over-enthusiastic host began introducing contestants, Jonathan felt Sherry gradually relax against him.

For the next thirty minutes, they lost themselves in the mundane spectacle of everyday people spinning wheels, solving puzzles, and celebrating small victories. They laughed at bad guesses, groaned at missed opportunities, and playfully argued over what they would do if they were contestants.

The sirens faded, replaced by the inane chatter of reality TV contestants. Jonathan and Sherry held each other close, stealing a moment of peace in a city on edge.

As the show's credits began to roll, Sherry lifted her head from Jonathan's shoulder. "Thank you," she said softly. "I needed that more than I realized."

Jonathan placed a gentle kiss on her forehead. "Anytime. That's what I'm here for."

Sherry sat up, stretching. "I should get back to work. But... maybe we could do this again later? Watch another episode before bed?"

"It's a date," Jonathan smiled.

As Sherry returned to her laptop and Jonathan began clearing the dinner dishes.

As they prepared for bed, the world outside their house continued to grapple with the day's shocking events. But in their small corner of New York, Jonathan and Sherry had found a balance – acknowledging the gravity of the situation while also cherishing the quiet moments of connection that sustained them.

Chapter Eight: Symmetry of Suspicion

A picture flashed on the TV of the UN headquarters. Scrolling across the bottom were the words 'In accordance with the established regional rotation, the President of this session of the General Assembly has been elected.'

"Breaking News," the anchor announced, "We are live now with the new UN President, Mr. Lucien Bennett. His presidency comes at a tumultuous time, but we are assured he has a plan to bring peace and stability back to our world."

The camera panned to a man standing behind a podium. There was an almost hypnotic quality to Bennett's presence on the screen. He exuded confidence and charisma, yet something about him - perhaps the too-perfect symmetry of his features or the utterly smooth texture of his skin - niggled at the edge of Jonathan's perception, feeding into his growing sense of unease.

Jonathan leaned in closer to the TV, trying to pinpoint what exactly felt off about the new UN President. As Lucien Bennett began to speak, his voice smooth and reassuring, Jonathan noticed a slight delay between the movement of his lips and the words coming out. It was barely perceptible, but once he saw it, he couldn't unsee it.

Bennett was a striking figure, perhaps in his early fifties, with smooth dark skin that seemed to glow under the studio lights. His closely cropped hair was mostly black, with distinguished streaks of silver at the temples.

Bennett's face was a study in contrasts. His features were strong and defined - a square jaw, high cheekbones, and a broad nose - yet there was a softness to his expression that put one instantly at ease. His eyes, a deep brown so dark they almost appeared black, sparkled with intelligence and warmth.

When he smiled, which he did often during the interview, deep dimples appeared in his cheeks, lending him a boyish charm that belied his powerful position. His teeth were perfectly straight and white, almost too perfect.

He wore a crisp, tailored charcoal suit that fit him impeccably, with a deep blue tie that brought out the richness of his skin tone. A small pin of the UN logo adorned his lapel, catching the light occasionally as he moved.

"We stand at a crossroads," Bennett was saying, his dark eyes fixed on the camera. "The challenges we face are unprecedented, but so too are our opportunities for unity and progress."

"You seeing this?" Jonathan called out to his wife, who was curled up on the other end of the couch, wrapped in a blanket and engrossed in her book.

"Hmm?" Sherry murmured, not looking up from the page. "Seeing what?"

Jonathan turned to her, his face pale. "I think... I think the new UN President might be that prophet we saw in Jerusalem.

Sherry looked up from her book, noticing the man on the TV in front of her.

"I am honored to accept this position and I will not let the memory of our fallen president be forgotten." Bennett said, "We will find peace, even if we must reach for the stars to find it."

"That can't be right," she muttered, watching the footage. "I... I believed he was really a prophet," she finally managed, her voice barely above a whisper. Sherry's eyes glistened with unshed tears.

"All this time? These past five years?"

"Until now. God, Jon, I'm so sorry."

With trembling fingers, she pulled up a file on her laptop, the one containing pictures from their Jerusalem trip five years ago. She scrolled quickly, her heart pounding, until she found what she was looking for.

There he was. The UN's new president was the prophet they had seen in Jerusalem.

"Lucien Bennett," Sherry said, letting her head drop, her face a mask of regret and shame.

The reporter had a rare smile on his face in the midst of so much turmoil. "Indeed, it seems Mr. Bennett is a man of his word, bringing change to the very corners of the world he promised to uplift."

But as Jonathan watched, he felt that same chill that had gripped him the first time he saw him in the marketplace.

The reporter ended the segment with a public invitation to see him speak. “And he’s here, at the UN embassy in New York.”

Sherry’s hand on his shoulder startled him out of his reverie, concern was etched on her face. “We have to go, Jon.”

The morning of the swearing-in ceremony dawned bright and clear, a stark contrast to the turbulent emotions swirling within Jonathan and Sherry.

They dressed in their finest clothes, a sense of occasion in the air. The streets were already filled with people.

They made their way to the square where Bennett would speak again. The crowd was even larger than before, a kaleidoscope of faces from all over the world.

The newly renovated General Assembly Hall gleamed in the sunlight, its sleek design a symbol of the reformed global order.

Security was tight, with a mix of human guards and advanced AI systems scanning every entrant. Jonathan and Sherry passed through,

Inside, the hall was a hive of activity. Delegates from every nation mingled, their conversations a babel of languages. Holographic displays showcased the achievements of the past five years: rebuilt cities, new clean energy initiatives, global cooperation indexes at all-time highs.

It all seemed so perfect, so hopeful. And yet, Jonathan thought, it was all built on a lie.

As they took their seats, Jonathan leaned close to Sherry, whispering, "Remember, we're here to observe. No matter what happens, we can't tip our hand."

Sherry nodded, her face a mask of professional composure. "Agreed. But Jon, if we see an opportunity..."

"We'll cross that bridge when we come to it," he finished.

The current Secretary-General, a tall, distinguished woman with silver hair and a commanding presence, stepped up to the podium. Her voice rang out clear and strong, filling the hall with an air of solemnity and purpose.

"Distinguished delegates, honored guests, citizens of the world. We gather here today to witness a historic moment. The swearing-in of our new United Nations President, a position that will lead us into a new era of global cooperation and peace."

Jonathan's eyes scanned the crowd, noting the positions of security personnel, the locations of exits. Beside him, he could feel Sherry doing the same.

"And now," the Secretary-General continued, "it is my great honor to introduce the man you have chosen to lead us forward. A visionary who guided us through our darkest hours, a beacon of hope in troubled times. Please welcome, President-elect Lucien Bennett."

The hall erupted in applause as Bennett strode to the podium. He moved with the confidence of someone who knew he held the world in the palm of his hand.

As the Secretary-General's words echoed through the hall, Jonathan and Sherry tensed imperceptibly in their seats. The moment they had been anticipating and dreading in equal measure had finally arrived.

When he spoke, his voice was warm, captivating. Bennett's hands, when they came into view, were large and well-manicured, moving with graceful precision as he emphasized his points. His gestures were smooth and practiced, each movement seemingly calculated for maximum effect.

"My fellow citizens," he began, "we stand at the dawn of a new age. An age where the artificial boundaries of nation-states fade away, where humanity comes together as one family."

As Bennett continued his speech, weaving a vision of a unified, peaceful world, Jonathan felt a chill run down his spine. The man's words were honey-sweet poison, and the assembled delegates were drinking it in.

It all seemed so perfect, so hopeful. And yet, Jonathan was sure it was all built on a lie.

Bennett's voice cut through Jonathan's thoughts. "And so, my friends, let us pledge ourselves anew to the great experiment of global governance. For in unity, we find strength. In cooperation, we find hope."

The assembly rose as one in a standing ovation. In the commotion, Jonathan made a split-second decision. He grabbed Sherry's hand, and together they slipped away from their seats, making their way towards the exit.

As they reached the exit, Jonathan cast one last look over his shoulder. There, on the giant screens behind the podium, was Bennett's face, larger than life. And for just a moment, Jonathan could have sworn he saw the mask slip, revealing something cold and calculating beneath.

As Jonathan and Sherry hurried away from the UN building, their minds reeling from the events they had just witnessed, the cool evening air hit their faces. The streets of New York were unusually quiet, as if the whole world was holding its breath in anticipation of the new era Bennett had promised.

They were at the stairs to their house when their elderly neighbor, Mr. Finley, called out to them from his front stoop. "Jonathan, Sherry! You've got to see this!" His voice trembled with excitement, or was it fear?

Exchanging a quick glance, they approached Mr. Finley, who was pointing frantically at the sky. "Look up there, just above the horizon. Tell me you see it too!"

Jonathan followed Mr. Finley's gaze, and what he saw made his blood run cold. There, shimmering against the darkening sky, was a binary star system - two stars locked in an eternal dance around each other. But Jonathan knew, with absolute certainty, that it shouldn't be there.

"My God," he whispered, his academic mind racing. "That's Sirius B."

Sherry looked at him, confusion etched on her face. "What's Sirius B?"

"It's a white dwarf star that orbits Sirius A," Jonathan explained, his voice low and urgent. "But it shouldn't be visible to the naked eye, let alone this bright. And it certainly shouldn't be in this part of the sky."

Mr. Finley nodded vigorously. "It just appeared about an hour ago. Everyone's talking about it online. Some are saying it's a sign from God, others think it's aliens. What do you think?"

Jonathan's mind was whirling. The impossible star in the sky, Bennett's speech about a new age, the sense of wrongness that had been gnawing at him for weeks - it all seemed connected, yet he couldn't quite grasp how.

"I don't know, Mr. Finley," he said carefully. "But I intend to find out."

As they bid goodnight to their neighbor and hurried into their house, Sherry gripped Jonathan's arm. "Jon, what does this mean?"

Jonathan shook his head, his eyes still drawn to the window, to the impossible stars shining outside. "I'm not sure, Sher. But I have a feeling we're about to find out just how deep this rabbit hole goes."

He turned to her, his face set with determination. "Whatever's happening, I think Bennett is somehow involved."

Jonathan and Sherry stepped away from the window, each gravitating towards their own space to process the information and attend to their individual tasks.

Jonathan settled at his desk near the window, pulling out his laptop. He opened a document filled with notes on the stars, his fingers hovering over the keyboard as he considered how to incorporate this new development into his research. The soft glow of the screen illuminated his furrowed brow as he began to type, occasionally pausing to reference an astronomical chart or consult his handwritten observations

Across the room, Sherry curled up in an armchair, her legal pad balanced on her knees. She flipped through pages of notes, her pen tapping thoughtfully against her chin. Every so often, her gaze would drift to the TV, still playing softly in the background, before she'd shake her head slightly and return to her work, jotting down ideas for her article on the city's rich cultural heritage.

The room fell into a comfortable silence, broken only by a sudden increase in volume from the room's television caught their attention. Jonathan's hand froze midway to his coffee mug, his eyes fixed on the television screen. Sherry leaned forward, her legal briefs forgotten on her lap. They turned in unison, drawn by the urgent tone of the news anchor's voice.

The screen displayed a "Breaking News" banner, its bold red letters contrasting sharply with the concerned face of the anchor. Behind her, a split-screen showed the star system shining brightly.

"We interrupt our regular programming to bring you this breaking news," the anchor announced, her voice taut with tension. "Scientists are baffled by the sudden appearance of binary star systems in the skies above major cities worldwide. Some are calling it a divine sign, others a cosmic coincidence. But as we continue to search for answers, the world watches with bated breath."

Jonathan's mind raced, his astrophysicist's training kicking into high gear. "This is impossible," he muttered, reaching for his phone. "Binary stars don't just appear out of nowhere, especially not in Earth's atmosphere."

"Think of the international ramifications," Sherry said, her voice a mix of awe and concern. "Airspace violations, light pollution laws, religious freedom claims... this could rewrite every book on international law."

As Jonathan furiously typed out messages to his colleagues at the university, Sherry's phone began to buzz incessantly. Clients from around the world were clamoring for advice, unsure of how these cosmic visitors might affect their global operations.

"I need to get to the observatory," Jonathan said, "If these really are binary stars, they should be emitting specific wavelengths of light. We need to analyze them before they disappear... if they disappear."

Sherry nodded, her mind clearly elsewhere. "I'll head to the office first thing in the morning. We need to start drafting statements, preparing for every possible scenario." She paused, looking up at Jonathan with a mix of excitement and trepidation. "Do you think... could this be related to the star you saw in Jerusalem?"

Jonathan froze, his hand on the doorknob. The memory of their trip years ago, of the strange lights he'd witnessed in the night sky over the holy city, came flooding back.

"I don't know," he said honestly. "But I don’t think so."

The binary stars, visible even in the daytime, pulsed with a rhythm that seemed almost... deliberate.

The room grew quiet as the news reporter said, “The star was not just a local phenomenon. It was global, and it was growing stronger.”

Jonathan turned to Sherry, his eyes reflecting the eerie glow from the impossible stars outside their window.

"I need to get to the bottom of this," he said, his voice filled with a mix of excitement and trepidation. "After work tomorrow, I'm heading to the observatory."

Sherry agreed, understanding the gravity of the situation. "Of course. Do you want me to come with you?"

Jonathan shook his head. "No, I think it's better if you go about your day as usual. We don't want to raise any suspicions. Plus, your connections in the legal world might come in handy if things... escalate."

"Alright," Sherry said, her eyes betraying her concern. "But promise me you'll be careful, Jon. Between Bennett's speech and now this... something big is happening."

"I know," Jonathan said, pulling her into a tight embrace. "I'll be careful, I promisc. But I might be late getting home tomorrow."

"I'll call you if I find out anything significant," he assured Sherry. "And if you hear any chatter about this at work, especially anything related to Bennett or the UN, let me know immediately."

As they prepared for bed, both of them found sleep elusive. The stars outside their window seemed to pulse with an otherworldly energy, a constant reminder of the mystery that lay before them. Jonathan's mind raced with theories and questions, each more outlandish than the last.

Jonathan woke up early to pack up his gear. As he stepped out of the bathroom, Sherry was already up. “I have a morning lecture, then the observatory. Don’t forget I will be out late.”

"I've got a full day ahead." Sherry said, "I guess I am going to spend the morning at the law library, and I have a trial at 2.”

Jonathan nodded, smiling at her lack of enthusiasm. "Sounds like a perfect way to spend the day," he said, kissing her forehead. "Learn something new, find some time to relax."

“You bet.” Sherry said.

He watched as she bustled around the room. Her plans were definitely different to his own day, which was to be filled with data and analysis, but he knew she had to do this.

For a Monday morning, the lecture hall at Columbia University was buzzing with an energy Jonathan hadn't felt in years. His Advanced Astrophysics class, usually a sea of drowsy faces and muffled yawns, was alive with whispers and furtive glances at smartphones. Jonathan couldn't blame them; he'd been fighting the urge to check his own phone every few minutes, but his interest was time.

Despite his excitement, Jonathan knew he had a job to do. He cleared his throat, drawing the attention of his students. "Alright, everyone," he began, his voice carrying a hint of the enthusiasm he was trying to contain. "I know there's a lot going on, but let's focus on the fascinating world of quantum gravitational effects in neutron stars for the next hour, shall we?"

As he launched into his lecture, he turned to the whiteboard, marker in hand, ready to delve into the intricacies of gravitational wave detection. But before he could write a single equation, a hand shot up in the back of the room.

"Yes?" Jonathan said, recognizing one of his brightest students.

Lisa Chen stood, her eyes bright with excitement. "Dr. Avery, I'm sorry, but... how can we talk about anything else when there are impossible stars in our sky? Shouldn't we be discussing binary systems?"

A murmur of agreement rippled through the class. Jonathan sighed, capping his marker. He'd known this was coming, had been both dreading and anticipating it.

"You're right, Ms. Chen," he conceded. "These are extraordinary circumstances. What would you like to know?"

The floodgates opened. Questions poured in from every corner of the room.

"Are they really stars, or some kind of atmospheric phenomenon?" "Could it be a mass hallucination?" "Is it true that they're emitting signals? Like, intelligent signals?"

Jonathan held up his hands, calling for quiet. "One at a time, please. Let's approach this scientifically." He moved to the center of the room, adopting a more informal stance. "First, to address Ms. Chen's question: yes, these appear to be genuine binary star systems. The spectral analysis confirms they're emitting light consistent with known stellar types. The impossible part is their proximity and apparent size."

He paused, letting that sink in. "As for atmospheric phenomena or hallucinations, we can rule those out. These objects have been independently verified by observatories around the world. They're real, they're there, and they defy everything we know about stellar dynamics and physics."

A student in the front row, Tom Fisher, leaned forward. "But Dr.? How is that possible? Stars can't just appear in our atmosphere. The heat alone would…"

"You're absolutely right, Mr. Fisher," Jonathan interrupted. "By all known laws of physics, this shouldn't be possible. And yet, here we are."

He took a deep breath, weighing his next words carefully. "As for the signals... There have been reports of patterns in the stars' pulsations. It's too early to claim they're intelligent in nature, but they do seem to be non-random."

The class erupted in excited chatter. Jonathan let it continue for a moment, his mind racing. He wondered how Sherry was handling the legal firestorm this must be creating.

"Dr. Avery?" Lisa Chen's voice cut through his thoughts. "What do you think this means? For us, for science... for everything?"

Jonathan looked out at the sea of eager faces, seeing in them the same mix of fear and excitement he felt. "I think," he said slowly, "that we're on the brink of something monumental. Whether it's first contact with an alien civilization, a fundamental shift in our understanding of the universe, or something we can't even conceive of yet... one thing is certain: the world as we know it is changing."

He moved back to the whiteboard, uncapping his marker with a purpose. "And that's why what we do here, what we learn and discover, is more important than ever. We need to be prepared to understand, to analyze, to question. So, let's start with what we know about binary star systems, and then we'll examine how these new visitors violate those principles."

As Jonathan began to sketch out diagrams and equations, he felt a surge of excitement. The mystery above their heads was daunting, perhaps even dangerous, but it was also the kind of challenge he'd spent his whole life preparing for.

Whatever these stars were, whatever their purpose, Jonathan was determined to uncover the truth.

Jonathan looked out at the eager faces of his students, an idea forming in his mind.

"Alright," he said, clapping his hands together. "Let's approach this systematically. We have an impossible phenomenon. Our job is to figure out why it's impossible and then hypothesize how it might be possible."

He began writing on the board, his marker squeaking against the surface.

"Let's break this down. What do we know about these binary stars that contradicts our current understanding of astrophysics?"

Hands shot up across the room. Jonathan pointed to a student in the middle row.

"They're too close to Earth," the student said. "Stars that close should have catastrophic effects on our planet."

"Excellent," Jonathan nodded, writing it down. "What else?"

Lisa Chen spoke up next. "Their apparent size is all wrong. They appear as large as our moon, but to be that size and that close, they'd have to be impossibly small for stars."

Jonathan added this to the growing list. "Good observation. Keep going."

For the next few minutes, the class called out observations: the stars' stable position defying orbital mechanics, the lack of extreme heat and radiation, the impossibility of their sudden appearance.

Once the board was filled, Jonathan stepped back. "Now, let's think outside the box. If these aren't stars as we know them, what could they be?"

The room fell silent for a moment before Tom Fisher hesitantly raised his hand. "What if... what if they're not actually there?"

Jonathan raised an eyebrow. "Explain your thinking, Mr. Fisher."

"Well," Tom continued, gaining confidence, "what if they're some kind of projection or hologram? It could explain why they're not affecting us physically."

Murmurs of discussion broke out. Jonathan nodded encouragingly. "Interesting theory. What technology could create such a convincing illusion on a global scale?"

Another student chimed in. "Maybe it's not technology as we know it. Could it be some kind of mass psychic phenomenon?"

"Or a glitch in the simulation, if you believe in that sort of thing," someone else added, half-jokingly.

Jonathan wrote each theory on the board, no matter how outlandish. "Good, good. Keep them coming. In situations like this, no idea is too crazy to consider."

As the brainstorming continued, Jonathan noticed Lisa Chen frowning at her tablet. "Ms. Chen? You look like you have something to say."

Lisa looked up, her brow furrowed. "I've been looking at the data from different observatories around the world. The stars appear identical everywhere... too identical. Real stars, even binary pairs, should show slight differences based on the viewing angle and atmospheric conditions."

Jonathan felt a surge of excitement. "Excellent catch, Lisa. What might that suggest?"

"That they're not physical objects," Lisa said slowly, "or at least, not where we think they are. Could they be... I don't know, some kind of quantum phenomenon? A projection from another dimension?"

The class erupted in excited discussion. Jonathan let it continue for a moment, his mind racing. This was the kind of innovative thinking that could crack the mystery wide open.

"Alright, settle down," he finally called out. "Let's organize these theories and start designing tests for each one. Remember, in science, being able to disprove a hypothesis is just as important as proving one."

As the class broke into groups, each tackling a different theory, Jonathan felt a renewed sense of purpose. They might not solve the mystery today, but they were asking the right questions, approaching the impossible with open minds and scientific rigor.

As he moved between the groups, guiding discussions and challenging assumptions, Jonathan couldn't shake the feeling that they were on the brink of a discovery that would change everything. And somehow, he knew that understanding these stars was only the beginning.

The real question was: what would happen when they finally unraveled the mystery? And would the world be ready for the answer?

As he stepped out into the university courtyard he stumbled upon an unexpected scene. The quad, typically a bastion of scholarly tranquility, was now a stage for a student protest against the latest round of security hikes. His heart skipped a beat as he saw the passionate faces.

Although he empathized with their plight, Jonathan had always been a non-confrontational soul. Raising his voice in protest was as foreign to him as the alien worlds he studied. So he walked right by them without saying a word.

The drive to the observatory was surreal. The streets were unusually quiet, with only a few early risers out and about. Many of them were staring up at the sky, pointing and talking in hushed tones. The binary star system was still visible, a glaring anomaly in the brightening sky.

As Jonathan pulled into the observatory parking lot, he saw a flurry of activity. Scientists and researchers were rushing in and out of the building, their faces a mix of excitement and confusion. He spotted Dr. Eliza Wright at the entrance, barking orders into a phone.

"Eliza!" Jonathan called out as he approached.

Dr. Wright turned, her eyes widening in recognition. "Jonathan! Thank God you're here. We've been trying to make sense of this all night."

They hurried inside, Wright leading him to the main research area. The room was a chaos of activity, with screens displaying various data readouts and star charts.

"What have you found?" Jonathan asked, his eyes darting from screen to screen.

Wright ran a hand through her disheveled hair. "It's... impossible, Jonathan. By all our calculations, that binary system shouldn't exist. Not there, not anywhere near us. It's as if someone just... placed it in our sky."

Jonathan felt a chill run down his spine. "Could it be some kind of massive projection? A hologram, maybe?"

Wright shook her head. "We've ruled that out. Whatever this is, it's real. We're picking up genuine stellar radiation, gravitational effects, everything. It's as if a chunk of space hundreds of light-years away suddenly decided to relocate to our backyard."

As they pored over the data, a young researcher burst into the room, his face pale. "Dr. Wright! You need to see this."

He pulled up a new image on the main screen. It showed the binary star system, but now there was something else. A shape, sleek and unmistakably artificial, was moving between the two stars.

"Is that..." Jonathan began, hardly daring to believe what he was seeing.

"A ship," Wright finished, her voice barely above a whisper. "An alien ship."

The room fell silent as the implications sank in. Humanity was not alone, and their visitors had made one hell of an entrance.

As the room buzzed with excited and fearful chatter about the alien ship, Jonathan's eyes remained fixed on the main screen. Suddenly, without warning, the sleek artificial shape that had been moving between the binary stars simply... vanished.

"What the—" Dr. Wright exclaimed, rushing to the console. "Where did it go?"

The young researcher who had alerted them earlier frantically tapped at his keyboard, bringing up different views and readouts. "It's... it's gone, Dr. Wright. No trace on any of our instruments."

The disappearance of the ship was almost more unsettling than its appearance. It suggested a level of technology far beyond anything humanity possessed—the ability to simply vanish from all detection.

"Could it have been a glitch?" Jonathan asked, though he already suspected the answer.

Dr. Wright shook her head, her face pale. "No, the readings were consistent across multiple instruments. It was there, and now it's not. But the binary star system remains."

The implications were staggering. Not only were they dealing with the inexplicable appearance of a star system where none should be, but now they had evidence—however brief—of an advanced alien presence.

Jonathan's phone felt heavy in his pocket, the mysterious text message from 'S' now taking on an even more ominous significance. He glanced at his watch. Fifty minutes until the proposed meeting time.

"Eliza," Jonathan said, his voice low and urgent, "I need to step out for a bit. There's something I have to do. Can you keep me updated if anything changes here?"

Dr. Wright looked at him quizzically but nodded. "Of course, but where are you going? We're in the middle of potentially the biggest discovery in human history!"

Jonathan hesitated, weighing his words carefully. "I... I might have a lead on what's going on. I can't say more right now, but I promise I'll fill you in as soon as I can."

As he turned to leave, the room still abuzz with theories and speculations about the vanished ship, Jonathan couldn't shake the feeling that he was walking into something far more complex and dangerous than he had ever anticipated. The binary stars continued to shine in the sky, a constant reminder that the world had changed irrevocably.

With one last look at the perplexed faces of the scientists, Jonathan headed for the exit, his mind racing.

Chapter Nine: Unanticipated Resolve

For weeks, Lucien Bennett had operated in the shadows of the UN, and now, with the world's attention focused on the stars' reappearance, he made his move.

Jonathan stood transfixed in the faculty break room. Surrounded by his colleagues, he watched a globally televised address that elicited shock, disbelief, and growing anger. The television screen flickered with images of Lucien Bennett, his face twisted in anger as he made his shocking statements.

Bennett unveiled what he purported to be classified information, detailing the energy being's alleged role in Earth's recent history. He painted a picture of a manipulative alien force that had been controlling human affairs for decades, culminating in the recent cosmic events.

"We've been pawns in an intergalactic game," Bennett declared, his voice resonating with carefully cultivated outrage. "The UN leadership has been complicit in this deception. They've sold out humanity's autonomy for a seat at an alien table!"

A collective gasp rippled through the room. Jonathan recognized the dangerous mix of truth and lies in Bennett's words. He had pieced together enough over the past weeks to know that while there was indeed an extraterrestrial presence, Bennett's narrative was a carefully constructed manipulation of the facts.

Dr. Parker, a late-arriving astrophysicist, turned to Jonathan, his eyes wide. "This can't be true, can it? The implications..."

Before Jonathan could respond, the television screen showed live footage of protests engulfing major cities worldwide. What had started as peaceful demonstrations were quickly devolving into chaos. Bennett's supporters, inflamed by his words, clashed violently with those who still believed in the UN's leadership.

"This is madness," muttered Professor Harding, a senior member of the Political Science department. "Bennett's fanning the flames of global unrest. If this continues, we could be looking at worldwide destabilization."

Jonathan watched the scenes of violence unfold, his mind racing as he grappled with how Bennett's dangerous narrative was taking an even deeper root.

Just then, his phone buzzed in his pocket. It was a text from Sherry: "Jon, it's happening. The protests have reached downtown. Be careful coming home. We need to talk ASAP."

As his colleagues debated the veracity of Bennett's claims and the potential fallout, Jonathan slipped out of the break room and made his way through the suddenly chaotic university campus. Students and faculty alike were glued to their phones, gathering in worried clusters, and he couldn't shake the feeling that they all stood on the precipice of something monumental.

The university corridors, typically buzzing with activity, now resonated with an eerie calm—the eye of a global storm. He leaned against the wall, his breath coming in short, sharp bursts as he tried to gather his thoughts.

Suddenly, a commotion erupted as a door flew open at the end of the hallway, and a student rushed out, his face a mix of shock and disbelief. Jonathan pushed himself off the wall, straining to hear what was happening.

"Turn on the news!" the student shouted. "Bennett's making an announcement!"

Heart pounding, Jonathan ran back to the faculty breakroom. The large screen on the wall was showing Bennett standing at a podium, his face grave but composed.

A reporter appeared on screen, her expression serious as she stood in front of the United Nations headquarters in New York City. The chyron below her read "UN Report Alleges Presidential Misconduct."

"Good evening. In a shocking turn of events, the United Nations has just released a comprehensive report detailing alleged misconduct by President Bennett during his time in office. The report, compiled over several months by an independent investigative committee, paints a troubling picture of abuse of power and ethical violations."

The camera cut to footage of the UN building as the reporter continued her voice-over. "According to the report, President Bennett has been accused of using his position to enrich himself and his allies through a series of questionable deals and policy decisions. The allegations include:

1. Diverting federal funds to personal business interests
2. Pressuring foreign leaders for personal favors
3. Obstructing international peacekeeping efforts for political gain
4. Manipulating intelligence reports to support controversial policies

The report cites multiple sources within the administration and includes documentary evidence supporting these claims."

The scene returned to the reporter, who was now holding a copy of the report.

"The UN Secretary-General has called for an emergency session to discuss the findings and potential consequences. Meanwhile, the White House has yet to respond to these allegations.

This unprecedented report has sent shockwaves through the international community and raised serious questions about the integrity of the current administration.

The reporter nodded solemnly as she transitioned to the next segment of her report.

"In light of these serious allegations, we now turn to President Lucien Bennett, who has agreed to address these claims directly. Mr. President, thank you for joining us.

The screen split to reveal Lucien Bennett, his face a mask of calm determination despite the gravity of the situation. He was seated in what appeared to be the Oval Office, the American flag visible behind him.

"Thank you for having me," Bennett began, his voice steady and authoritative. "I want to address the American people directly regarding this UN report."

The reporter interjected, "Mr. President, these are very serious allegations. How do you respond?"

Bennett leaned forward slightly, his gaze unwavering. "My fellow citizens of the world," Bennett began, his voice carrying a note of indignation. "I stand before you today to address the baseless allegations that have been leveled against me and the subsequent unrest that has gripped our global community."

A tense silence fell over the room as everyone leaned in to listen.

Bennett continued, his tone growing more forceful, "Let me be clear: Although I am asked to step down, I categorically deny any and all accusations of wrongdoing. The attacks on my character and leadership are nothing more than a coordinated effort to undermine the progress we have made together."

Jonathan felt a knot form in his stomach. This was not the admission or resignation he had anticipated.

"Despite these false claims," Bennett continued, "I remain committed to the principles that have guided us thus far. I will not bow to pressure based on lies and misinformation. We have come too far to let unfounded accusations derail our mission for global unity and progress."

The screen panned back to the reporter, “As this story develops, we'll continue to bring you updates. Back to you in the studio."

As the denial rang out, Jonathan's mind whirled; this defiant stance complicated matters even further, and the room buzzed with murmurs of disbelief and confusion.

Lucien Bennett, once a beacon of hope, now stood with his credibility in tatters and his support base crumbling. UN security forces swiftly moved in to apprehend him. As he was led away, the look of defeat on his face told the story of a man whose grand ambitions had led to his downfall.

"I can't believe it," Professor Harding muttered, his voice a mix of awe and horror. "To think how close he came to plunging the whole world into chaos."

Dr. Wheeler turned to Jonathan, her eyes narrowed with suspicion. "You don't seem as surprised as the rest of us, Jon. Did you know something about this?"

Jonathan hesitated, weighing his words carefully. He had been involved in uncovering the truth behind Bennett's deception, but the full story was far more complex than what was being reported on the news.

"Let's just say I had my suspicions," he replied cautiously. "Bennett's story never quite added up, especially after the appearance and disappearance of that binary star system."

A heavy silence descended upon the room as everyone grappled with the news. The past few weeks had unleashed a maelstrom of revelations, conspiracies, and cosmic events, shattering humanity's understanding of its place in the universe.

"So what happens now?" asked a young adjunct professor, her voice tinged with curiosity, giving a voice to the question hanging in everyone's minds.

Jonathan's gaze swept across his colleagues, their faces a canvas of confusion and wonder. He realized that while Bennett's capture marked the end of one chapter, it was far from the end of the story.

"Now," Jonathan declared, his voice resonating with determination, "we start asking the right questions—about our place in the universe, the nature of the beings we've encountered, and our own untapped potential as a species."

Bennett's downfall marked only the beginning of humanity's journey into a new reality—a universe now known to be teeming with intelligent life.

Suddenly, Jonathan felt a hand on his shoulder. He turned to see June Cragen, her familiar face now full of concern. Jonathan recognized June, a colleague from the University's cybersecurity unit, known for her kind demeanor and aversion to conflict.

"Jon," she whispered, her voice barely audible over the murmurs in the room, "we need to talk. Privately, if possible."

Jonathan nodded, recognizing the urgency in her tone despite her characteristically calm demeanor. As they quietly made their way out of the crowded breakroom, Bennett's voice faded behind them, replaced by the hushed, bewildered conversations of their colleagues.

June guided Jonathan to a secluded nook in the hallway, safely out of earshot from curious onlookers. Her gentle nature seemed at odds with the gravity of the situation, but Jonathan could see the resolve in her eyes.

"I'm sorry to pull you away likc this," June began, her voice low and measured. "I know you're not one for stirring up trouble, and neither am I, but..." She paused, glancing around to ensure they were alone. "There's something you need to know. Something that might shed light on what's really going on with Bennett and these allegations."

Jonathan leaned in closer, intrigued by June's uncharacteristic behavior; she had always been thorough and cautious in her work, never one to jump to conclusions or spread unsubstantiated rumors.

"What is it, June?" Jonathan prompted gently, sensing her hesitation.

June inhaled deeply, her usually unflappable demeanor cracking under the weight of anxiety. "It's about some anomalies I've detected in our global communication monitoring systems. At first, I thought it was just a glitch, but now... Jon, if what I've found is correct, it could change everything we think we know about Bennett and these recent events."

As June began to explain her findings, Jonathan's heart raced with a potent mixture of anticipation and dread. Whatever June had discovered, he realized, could be the key to unraveling the mystery that had been haunting him. But it also meant that the situation was likely far more complex – and potentially dangerous – than he had initially considered.

June's eyes darted nervously around the hallway once more before she continued, her voice barely above a whisper. "Jon, I've been monitoring some unusual patterns in global communications, especially those related to Bennett's office. At first, there was just increased chatter due to the recent events, but..." She paused, swallowing hard. "There's something off about the data streams. They don't match up with official records."

Jonathan leaned in closer, his curiosity piqued. "What do you mean, June? How don't they match up?"

"There are two distinct communication streams," June explained. "One aligns with public information, but the other... It's encrypted and seems to originate from Bennett's inner circle. It paints a very different picture."

Jonathan's mind raced with the implications. "Have you decrypted any of it?" he asked urgently.

June shook her head. "Not yet. The encryption is unlike anything I've seen before. But the timing of these communications... They coincide perfectly with major events. The assassination, the riots, even Bennett's speech just now."

"Are you saying Bennett might be orchestrating all of this?" Jonathan asked, his voice a mix of disbelief and growing suspicion.

"I'm not saying anything definitive," June replied, her natural caution evident. "But something isn't right, Jon. And given your position and... well, your history with investigations, I thought you should know."

Jonathan nodded slowly, processing the information. "Thank you, June. I know this isn't easy for you. What do you think we should do?"

June bit her lip, clearly uncomfortable with the weight of the situation. "I... I don't know, Jon. Part of me wants to report this up the chain, but given how high this goes... I'm not sure who we can trust."

Then, seeming to make a decision, she reached into her bag and pulled out a tablet. "I brought this. It's a secure device, off the main networks. I want to show you what I've found."

As June powered on the tablet, the screen came to life, displaying a complex series of graphs and data streams.

"Look here," June said, pointing to a particular set of data points. "These are the official communication logs from Bennett's office." She swiped to another screen. "And these are the anomalous data streams I detected."

Jonathan leaned in, eyes darting between the screens, his brow furrowed in concentration. Even to his untrained eye, the discrepancies were glaring. "They don't match at all," he breathed, disbelief coloring his voice.

June nodded grimly. "Exactly. And look at the timestamps. The unofficial communications spike just before every major event we've seen unfold."

As they pored over the data, a chill ran down Jonathan's spine. The implications were staggering. If this information was accurate, it suggested a level of orchestration that was almost unthinkable.

"June," he said slowly, "if what we're seeing is real, it means—"

Suddenly, the tablet screen flickered, then went black. June tapped it frantically, but it remained unresponsive.

"That's impossible," she whispered, her face draining of color. "This device is completely isolated. Unless..."

Their eyes met, a shared realization dawning. If someone had managed to remotely access and disable the tablet, it meant their conversation was no longer private. It meant they were being watched.

June held the disabled tablet between them as they exchanged worried glances, processing the compromised security.

As the gravity of the situation settled over them like a heavy fog, a sudden commotion jolted their attention. People were pouring out into the hallway, their faces a mix of confusion and concern.

June leaned in, her voice barely audible. "Be careful, Jon. I'll keep digging on my end. Whatever's happening, it's clear we're only seeing the tip of the iceberg."

As she walked away, Jonathan checked his watch. Sherry would still be at work, he had some time he hoped would bring some clarity to his jumbled thoughts.

As Jonathan headed for the door, his mind raced ahead. He straightened his shoulders, determination etching itself across his face. *I have no choice,* he thought. *It's time for people to face reality, no matter how difficult it might be.*

Casting a final glance at the swirling chaos around him, Jonathan steeled himself for what could be the most pivotal meeting of his life.

As Jonathan exited the building, June's revelation echoed in his mind, the weight of the information pressing down on him with each step. The city was alive with a mix of celebration and lingering tension following Bennett's arrest.

Bennett's speech was plastered across every digital billboard and news ticker, yet the streets were quiet, as if the world was collectively holding its breath.

Needing time to process before heading home, he decided to stop at The Rusty Nail, a local pub he occasionally frequented.

As Jonathan pushed open the weathered wooden door, a wave of familiar scents washed over him—the sharp tang of hops mingling with the Earthy aroma of worn leather. The pub buzzed with an unusual energy, its patrons huddled in animated clusters, all engrossed in discussing the day's Earth-shattering events. Jonathan made his way to the bar, nodding at a few familiar faces.

"The usual?" Mike, the bartender, asked with a knowing smile.

"Please," Jonathan replied, settling onto a stool with a weary sigh.

As Mike poured his drink, Jonathan couldn't help but tune into the animated conversations surrounding him.

"I'm telling you," a man in a rumpled suit leaned in, his voice a conspiratorial whisper, "this whole Bennett arrest? It's all smoke and mirrors. Mark my words—he'll be out before the week's end."

"You really think so?" his friend replied, arching an eyebrow in skepticism.

The man in the suit nodded emphatically. "Of course! The man knows too much. They can't risk a public trial. He'll make some kind of deal, you'll see."

Jonathan nursed his drink, the amber liquid swirling in his glass as he tuned into the conversations around him. At a nearby table, a group of students from the university were engaged in their own heated discussion.

"But what if Bennett was right?" one of them asked, her eyes wide with speculation. "What if there really is some alien influence controlling everything?"

"Don't be ridiculous," another scoffed, rolling his eyes. "Next you'll be saying the moon landing was faked."

As the debates swirled around him like eddies in a turbulent river, Jonathan found himself caught between amusement and frustration, a wry smile playing at the corners of his mouth. If only they knew the truth—or at least, the fragments of truth he had been privy to.

"Quite the day, eh?" Mike said with a grin, wiping down the bar with a practiced hand. He leaned in, curiosity gleaming in his eyes. "What do you make of all this hullabaloo?"

Jonathan paused, considering his words carefully. "I think," he said slowly, weighing each word, "that the truth is probably more complex than any of us realize."

Mike nodded sagely, a knowing glint in his eye. "Ain't that always the way?"

As Jonathan drank the last of his drink and prepared to leave, he couldn't shake the feeling that despite Bennett's arrest, this was far from over. The speculation he'd overheard in the pub only reinforced his sense that there were more revelations to come—revelations that would shake the very foundations of human understanding.

Jonathan emerged from the warmth of the pub into the cool embrace of the night, the city's lights twinkling like earthbound stars. He started his trip home knowing that his impending conversation with Sherry would be a pivotal one.

Pulling into his driveway, he saw the warm glow of lights from inside his house. A wave of relief washed over him at the thought of seeing Sherry. If anyone could help him make sense of this chaos, it was her.

Jonathan found Sherry in the living room, curled up on the couch amidst a sea of scattered case files. She looked up as he entered, her face a mix of concern and relief.

"Jon," Sherry said, rising to embrace him, "I've been worried sick. Bennett's news... it's consumed everyone's conversations."

Jonathan held her tightly, drawing comfort from her presence. "It's been a hell of a day, Sher," he murmured, his voice muffled against her shoulder.

They settled on the couch, Sherry clearing away some files to make space, as Jonathan began to recount the day's tumultuous events. He told her about Bennett's defiant speech, the encounter with June, and finally, the meeting with June.

Sherry listened intently, her lawyer's mind picking up on details Jonathan hadn't even considered. When he finished, she was quiet for a moment, processing everything.

"Jon," she said finally, her voice grave, "this is big. Bigger than anything we've dealt with before. Are you sure you want to get involved?"

Jonathan sighed, running a hand through his hair. "I'm not surc I havc a choicc anymorc. Junc and I... we've seen things we can't unsee."

Sherry nodded, understanding in her eyes. "Just promise me you'll be careful. And keep me in the loop. My contacts in the legal world might be able to help if things get... complicated."

As they sat there, the weight of the situation settling over them like a heavy blanket, Jonathan felt a mix of fear and determination. Whatever lay ahead, he knew he had Sherry's support, and that gave him strength.

As they moved to the kitchen, Jonathan managed a small smile, grateful for her steady presence in the midst of the growing storm.

Chapter Ten: Cryptic Summons

A year had passed since the star system incident, with Jonathan and Sherry immersing themselves in their careers, yet the topic lingered in their conversations. Occasionally, they found themselves speculating about the system, Bennett, and the potential repercussions of those events.

They would soon find out. An email arrived that would alter the trajectory of Jonathan's life. The sender, Colonel Donald Sultrier, a senior Pentagon official, had crafted a message both concise and pointed: the government had encountered something beyond human or machine comprehension, an enigma that defied explanation. They sought Jonathan's expertise, a request not made lightly given the gravity of the situation.

The implications of the email were as stark as the black text staring back at him from the screen. The Pentagon's interest in his work was simultaneously flattering and terrifying. Jonathan knew the extent of their resources and the depth of their secrets. The prospect of involvement in such a clandestine matter sent a shiver down his spine, yet the allure of discovery was impossible to ignore.

After a night of fitful sleep, Jonathan sat before his computer, composing a careful reply. His fingers hovered over the keyboard, with a slight hesitation.

Finally, with a deep breath, he sent his acceptance. The universe had presented him with an unprecedented opportunity to explore the most profound mystery of all: the whispers of the stars, now echoing in the halls of power.

As days stretched into weeks without a response, Jonathan's initial anticipation congealed into a thick, cloying doubt. He second-guessed himself, wondering if he'd misinterpreted the email or if Colonel Sultrier had reconsidered his request. Maybe the artifact was no longer a concern, or perhaps they'd solved the mystery without him.

Jonathan settled into his chair for his daily email check, the routine now tinged with a hint of resigned expectation. His eyes scanned the inbox, pausing abruptly at the third message down. The sender's name leapt out at him: Colonel Donald Sultrier. The subject line, 'Further Instructions', seemed to pulse on the screen, laden with possibility and potential danger.

His heart racing, Jonathan's cursor hovered over the email. The simple act of opening a message had never felt so momentous. He took a deep breath, steadying himself, then clicked. As the email unfurled before him, Jonathan felt the weight of anticipation pressing down, knowing that its contents could irrevocably alter the course of his life.

From: Colonel Donald.Sultrier@pentagon.gov Subject: Further Instructions
Dr. Jonathan Avery,
Thank you for your prompt response and willingness to assist us in this matter of utmost national security. Your expertise is invaluable to our ongoing investigation. Remember, the safety of our nation and potentially the world rests on the discretion and success of this mission. Godspeed, Dr. Avery. Colonel Donald Sultrier Senior Official, Pentagon Office of Special Investigations

Attached was an encrypted link that led to a secure government server, and with a trembling hand, Jonathan clicked it open.

He read through the documents. The set of instructions were clear and precise.

Please be advised of the following:

1. You are to report to Andrews Air Force Base at 0600 hours this coming Tuesday. Your transportation will be provided at precisely 0200 under cover of night. A military transport will be waiting for you.
2. All necessary clothing and equipment will be provided.
3. You are not to discuss this matter with anyone, including family members. A cover story for

your absence has been prepared and will be provided upon your arrival.

4. Upon arrival at the base, you will be briefed on the full nature of the situation and your role in the investigation.
5. You will be provided a top secret government clearance.
6. For security purposes, this will be our last direct communication until we meet in person.

Jonathan sank back in his chair, the email weighing heavily on him, its meaning creeping into every part of his thoughts. The vague yet threatening tone, the requests for secrecy, and the mention of national security hinted at something much larger than his usual academic work.

His mind raced with questions: What groundbreaking discovery had led to this secret message? How did it connect to his years of research? And most importantly, how could he explain this to Sherry?

"Jon? Are you home?" Sherry's voice broke through his thoughts as she entered, her footsteps resonating in the hallway.

Jonathan quickly closed the email and jumped up, his heart racing. Sweat trickled down his forehead as he faced a tough choice in the brief moments before

Sherry arrived. The email had clearly told him not to share this with anyone, but this was Sherry—his partner, his confidant, the one person he had always told everything. How could he hide something so significant from her?

As Sherry approached, Jonathan felt torn between two strong forces: his duty to scientific integrity and national security on one side, and the trust in his marriage on the other.

Jonathan made a split-second decision. He would tell her the bare minimum - that he had been called away on a consulting job. It wasn't a complete lie, but it felt wrong to withhold the full truth from her.

"In here, Sher," he called out, trying to keep his voice steady.

As she entered the room, he forced a smile, all the while feeling the weight of secrets beginning to form a barrier between them.

As Sherry entered the study, Jonathan's forced smile wavered slightly. She knew him too well, and he could see the concern immediately flicker across her face.

"Jon? What's wrong?" she asked, her lawyer's intuition kicking in.

Jonathan took a deep breath. "I... I've been offered a consulting job. It's rather sudden, and I'll have to leave for a while."

Sherry's eyes narrowed. "A consulting job? For whom?"

"I can't say much about it," Jonathan replied, hating the taste of half-truths in his mouth. “It's a government contract. Very hush-hush."

Sherry was silent for a moment, studying his face. "This has something to do with Bennett."

Jonathan felt a mix of pride and frustration at her perceptiveness. "I honestly don't know, Sher. They haven't told me much. But... It's important. Really important."

She nodded slowly, her expression a mix of worry and understanding. "When do you leave?"

"Tuesday morning. Early."

Sherry moved closer, taking his hands in hers. "Promise me you'll be careful, Jon. Whatever this is... it feels big."

Jonathan pulled her into a tight embrace, breathing in her familiar scent. "I promise," he whispered, wishing he could tell her everything.

The next few days passed in a blur of preparation and barely concealed anxiety. Jonathan packed as instructed, said goodbye to his colleagues at the university under the guise of a sudden sabbatical, and spent every moment he could with Sherry.

Tuesday morning arrived all too soon. As Jonathan prepared to leave for Andrews Air Force Base, Sherry stood in the doorway of their bedroom, watching him with a mix of love and concern. "Just come back to me, okay?"

"I'll call as soon as I can," Jonathan promised, though he wasn't sure when or if that would be possible.

Sherry nodded, pulling him in for one last kiss.

At exactly 0200 hours, just as planned, the unmarked black car pulled up outside his house. The headlights didn't shine, the engine was almost silent.

Jonathan looked over at Sherry, who was sitting on the couch, her eyes glued to the TV, pretending not to hear the car.

"It's time," he said softly.

Three men in sharp suits knocked on the door, their faces stern and unreadable. They didn't introduce themselves, they didn't need to. The badges on their chests were all the identification necessary.

He looked back at Sherry, her eyes brimming with fear and pride. Whatever lay ahead, Jonathan knew that his life was about to change irrevocably. Now, all that remained was to face whatever mystery awaited him at Andrews Air Force Base.

"Call me when you can," she said, her voice trembling.

He picked up his bag, and followed the men out into the night. No questions, no explanations, just a simple order to bring his clothes and his expertise.

The car door shut with a solid thud, cutting off the outside world, and the vehicle glided away from the curb, swallowed by the shadows. Jonathan felt the weight of his decision pressing down on him, as the car sped through the quiet streets, the neon lights of the town fading into the distance.

The men didn't speak, their eyes focused on the road ahead. The silence was thick, punctuated only by the sound the soft hum of the engine made.

The trip was a blur of darkened highways and occasional patches of rural countryside, the city lights giving way to the night. Jonathan arrived at Andrews Air Force Base at 0600.

The car stopped before a sleek military jet, its engines idling, a ramp lowered expectantly. The men escorted him out, their grip firm but not unkind.

"This is where we part ways, Dr. Avery." one of them said, and the car pulled away, leaving him alone with the looming aircraft.

Jonathan took a deep breath, the cool night air filling his lungs as he climbed the ramp.

He was immediately met by stern-faced military personnel who efficiently processed his arrival.

As he boarded the aircraft, a tall, distinguished man in a crisp uniform approached him.

"Dr. Avery? I'm Dr. Gray. Welcome aboard. We have much to discuss during our flight."

Jonathan nodded, his throat suddenly dry. "Where exactly are we going?"

The man's face remained impassive. "To the place where it all began, Dr. Avery. To the heart of the mystery."

As the plane's engines roared to life, Jonathan settled into his seat, his mind racing with possibilities. his mind raced with questions, but he knew better than to ask.

The destination remained unknown, shrouded in mystery, a secret shared only by the government officials who had come for him. Whatever lay ahead, he knew that the answers he sought were waiting for him at the end of this journey.

The plane leveled off at cruising altitude, Dr. Gray settled into the seat across from Jonathan. His piercing blue eyes studied Jonathan intently before he spoke.

"Dr. Avery, what I'm about to tell you is classified at the highest levels. Are you prepared for that responsibility?"

Jonathan nodded solemnly. "I am."

Dr. Gray produced a tablet from his briefcase and handed it to Jonathan. "This contains the full briefing on what we've discovered. I suggest you start reading now. We'll discuss your questions when you're done."

With slightly trembling hands, Jonathan activated the tablet. As he began to read, his eyes widened in disbelief.

The report detailed the discovery of an ancient artifact, uncovered during a classified deep-sea expedition in the Mariana Trench. The object, composed of an unknown material, appeared to be of extraterrestrial origin and predated any known human civilization by millions of years.

Most astoundingly, the artifact seemed to be the source of intermittent energy pulses that matched the frequency of the mysterious binary star system that had appeared and vanished over a year ago.

As Dr. Jonathan Avery delved deeper into the report on the tablet, he learned of the government's attempts to study and activate the artifact, all of which had failed. The most brilliant minds in physics, engineering, and computer science had been stumped by its complexity; he found a detailed analysis of the binary star system that had appeared and vanished over a year ago. The report included complex astronomical data, spectral analyses, and gravitational measurements that defied conventional understanding of stellar physics.

Most intriguing, the report detailed intermittent energy pulses detected from Earth that seemed to correlate with the binary star system's appearance and disappearance. These pulses, the report suggested, originated from an unknown source deep within the Mariana Trench.

Jonathan looked up from the tablet, his mind racing. "This energy source in the Mariana Trench – have you recovered it?"

Dr. Gray nodded gravely. "That's precisely why you're here, Dr. Avery. We've retrieved an artifact from the depths of the trench. It's unlike anything we've ever seen, and it seems to be the source of these energy pulses."

"And you think this artifact is connected to the binary star system?" Jonathan asked, though he already suspected the answer.

"We're certain of it," Dr. Gray replied. "But that's not all. The artifact seems to be of extraterrestrial origin, predating any known human civilization by millions of years. And most importantly, it's... reactive."

Jonathan's brow furrowed. "Reactive? In what way?"

Dr. Gray leaned forward, his voice low. "It responds to certain individuals, Dr. Avery. And it responds most strongly to your biometric data. That's why you're here. We need you to help us understand this artifact and its connection to the star system."

"Now you understand why we need you, Dr. Avery," Dr. Gray said quietly.

Jonathan's throat felt dry. "This is... incredible. But why me? Surely there are others more qualified—"

Dr. Gray cut him off. "Because the artifact responded to you, Dr. Avery. When we ran your biometric data through our systems, it pulsed in a way we've never seen before. It's as if it's been waiting for you."

The full weight of his situation crashed over him. Thoughts of Sherry and the life he'd left behind collided with what he'd just learned. The universe suddenly seemed both infinitely larger and unsettlingly focused on him.

"What exactly do you want me to do?" Jonathan asked, his voice a hoarse whisper, tension etched in every line of his face.

Dr. Gray leaned forward, his eyes burning with an intensity that made Jonathan want to shrink back. "We need you to communicate with the artifact, Dr. Avery. Unlock its secrets, help us understand our place in the cosmos. The fate of humanity may very well rest on what we learn from this... object."

Jonathan swallowed hard, his mouth suddenly dry. "I understand. But I have to ask - does this relate to Lucien Bennett and the events of last year?"

Dr. Gray's expression tightened, a flicker of something—anger? fear?—crossing his features. "Bennett was... a dangerous complication," he said, his jaw clenching. "He stumbled upon fragments of information about the artifact and, in his arrogance, twisted them to suit his own misguided agenda. The damage he caused..." He trailed off, shaking his head.

"And now?" Jonathan pressed, sensing there was more to the story.

Dr. Gray's gaze bore into Jonathan. "Now, we have a chance to set things right. To understand the truth that Bennett nearly destroyed. But we need your help, Dr. Avery. Your unique insights might be the key to unlocking everything."

Jonathan felt the weight of responsibility settle on his shoulders like a physical burden. He was standing on the precipice of something monumental, something that could change the course of human history. And yet, a small voice in the back of his mind whispered a warning—about the dangers of unchecked knowledge, about the cost of secrets kept from those we love.

Jonathan's mind raced, connecting dots he hadn't even realized were there. "So the binary star system, the ship we saw - were they projections from the artifact?"

"We believe so," Dr. Gray confirmed. "But that's just scratching the surface of what this object seems capable of. That's why we need you, Dr. Avery. Your unique perspective might be the key to understanding it all."

As the plane began its descent, Jonathan gazed out the window at the unfamiliar landscape below. Desert stretched as far as the eye could see, broken only by what appeared to be a massive, state-of-the-art facility gleaming in the distance.

"Welcome to Area 52, Dr. Avery," Dr. Gray said, following Jonathan's gaze. "Your new home for the foreseeable future."

Jonathan's heart raced with anticipation. As the plane touched down. Whatever happened next would change everything - not just for him, but potentially for all of humanity.

Jonathan squared his shoulders, ready to face whatever challenges lay ahead. With a mix of excitement and trepidation, Jonathan prepared himself for whatever challenges lay ahead, knowing that the next few days, weeks, or even months could change the course of human history forever.

Dr. Gray ushered Jonathan off the aircraft, the heat of the desert immediately enveloping them. A sleek black vehicle with heavily tinted windows awaited, its engine purring quietly in the stillness of the remote location. As they slipped into the cool interior, Jonathan caught a glimpse of armed guards discreetly positioned around the perimeter.

After a short drive through the sun-baked landscape, they arrived at the heart of Area 52. Stark, angular buildings of glass and steel rose from the desert floor, their surfaces reflecting the harsh sunlight. Jonathan noted the subtle shimmer of advanced force fields and the silent swivel of camouflaged security cameras—clear indicators of the facility's critical importance.

"This will be your home for the duration of the project, Dr. Avery," Dr. Gray explained as they entered one of the buildings. The air inside was cool and crisp, a stark contrast to the scorching heat outside. They walked down a corridor lined with doors, each marked with a nameplate. The soft hum of advanced technology permeated the air, a constant reminder of the cutting-edge nature of their work.

Jonathan's fingers twitched at his side, eager to begin his investigation. As they approached a door marked "Dr. Jonathan Avery," he felt a surge of excitement and trepidation. Behind that door lay the first step in a journey that could change everything—for him, for science, and for humanity's understanding of its place in the universe.

Stopping at one of the doors, Dr. Gray produced a key card and handed it to Jonathan. "This is your quarters. We've tried to make it as comfortable as possible, given the circumstances."

As Jonathan swiped the card and stepped inside, he was immediately struck by the unexpected luxury of the space. The room unfolded before him, surprisingly spacious and well-appointed, more reminiscent of a high-end hotel suite than the spartan quarters he had anticipated. A comfortable-looking bed dominated one side of the room, while a small sitting area with a plush couch and armchair occupied another. A sleek desk equipped with a state-of-the-art computer caught his eye, and he noted a door leading to what he assumed was a private bathroom.

"You'll find everything you need here," Dr. Gray continued, gesturing around the room. "The closet has been stocked with uniforms in your size."

Jonathan's eyebrows rose in surprise. He hadn't even thought about uniforms.

Dr. Gray nodded toward the desk. "There's a tablet there with secure access to any research materials you might need. The cafeteria is open 24/7, and there's a small gym and recreation area down the hall."

Jonathan nodded slowly, his eyes sweeping the room once more. The reality of his situation was beginning to sink in. "Thank you," he said, his voice slightly hoarse. "This is... more than I expected. It's almost unsettling how prepared you are."

Dr. Gray's expression softened slightly, a flicker of understanding crossing his features. "We understand the sacrifice you're making by being here, Dr. Avery. The least we can do is ensure your comfort." He paused, his tone becoming more serious. "Get some rest tonight. Tomorrow, we'll begin the real work."

The luxurious accommodations suddenly felt like a gilded cage, a comfort offered in exchange for his complete dedication to unraveling cosmic mysteries.

The soft click of the door closing behind Dr. Gray echoed in the sudden silence. Jonathan sank onto the edge of the bed, his eyes roaming the room that would be his home for an indeterminate future. Tomorrow, he would begin to probe the secrets of the universe – but at what cost to his own life and relationships?

The room, for all its luxuries, felt sterile and impersonal—a gilded cage. With a heavy sigh, Jonathan forced himself to his feet and began to unpack. His hands trembled slightly as he placed a framed photo of Sherry on the nightstand, her frozen smile a bittersweet reminder of the life he'd left behind. The sight of her face brought a lump to his throat, and he swallowed hard against the sudden surge of emotion.

The soft chime of the room's intercom cut through his restless night's sleep, dragging him back to consciousness. A static filled voice he didn't recognize informed him to be at breakfast in 30 minutes, followed by a meeting with Dr. Gray.

With a groan, Jonathan hauled himself out of bed. The shower's hot water did little to wash away his apprehension, but it at least helped clear the fog from his mind. As he dressed in the provided clothing—a simple but well-fitted dark blue jumpsuit with his name embroidered on the chest, further separating him from his old life.

Jonathan stepped out into the hallway, the door hissing shut behind him. The corridor stretched before him, its stark white walls and shiny floors emphasized its clinical nature. An eerie quiet permeated the air, broken only by the soft hum of hidden machinery and the occasional echo of distant footsteps.

Jonathan passed a few researchers and security personnel. Their curt nods and averted gazes did nothing to alleviate his sense of isolation. Each person he encountered seemed wrapped in their own world of secrets and responsibilities, reinforcing the clandestine nature of the facility.

Approaching the cafeteria, Jonathan took a deep breath, steeling himself for whatever the day might bring. He knew that beyond those doors lay not just breakfast, but the beginning of a journey that would challenge everything he thought he knew about the universe—and perhaps about himself.

Inside, Jonathan found himself surrounded by a small group of other scientists, all wearing similar jumpsuits. The atmosphere was tense, with hushed conversations taking place over steaming cups of coffee. He couldn't help but wonder if these were the "brilliant minds" that had been stumped by the artifact.

As he finished his breakfast, Dr. Gray appeared at his table. "Ready for your first look, Dr. Avery?"

Jonathan nodded, his heart rate quickening. "As ready as I'll ever be."

Dr. Gray led him through a series of security checkpoints, each more stringent than the last. Finally, they arrived at a massive reinforced door. Dr. Gray placed his hand on a biometric scanner, and the door slowly swung open.

The room beyond was filled with an array of advanced scientific equipment. But Jonathan's eyes were immediately drawn to the glowing object that hovered inside a transparent containment field.

The artifact was unlike anything Jonathan had ever seen. It was roughly spherical, about the size of a baseball, with an iridescent surface that seemed to shift and change as he looked at it. Strange, intricate patterns flowed across its surface, reminiscent of the complex equations he'd spent his career studying.

As Jonathan approached, he felt a strange sensation - a sort of humming in his bones, a pull that he couldn't quite explain. The artifact seemed to pulse gently, its glow intensifying slightly.

Dr. Gray watched him closely. "What do you feel, Dr. Avery?"

Jonathan struggled to find the words. "It's... calling to me. Somehow." He turned to Dr. Gray, his eyes wide with wonder and a hint of fear. "What is it?"

"That, Dr. Avery," Dr. Gray said solemnly, "is what we're hoping you can tell us. Because right now, that object might be the most important thing on this planet - and possibly beyond."

As Jonathan stood there, mesmerized by the artifact, he knew that his life's work had led him to this moment and whatever secrets this object held.

Jonathan approached the artifact cautiously, his eyes never leaving its shifting surface. As he drew closer, the humming sensation in his bones intensified, and he could swear he heard whispers at the edge of his consciousness.

"Remarkable," he murmured, circling the containment field. "Have you tried—"

Suddenly, the artifact pulsed brightly, its glow intensifying to an almost blinding level. The patterns on its surface began to move more rapidly, forming complex shapes that seemed almost familiar to Jonathan.

Alarms blared throughout the facility. Scientists and security personnel rushed into the room.

"Dr. Avery, step back!" Dr. Gray shouted, but Jonathan found himself rooted to the spot, transfixed by the object before him.

Without warning, a beam of energy shot from the artifact, enveloping Jonathan in a cocoon of shimmering light. He felt no pain, only a sensation of weightlessness and a flood of information pouring into his mind.

As quickly as it began, the energy field dissipated. Jonathan collapsed to his knees, gasping for air. The room around him was in chaos, but he barely noticed. His mind was reeling from what he'd experienced.

Chapter Eleven: The Cosmic Script

As the commotion in the facility began to settle, Jonathan felt a vibration in his pocket. He pulled out the secure phone he'd been given upon arrival. An unknown number flashed on the screen—unusual given the facility's strict security protocols.

With a glance at Dr. Gray, who nodded his approval, Jonathan answered. "Dr. Avery speaking," he said, his voice still shaky from the recent event.

"Jonathan," Colonel Sultrier's voice came through, tense and urgent. "I've just been briefed on what happened. Are you alright?"

Though he'd never heard it aloud before, Jonathan instantly recognized Colonel Sultrier's voice. "I'm fine, Colonel Sultrier," Jonathan replied, trying to steady his voice. "It was... intense, but I'm unharmed."

Jonathan scanned the room, noting that Dr. Gray and the others were engrossed in their own discussions, paying him no mind. He lowered his voice. "What do you know about what happened?"

"I know that the artifact showed you things, Dr. Avery. Things about our past, our future. About the true nature of humanity's place in the cosmos."

A chill ran down Jonathan's spine—how could he already know about his vision?

"Good, good," Colonel Sultrier said, though he didn't sound entirely relieved. "Listen carefully, Jonathan. What you experienced—what you saw—it's of utmost importance. We need you to document everything, every detail, no matter how small or seemingly insignificant."

Jonathan nodded, even though Colonel Sultrier couldn't see him. "Of course. I was just about to suggest that we—"

"There's more," Colonel Sultrier interrupted. "We're detecting unusual activity in the upper atmosphere. It started right after your... encounter with the artifact. We think they might be related."

Jonathan's heart raced. "Activity? What kind of activity?"

There was a pause on the other end of the line. "We're not entirely sure. But it bears a striking resemblance to the energy signatures we recorded when the binary star system appeared last year."

The implications slammed into Jonathan, nearly knocking the breath from his lungs. "You think it's coming back? The star system?"

"We don't know," Colonel Sultrier admitted. "But whatever's happening, it's big."

Jonathan inhaled sharply, his mind reeling as he tried to process the flood of information. "What do you need me to do?"

"For now, work with the team there. Share what you've learned. Try to establish some kind of communication with the artifact if you can. We need answers, and we need them fast."

"Understood," Jonathan said, his mind already racing with possibilities.

As he ended the call, Jonathan turned to find Dr. Gray and the rest of the team watching him intently. He paused, gathering his thoughts before addressing them.

"Dr. Avery?" Dr. Gray's voice snapped him back to reality. "Is everything alright?"

"Yes, I... I just needed a moment to collect my thoughts."

As he rejoined the group, Jonathan's mind raced with questions. *How did he know about my experience with the artifact? And what did he mean about my greater purpose?*

"Ladies and gentlemen," Dr. Gray began, his voice growing stronger with each word, "we're on the brink of something monumental. The artifact, the binary star system, the atmospheric activity—they're all connected. And we need to figure out how, why, and what it means for humanity."

He paused, meeting each person's gaze. "I know you all have questions. So do I. But right now, we need to focus. We're not just scientists anymore. We're humanity's first line of defense—and possibly its ambassadors to whatever's out there."

"Let's get to work," he said, turning back to the artifact. "We have a universe to understand."

They stopped before a massive, reinforced gate. The men exchanged a knowing glance as Dr. Gray typed a sequence of codes into a keypad.

"Impressive, isn't it?" Dr. Gray said as the gate hissed open.

Jonathan's eyes widened in amazement as he took in the laboratory, wonder etched across his face. The room hummed with energy, filled with technology he'd only dreamed of—quantum computers, gravitational wave detectors, and holographic star maps that seemed to float in mid-air.

The air crackled with an energy that made the hairs on Jonathan's arms stand on end.

The gate closed behind him with a loud clang, the sound reverberating through the room.

For a moment, Jonathan just stood there, the cold metal of the door at his back, absorbing the scene before him. The room was a flurry of activity. Scientists in blue jumpsuits and white lab coats moved with purpose, their eyes glued to screens and monitors, their fingers flying over keyboards and consoles. It was a symphony of clicks and beeps, punctuated by the occasional sharp intake of breath.

"Welcome to the facility, Dr. Avery," Dr. Gray said, gesturing broadly. "Let's just say we're somewhere the stars can speak to us without interference. Now, let me show you around."

As Dr. Gray guided Jonathan through the lab, explaining the purpose of various instruments, Jonathan's mind reeled at the implications of what he was seeing. This was beyond cutting-edge; it was revolutionary.

Dr. Gray's smile softened as he turned to a woman in a lab coat. She was bent over a microscope, her eyes glued to the slides. Her auburn hair was pulled into a tight bun, with stray strands curling at her neck. Glasses perched on the tip of her nose.

The woman looked up from her work, her piercing, intelligent eyes scanning Jonathan. He couldn't help but feel like a specimen under her scrutiny. She straightened, her posture perfect despite the long hours she must have spent hunched over her work.

"And here," Dr. Gray said, gesturing to the woman, "is Dr. Sarah Mitchell. She'll be your assistant on this project."

"We're expecting great things from you, Dr. Avery." Dr. Mitchell said.

Her voice was cool and professional as she offered her hand. Her grip was firm, but not as rough as Dr. Gray's.

As Dr. Gray continued the tour, Dr. Mitchell fell into step beside them. In a low voice, she murmured to Jonathan, "Don't you find it odd that the government is suddenly pouring unlimited resources into studying 'whispering' stones?"

Jonathan glanced at her, surprised by her directness. "You think there's more to this?"

Dr. Mitchell's eyes darted around before meeting his. "I think they're using this to cover something up. Something big."

Before Jonathan could respond, Dr. Gray called their attention to a massive screen displaying real-time data from various stars.

As Jonathan and Dr. Mitchell turned to the screen, a sudden flurry of activity erupted among the monitoring scientists. The display began to flicker, showing rapid fluctuations in the stellar readings.

"What's happening?" Dr. Gray's voice was sharp with concern.

One of the technicians responded, his fingers flying over the keyboard. "Sir, we're detecting an anomaly in the Sirius system. The readings are off the charts!"

Jonathan stepped closer to the screen, his eyes widening as he took in the data. The numbers and graphs were shifting at an impossible rate, defying everything he knew about stellar physics.

"This can't be right," he muttered, more to himself than anyone else.

Dr. Mitchell leaned in, her voice low and urgent. "Dr. Avery, look at the spectrographic analysis. Does that pattern seem familiar to you?"

As Jonathan focused on the spectrograph, he felt a jolt of recognition. The pattern was eerily similar to the one he had seen on the artifact during his strange vision.

Suddenly, alarms blared throughout the facility. Dr. Gray barked orders into his communicator, while other scientists rushed to their stations.

"Everyone, stay calm!" Dr. Gray shouted over the noise. "We need to analyze this data immediately. Dr. Avery, Dr. Mitchell, I need your expertise on this now!"

As Jonathan approached the central console, Dr. Mitchell gripped his arm. "Remember what I said," she whispered. "There's more going on here than they're telling us. Keep your eyes open."

The stars were no longer whispering but screaming, thrusting Jonathan Avery into a cosmic mystery that threatened to upend everything he knew about the universe.

Jonathan's gaze flickered between the stellar data on the main screen and the artifact in its containment field. As if responding to his attention, the artifact suddenly pulsed with an intense light, its surface patterns shifting rapidly.

"Dr. Avery!" a technician called out. "The artifact—it's becoming highly active!"

Jonathan rushed to the containment field, Dr. Mitchell close behind. As they approached, the artifact's glow intensified, and the humming sensation Jonathan had felt earlier returned, stronger than ever.

"It's reacting to the stellar event," Jonathan muttered, his eyes fixed on the shifting patterns. "No, not just reacting—it's... communicating."

Dr. Mitchell's eyes widened. "Communicating? With what?"

Before Jonathan could respond, the artifact emitted a powerful energy pulse that momentarily overloaded the facility's systems. As the lights flickered back on, Jonathan gasped at the main screen.

The energy surge from Sirius had changed course. It was no longer headed directly for Earth, but seemed to be forming a complex pattern in space—a pattern that mirrored the one on the artifact's surface.

"My God. What's happening?" Dr. Gray joined them at the containment field.

Jonathan's mind raced, trying to piece together the puzzle before him. "I think... I think the artifact is acting as some kind of beacon or translator. It's communicating with whatever is causing the disturbance in the Sirius system."

Dr. Mitchell stepped forward, her face a mask of concern and determination. "Can you understand what it's saying, Dr. Avery? Is it a threat?"

Jonathan shook his head, frustration evident in his voice. "I can't decipher it completely, but it doesn't feel threatening. It's more like... an invitation."

"An invitation to what?" Dr. Mitchell asked, her voice barely above a whisper.

As if in response to her question, the artifact's glow suddenly enveloped Jonathan. He felt a rush of information flood his mind, similar to his earlier experience but more focused, more urgent.

When the light faded, Jonathan stumbled back, steadied by Dr. Mitchell's quick reflexes.

"Dr. Avery!" Dr. Gray exclaimed. "Are you alright? What happened?"

Jonathan looked up, his eyes wide in awe and disbelief. "I know what it wants," he said, his voice shaking slightly. "It's not just an invitation—it's a summons. And I think... I think I'm meant to answer it."

The room fell silent as Jonathan's words sank in. The artifact pulsed gently in its containment field, as if awaiting a response to its cosmic call. Jonathan stood at the crossroads of human knowledge and the unknown, faced with a decision that could alter the course of human history.

As the facility buzzed with renewed activity and urgent discussions, Jonathan couldn't help but wonder: was this the government's plan all along? Or were they, like him, merely pawns in a game of cosmic proportions?

Dr. Gray's expression shifted from concern to intense curiosity. "A summons? From whom? To where?"

Jonathan shook his head, struggling to put the flood of information into words. "I'm not entirely sure. But it's connected to the Sirius system, to the energy patterns we're seeing. It's like a doorway is opening, and I'm being called to step through."

Dr. Mitchell gripped Jonathan's arm, her voice low and urgent. "Dr. Avery, you can't seriously be considering this. We have no idea what's on the other side."

Dr. Gray interjected, his voice tense. "This is unprecedented. We need to inform the higher-ups immediately."

"Dr. Gray, what's our protocol for this kind of situation?"

Dr. Gray's eyes never left Jonathan as he replied, "There is no protocol for this. We're in uncharted territory." He paused, then addressed Jonathan directly. "Dr. Avery, I need you to tell us everything you experienced, every detail. We need to understand what we're dealing with before we make any decisions."

As Jonathan began to recount his experience, the artifact pulsed gently in its containment field, as if punctuating his words. The stellar data on the main screen continued to show the complex pattern forming near Sirius, a cosmic door seemingly waiting to be opened.

The government's secretive behavior, Dr. Mitchell's warnings, the artifact's mysterious origins—all of it swirled in his mind as he tried to make sense of the cosmic summons he'd received.

As he spoke, Jonathan realized that his next decision could alter the course of human history. Would he heed the call of the stars, risking everything to unveil the mysteries of the universe? Or would he err on the side of caution, potentially missing humanity's greatest opportunity for advancement?

With every eye in the room upon him and the weight of the cosmos on his shoulders, Dr. Jonathan Avery prepared to make a choice that would reshape his understanding of reality itself.

Jonathan stared at the screen, his mind racing with possibilities. As he began to grasp the magnitude of the task before him, he couldn't shake Dr. Mitchell's words from his mind. What if this was more than just an astronomical anomaly? What if the government was hiding something?

Over the next few weeks, Jonathan immersed himself in the data. Thc artifact's behavior defied conventional explanation. The signals weren't radio waves or any known form of stellar emission; they seemed to exist in a realm between traditional physics and something else entirely.

A little past midnight, they were alone in the lab. Jonathan was analyzing spectral data when he noticed an anomaly.

"Dr. Mitchell, come look at this," he called out, his voice tinged with excitement and confusion.

Dr. Mitchell hurried over, leaning in to examine the screen. "What am I looking at?"

Jonathan pointed to a series of irregular peaks in the data. "These patterns of the artifact are not random. There's a structure here that doesn't match any known stellar phenomenon."

Dr. Mitchell's brow furrowed as she studied the data. Suddenly, her eyes widened. "Wait a second..."

She quickly pulled up another set of data on her tablet. "I segregated the star patterns. Look at this side by side."

As they compared the two sets of data, an astonishing correlation emerged. The patterns in the stellar emissions matched the structure of complex language systems.

"It's a language. The stars are speaking to the artifact," Dr. Mitchell whispered.

They worked feverishly through the night, cross-referencing the stellar data with every known human language and communication system. Nothing matched.

As the first rays of dawn broke through the lab windows, Jonathan sat back, running his hands through his disheveled hair. "Dr. Mitchell, do you realize what this means?"

She nodded slowly, the weight of the discovery evident in her voice. "It's not just a stellar phenomenon. It's not a government conspiracy. It's..."

"Alien," Jonathan finished. "We're picking up an alien language transmitting from the stars themselves."

As the information began to sink in, Jonathan realized that the truth about humanity's place in the cosmos was far more complex and astounding than anyone had ever dreamed. Images flashed before his eyes: the binary star system, alien cities, cosmic events beyond human comprehension.

Dr. Mitchell reached for the comm panel. "We need to tell Dr. Gray. The whole project needs to be reoriented."

As Jonathan watched her make the call, they shared a look of anticipation. They had unlocked the first key to understanding what was happening, but the real challenge lay ahead: They had to communicate with whoever—or whatever—was reaching out to the artifact from the depths of space.

Jonathan's mind was already racing with ideas and theories. He felt his breath catch in his throat. This was it. This was the puzzle he had been invited to solve, the enigma that had piqued the interest of the most powerful nation on Earth.

"We need to see it up close," he said, his voice steady.

Dr. Gray looked at him for a moment, his gaze searching for any signs of doubt. "You know the risks," Dr. Gray warned.

"I need to hear it without any interference. I need to be closer to it. To understand it better," Jonathan replied firmly.

"Fine, I'll arrange that for you," Dr. Gray said tightly. "But you're going in alone, and you're on a strict time limit. If anything goes wrong, we pull you out. Understood?"

Jonathan nodded, his heart racing. "Fascinating."

Dr. Gray clapped him on the shoulder. "That's an understatement. But come, let's talk in my office. There's a lot I need to catch you up on."

Dr. Gray led Jonathan through the lab's maze, their footsteps echoing off the gleaming floors. Finally, they reached a small office amidst the chaos. The room was a familiar disarray of books, papers, and half-empty coffee cups, a testament to Dr. Gray's inability to maintain a neat workspace. The walls were adorned with degrees and certificates earned from the man's years of dedication to his field.

The desk was cluttered with paperwork and models of various scientific theories, each more complex than the last, yet a sense of orderliness prevailed—each item placed with purpose.

Dr. Gray gestured for Jonathan to sit, his own gaze lingering on the screen through the window that looked out into the lab.

"We've tried everything. Every codebreaker, every linguist, every computer program we have at our disposal to see what the artifact was doing. Nothing."

Jonathan nodded, swallowing the lump in his throat. "Because it's speaking directly to the stars, we can't understand it."

The rest of the day flew by in a blur of research and discussion as he worked to piece together the patterns of language. As the sun began to set, casting a warm glow through the lab's windows, Jonathan finally sat back in his chair, his eyes bleary with fatigue.

Sherry waited back home, her eyes glued to the phone, her heart in her throat waiting for it to ring.

"I can't tell you everything, Sherry, but it's incredible. And terrifying. And beautiful. And everything in between," he said.

"Be safe, Jon," she replied, her voice crackling with the static of a long-distance call.

"Always," he promised.

"And come back to me."

As he ended the call, Jonathan couldn't help but think about the light at the end of the tunnel he and Sherry had always talked about. It had once seemed so distant, a mere pinprick in the vast darkness of the unknown. But now, with the star before him, that light was growing brighter, and the train was definitely approaching.

Jonathan rubbed his tired eyes, staring at the holographic display of quantum entanglements. Dr. Mitchell walked in, carrying two mugs of coffee.

"Any progress?" she asked, handing him a mug.

Jonathan sighed, taking a sip. "Some. I think I'm starting to understand how they perceive time. It's not linear for them. Past, present, future, it's all accessible."

Dr. Mitchell nodded, her eyes bright with excitement despite the late hour. "That tracks with what I've been finding in the linguistic patterns. Their language isn't just communication—it's a transfer of entire concepts, memories, even possible futures."

They worked in silence for a while, occasionally bouncing ideas off each other. Jonathan noticed a significant change in Dr. Mitchell's demeanor. The initial skepticism she had harbored about the project had transformed into a driven curiosity. Her eyes were alight with a newfound intensity as she processed the information.

"Dr. Avery," Dr. Mitchell said, "the patterns, the energy signatures - they're not just random anomalies. They're a form of alien communication, aren't they?"

Jonathan nodded, relieved to see that Dr. Mitchell was now fully engaged. "I think so, yes. It's as if the artifact is acting as a translator between us and whatever is out there."

"Look. I've found something," he whispered, glancing nervously over his shoulder before he handed her a tablet. On it was a classified government memo, dated years before the first star system was detected.

Dr. Mitchell's brow furrowed as she read. "Project B... attempts to communicate with advanced civilizations... quantum entanglement on a stellar scale?"

She looked up at Jonathan. "How did you find this?"

He smiled grimly. "I have my ways. But don't you see? They knew this was coming. The government didn't just stumble onto this."

"If this is true, then what we're hearing..."

"We might be on the brink of first contact." Dr. Mitchell finished.

As Jonathan began to explain, Dr. Mitchell's mind raced. The artifact was definitely answering to something. And whatever was out there was on its way to Earth.

Suddenly, Jonathan sat up straight. "Dr. Mitchell, look at this!" He manipulated the holographic display, zooming in on a particular entanglement pattern. "See how this node pulsates? I think it's trying to show us something."

Dr. Mitchell leaned in, her shoulder brushing against Jonathan's as she studied the pattern. "It's like a heartbeat," she murmured. "But not just one. Millions, billions of them, all in sync."

Realization dawned on them simultaneously. Jonathan breathed. "This entire system is connected to life itself. Every living being in the galaxy."

"...is part of the network," Dr. Mitchell finished. "That's how they perceive everything at once. They're tapped into the very essence of life."

If they could learn to access this network, to truly communicate through it, the potential for human advancement was staggering.

Just then, the entanglement pattern shifted dramatically. New connections formed, pulsing with an urgency they hadn't seen before.

"Something's happening," Dr. Mitchell said, her fingers flying over the controls to capture the data.

Jonathan felt a presence in his mind. Images flashed through his consciousness: a distant star system, a massive stellar event about to occur, the potential destruction of an entire civilization.

He gasped as the connection broke. "They're coming," he said, still reeling from the experience.

Jonathan stood up, a plan already forming in his mind. "We don't need to understand it all yet. We just need to trust in what we've learned so far." He turned to Dr. Mitchell, extending his hand. "Are you with me?"

Dr. Mitchell stared at him, "But how? We barely understand this technology, let alone have the means to stop it."

"It's not just patterns anymore," Jonathan explained, his face pale. "It's a message. I'm translating it now."

As they watched, words began to appear on the screen:

"WE HAVE HEARD YOU. WE ARE COMING."

The question now was: were they coming as friends or foes? And was humanity ready for either possibility?

Jonathan glanced at Dr. Mitchell, seeing his own mix of fear and excitement mirrored in her eyes. Whatever was coming, they were at the forefront of perhaps the most significant moment in human history.

The main screen was alive with activity. The whispers had changed, becoming more intense, more focused.

In the days following the discovery, Jonathan and Dr. Mitchell worked tirelessly to understand and communicate with the alien intelligence they now called Project C.

Jonathan turned to Dr. Mitchell with his grave expression. "I think it's time they told the whole truth about Project B."

The bustling activity of the facility seemed to fade into the background as Jonathan's words hung in the air. Dr. Mitchell's eyes widened slightly, her posture tensing as she processed the implications of what he had just said.

"I've been piecing things together. The way Dr. Gray avoids speaking when certain topics come up, the redacted sections in some of the reports we've been given. There's a whole other layer to this operation that they're keeping from us."

Dr. Mitchell leaned in closer, her voice barely audible. "What do you think it is?"

"I'm not entirely sure," Jonathan admitted, "but I have a theory. Remember how the artifact seemed to recognize me specifically? How it responded to my presence? I don't think that was a coincidence."

Dr. Mitchell's brow furrowed as she caught on to his train of thought. "You think Project B has something to do with you? Why you were chosen for this?"

Jonathan nodded again. "And not just me. I think there might be others. People who have some sort of connection to whatever intelligence is trying to communicate with us."

Dr. Mitchell took a deep breath, processing this new information. "If you're right, this goes far beyond just studying a star or an artifact. They could be experimenting on people, manipulating genetics. The ethical implications alone are staggering."

"Exactly," Jonathan agreed. "And that's why I think it's time they came clean. We can't hope to establish meaningful communication with an alien intelligence if we're keeping secrets from each other."

Dr. Mitchell studied Jonathan's face for a moment before speaking. "You're planning to confront Dr. Gray about this, aren't you?"

"I think we have to," Jonathan replied. "For the sake of the project, for the sake of whatever's out there and for our own sakes. We deserve to know the whole truth."

Dr. Mitchell nodded, a determined look settling on her face. "You're right. And I'm with you on this, Dr. Avery. Whatever happens, we're in this together."

As they prepared to seek out Dr. Gray and demand answers about Project B, Jonathan and Dr. Mitchell knew they were about to cross a line.

Chapter Twelve: System of the Stars

The echo of their footsteps ricocheted off the walls as Jonathan and Dr. Mitchell approached Dr. Gray's office, Jonathan's hand hovered over the door handle, a moment of hesitation betraying his inner turmoil.

Dr. Mitchell turned to Jonathan, her eyes searching his face. "Are you absolutely sure about this?" she whispered, her voice taut with tension. "Once we do this, there's no going back."

"We've come too far to back down now. Whatever the consequences, we need to know the truth." Jonathan took one more look at Dr. Mitchell and knocked on the door.

"Come in," Dr. Gray's voice called from inside.

They entered to find Dr. Gray hunched over his desk, surrounded by stacks of papers and holographic displays. He looked up, his expression shifting from surprise to concern as he registered the serious looks on their faces.

"Dr. Avery, Dr. Mitchell," he greeted them, his voice cautious, a flicker of unease crossing his features. "What can I do for you?"

Jonathan stepped forward, his heart racing. "Dr. Gray, we need to talk about Project B."

The color drained from Dr. Gray's face as he quickly tapped a button on his desk, filling the room with the faint hum of a privacy field.

"How do you know about that?" he asked, his voice barely above a whisper.

"We've pieced things together," Dr. Mitchell replied, her tone firm. "The redacted reports, the secret meetings, the way the artifact responded to Jonathan. It's time for the truth, Dr. Gray. What is Project B, and what does it have to do with alien life?"

Dr. Gray sank back into his chair, suddenly looking much older. "You have no idea what you're getting into," he said, his voice heavy with resignation. “Come with me.”

Dr. Gray led Jonathan and Dr. Mitchell to a secure room deep within the facility. As the heavy door sealed behind them, he activated a holographic display showing a complex network of quantum entangled particles stretching across the galaxy.

Jonathan and Dr. Mitchell exchanged bewildered glances as Dr. Gray continued. "What I'm about to tell you must not leave this room. Project B isn't just about alien life - it's about human evolution."

"We've known about extraterrestrial intelligence for decades. But more importantly, we discovered that certain individuals on Earth possess a unique genetic marker - one that allows them to interface with alien technology. You, Dr. Avery, are one of those individuals."

"Project B was meant to prepare humanity for this moment - first contact. But something's gone wrong. The aliens we were communicating with - they're not all friendly. We need to proceed with caution."

Dr. Mitchell listened intently, her brow furrowed in concentration. "If what you're saying is true…"

Jonathan, who had been quietly observing, finally spoke up. "Caution? With all due respect, Dr. Gray, if you know a way to make contact with an advanced alien civilization, we need to seize it immediately."

Dr. Mitchell found herself nodding in agreement with Dr. Gray. "He's right. As much as I feel compelled to answer this call, we can't rush into this blindly. We need more data."

"Alright, here's what we're going to do. Dr. Avery, I want you and Dr. Mitchell to work together on deciphering more of the artifact's patterns. See if you can establish a clearer line of communication. I will coordinate with our orbital satellites. I want constant monitoring of the system and any anomalies in our local space."

As they dispersed to their assigned tasks, Jonathan turned to Dr. Mitchell, "you were skeptical about this whole project," he said quietly.

Dr. Mitchell looked up at him, a small smile playing on her lips. "I still have my doubts about the government's true motives, Dr. Avery. But I can't deny the evidence in front of me. Whatever's happening here, it's real, and it's bigger than any of us. I intend to see it through."

Jonathan nodded, feeling a sense of camaraderie with his colleague. As they began their work, the artifact pulsed gently in its containment field, then suddenly there was another violent tremor that shook the facility, more powerful than the last. As if responding to the seismic activity, the artifact suddenly burst to life, shooting out brilliant beams of light in all directions. The radiance was blinding, forcing everyone in the chamber to shield their eyes.

As the chaos unfolded around them, the artifact suddenly went dark, its pulsing glow fading to nothing. The screens monitoring the star system they had been studying likewise went blank, plunging the room into an eerie silence that contrasted sharply with the alarms still blaring throughout the facility.

Jonathan's eyes widened as he processed this sudden change. "The artifact... the star... they've gone silent," he muttered, his voice barely audible over the commotion.

Dr. Gray turned to him, confusion evident on his face. "What? How is that possible?"

Jonathan's mind raced, connecting dots that only he seemed to see.

Jonathan, blinking away the afterimages, turned to Dr. Mitchell, his voice urgent. "We have to get to the observatory right away. Now!"

Dr. Gray, still visibly shaken by the artifact's display, looked at Jonathan in confusion. "The observatory? Dr. Avery, we've just experienced a potentially catastrophic event. We need to secure the artifact and—"

"You don't understand," Jonathan interrupted, his tone brooking no argument. "Those light beams, the earthquake, the silence – it's all connected. Whatever's happening here is tied to something much bigger. We need a clear view of those stars immediately."

Dr. Mitchell, who had been checking the now-silent equipment, joined them. "He's right, Dr. Gray. Jonathan's insights have been crucial so far. If he thinks we need to get to the observatory, we should trust him."

Dr. Gray hesitated, looking from the darkened artifact to the still-smoldering wall where unknown entities threatened to break through. Finally, he nodded. "Alright, but we need to move fast. The facility will go into complete lockdown in less than five minutes."

As they turned to leave, Jonathan cast one last glance at the silent artifact. "Whatever's coming," he said quietly, "I have a feeling it's bigger than anything we've imagined."

The trio rushed out of the chamber, navigating through panicked staff and failing systems. As they raced against time to reach the observatory,

The image of those light beams shooting from the artifact played over and over in Jonathan’s head. Had he just witnessed some kind of signal – or perhaps a warning?

As they neared the exit, Jonathan suddenly halted, causing Dr. Gray and Dr. Mitchell to nearly collide with him. His face was etched with determination and a hint of regret as he turned to face them.

"Wait," Jonathan said, his voice firm but tinged with urgency. "You two need to stay behind."

Dr. Gray's brow furrowed in confusion. "What? Dr. Avery, we don't have time for this. We need to—"

Jonathan cut him off, shaking his head. "No, listen to me. If the artifact and the star system start communicating again, you two are the only ones who can decipher it. You need to stay here and monitor the situation."

Dr. Mitchell stepped forward, her eyes searching Jonathan's face. "But Jon, we're a team. We should face this together."

"I know," Jonathan replied, his voice softening slightly. "But think about it. If something happens up there, if what I suspect is true, we can't risk losing all of our expertise in one place. You two are vital to understanding the artifact and the star system. If they reactivate, we need you here to interpret."

Dr. Gray nodded slowly, beginning to understand. "You're right. As much as I hate to admit it, you're right. But what about you? What do you expect to find in the observatory?"

Jonathan's eyes flickered with a mix of excitement and apprehension. "I'm not sure. But those light beams from the artifact, I think they were a signal. Whatever's coming, I have a feeling it's going to be visible in this night sky. And someone needs to be there to witness it firsthand."

Dr. Mitchell reached out and grasped Jonathan's hand. "Be careful, Jon. We still don't know what we're dealing with."

Jonathan squeezed her hand in return, offering a small smile. "I will. And I'll contact you as soon as I can. If anything changes down here, if the artifact or the star system show any signs of activity, let me know immediately."

Dr. Gray placed a hand on Jonathan's shoulder. "Good luck, Dr. Avery. I have a feeling we're all going to need it."

With a final nod to his colleagues, Jonathan turned and sprinted towards the exit. As he ran, the weight of responsibility settled on his shoulders. He was potentially the only person prepared to witness whatever cosmic event was about to unfold, and he silently prayed he was ready for it.

Behind him, Dr. Mitchell and Dr. Gray exchanged a worried glance before hurrying back to the artifact chamber, ready to face whatever challenges awaited them there. The fate of humanity's understanding of the cosmos now rested in their hands, split between two locations in a race against time and the unknown.

The car was waiting when he emerged from the lab. The driver eyed him with curiosity. "You're going to the observatory?" he asked, his voice thick with an accent.

Jonathan nodded as he was putting on his seatbelt.

"To see the star system?" The driver asked, a knowing smile playing on his lips.

"Yes," Jonathan said, his voice firm.

"You're not the first," he said, as if sharing a secret. "Many have been there in the last few days. All looking for answers in the sky."

The trip was silent, the car weaving through the dark streets.

The observatory stood on the other side of Area 52, a bastion of science and technology amidst the landscape. The structure stood against the backdrop of the desert, gleaming white against the burgeoning light of the dawn.

The guards at the gate eyed him warily, checking his credentials before letting him through. Inside, the air was alive with the hum of computers and the murmur of scientists, all focused on the star system.

The observatory director, a stoic man named Dr. Mark Mizrahi greeted him with a firm handshake. "Welcome, Dr. Avery," he said, his eyes flickering to the sky. "We're expecting quite a show tonight."

Throughout the facility, the buzz of conversation about the star system filled the air. Scientists were talking in hushed, excited tones. Jonathan wondered if they knew the situation at hand as he tried to focus on his preparations for the observation, but the talk of prophecy and divine intervention kept pulling him from his calculations.

A couple of scientists at the table were talking about a leader who would come with a star system to usher in peace. And here he was searching for answers about a star system that defied all natural laws.

Dr. Mizrahi noticed Jonathan's distraction, his gaze sharpening. "You're not one to indulge in the myths and legends, are you?" he said, his voice low.

Jonathan looked up from his notebook. "I'm an astrophysicist," he said. "I deal in facts and data."

Dr. Mizrahi nodded. "Good," he said. "Because there's something about this star system that doesn't sit well with me either. These people sure think that the star system is a sign of a leader coming. Makes no sense."

The doctor's expression grew solemn. "It means we have to be careful. This isn't just about science anymore. It's about perception, and how that perception can shape reality."

The words lingered in the air as they returned to their stations, the countdown to the observation time ticking down. The director's words echoed in his mind as he worked alongside the other astronomers, setting up the telescopes and calibrating the instruments. Yet, despite the seriousness of why they were there, the atmosphere was electric with excitement. Everyone was eager to get a closer look at the star system that had captured the world's attention.

The time passed in a blur of conversations, data and calculations, the star system's movements mapped out with precision.

As the night grew colder, the other scientists grew more jovial, sharing stories and theories. But Dr. Mizrahi remained silent, his eyes never leaving the sky.

When the time came for the observation, Jonathan took his place at his assigned telescope, his heart racing.

Dr. Mizrahi input the coordinates of the star system into the computer, his fingers trembling slightly.

The room fell silent as the telescopes whirred to life, the dome sliding open to reveal the night sky. The moment was surreal, the star systems above seemingly within his grasp.

He looked through his eyepiece and gasped. The star system was closer than he had ever seen it, its fiery surface boiling with an intensity that took his breath away. But no matter how much data he had gathered, the star system's behavior remained inexplicable.

The star system began to pulse, the rhythm growing faster and faster until it was a blur of light and color.

And in that moment the star system grew, swelling in the sky until it was all he could see, consuming his vision.

But when he blinked, it was gone, the sky returning to its usual array of celestial bodies.

Dr. Mizrahi looked at him, his brow furrowed. "What did we just see?"

Jonathan took a deep breath, trying to find the words. "I saw something," he said. "I'm not sure. It vanished."

The doctor's eyes widened, his face a mask of disbelief. "Vanished? That's impossible," he murmured.

But Jonathan knew what he had seen, and he knew that it was anything but impossible.

The evening grew late, and the other scientists began to drift away, leaving Jonathan and Dr. Mizrahi alone in the control room. The silence was broken only by the hum of the computers and the occasional crackle of static on the speakers.

Dr. Mizrahi leaned in closer, his gaze never leaving the screens. "There's something about that star system," he said, his voice low. "It's not just a star system."

Jonathan's heart raced, he knew the answer but was not at liberty to say anything. Not yet anyways. "I agree"

Dr. Mizrahi turned to him, his eyes serious. "The patterns, the movement…"

Jonathan was gathering his belongings, shoving the last papers in his backpack when he looked up to find Dr. Mizrahi standing beside him. His face was a mask of determination. "We need to get closer," he said. "Much closer."

The decision was made swiftly, a risky plan hatched in the heart of the night. They would use one of the observatory's highest powered telescopes, one that had been off limits to without a special clearance since its inception.

As they approached the restricted area Dr. Mizrahi swiped his badge. The heavy door groaned open and the lights flickered on. The room was much smaller than Jonathan expected, but the sense of power within it was chiling. Every wall was filled with screens and complex machinery. Each breath he took had the scent of oil and metal.

Jonathan's heart was racing as the door hissed shut behind them. In the very center of the room, the gleaming monstrosity of the telescope. A high-powered marvel of engineering, its gleaming metal body a testament to humanity's quest for knowledge. The lens was the size of a small car, and the frame that held it looked like it could withstand a small meteor shower. He ran his hand along the cool metal, feeling the vibrations of the machinery beneath his fingertips.

He had read about this kind of technology, but never had he been so close to something so powerful.

The control panel was a symphony of buttons and screens, each one telling a different story about the cosmos. Dr. Mizrahi's hand hovered over the controls, an audible countdown began, the screens in front of them flickering to life, and they both took deep breaths, steeling themselves for what they might discover.

"Ready?" he asked, and without waiting for a response, he began the sequence to align the telescope.

The floor trembled beneath them as the massive instrument swiveled and adjusted, pointing towards the heavens with unerring accuracy.

Jonathan took a step back, his heart racing. This was it. This was the moment they would see the ship up close.

The anticipation was electric, the tension in the room almost tangible as the doctor's hand hovered over the final button.

He pressed it. The room plunged into darkness, and for a brief moment, Jonathan held his breath.

Then, light, blinding and brilliant, filled the room, and the star system was once again in their sights. Only this time, it was closer, its fiery dance magnified to a terrifying degree.

They stared into the abyss, searching for answers in the heart of the cosmic anomaly that had brought them together, watching as the star system grew even larger. Its fiery tendrils reaching out towards them.

And then, as suddenly as it had appeared, the star system winked out of existence, leaving them in the cold, black emptiness of space.

The silence was deafening, the screens in front of them now showing only the void where the star system had been.

Jonathan and Dr. Mizrahi exchanged a look of sheer astonishment as the star systems began to align themselves to match the binary map that lay in front of them.

As they watched Jonathan heard something. It was faint, almost imperceptible, but it was there—a whisper, a murmur that seemed to come from nowhere and everywhere at once.

"Did you hear that?" Jonathan asked, his voice low.

Dr. Mizrahi nodded, his eyes searching the shadows.

They looked around the room, searching for the source of the sound, but saw no one. The door was closed. They were alone. Only the maintenance team was anywhere in the building, and they had passed them working in the Planetarium Dome room.

The whisper grew louder, the words discernible. “We are coming.”

They exchanged a confused glance, their hearts pounding in their chests. The urgency of the voice was impossible to ignore.

Dr. Mizrahi's hand hovered over the controls, his eyes searching the sky.

Suddenly, the star system returned, its light grew brighter, the whispers grew clearer. "Look," it said again, more urgently this time. "Look to the east."

Dr. Mizrahi turned the telescope, their eyes scanning the horizon. There, where the sky met the desert, they saw it—a second point of light, moving towards the city.

Their eyes widened in shock. It was another star system, similar to the binary star system, but different. This one was a deep blue, and it was approaching rapidly.

Jonathan's mind raced with the implications. "It can't be," he murmured.

Jonathan was trying to make sense of what they were seeing and hearing. He looked away for a moment and the whispers grew softer. He looked through the telescope to find the light of the new star system had dimmed slightly as if retreating.

“We need to get closer!” Dr. Mizrahi's voice boomed.

Then with a few more buttons pushed the telescope zoomed out then back in, further revealing a pattern in its light that danced and swirled before their eyes.

A pattern that spoke of something ancient and powerful.

The whispers grew louder, guiding them even closer, and the pattern grew clearer. It was a map, a cosmic blueprint that pointed not just to the heavens, but to the very heart of human existence.

Jonathan stared in awe as the star system's light enveloped them, the whispers becoming a cacophony of voices, all speaking in unison. The voices grew deafening, and the light blinding.

The pattern grew more intricate, revealing itself to be a series of symbols, each one more ancient and enigmatic than the last.

Jonathan's mind raced as he sketched out the symbols in his notebook, his mind swirling with the star system's light as the whispers grew into a crescendo, the voices urging them to get even closer, and suddenly, they were in the heart of the star system.

The star system's core was a maelstrom of light and energy, and within it, the whispers coalesced into a single, clear voice. “What is ours…”

Jonathan and Dr. Mizrahi looked at each other, their eyes wide with astonishment.

What does that mean? Jonathan thought to himself.

As they searched in the heart of the celestial fire, the voice grew softer, the light dimming. They realized that the star system was speaking of a time when the universe would face a great reckoning, and how their world was but a speck in the vast tapestry of cosmic events.

The whispers grew fainter, the light of the star system receding. As it pulled away from the cosmic embrace, the voice spoke in barely a whisper. Jonathan strained to hear, “Coming. Ours. Soon."

With that, the star system's light dimmed, and the whispers ceased. The telescope's instruments went dark, and for a moment, Jonathan and Dr. Mizrahi were looking at a sea of blackness.

The sky returned to its usual constellation of stars. The data Jonathan had collected was invaluable, the experience indescribable.

Chapter Thirteen: The Interstellar Liaison

Jonathan burst through the lab doors, his chest heaving as he gasped for air. His sudden entrance startled Dr. Mitchell and Dr. Gray, who were bent over the still-silent artifact.

"Jon!" Dr. Mitchell exclaimed, rushing to his side. "What happened? What did you see?"

Jonathan leaned against a nearby console as he tried to catch his breath. "A ship," he managed to say between gulps of air. "I saw a ship... in a second star."

Dr. Gray approached quickly, his face a mask of confusion and intrigue. "A second star? What do you mean? How did you—"

Jonathan waved off the question. There was no time to explain the intricate process of how he'd managed to use the high-powered telescope to observe something so distant and seemingly impossible. "No time," he panted. "But that's not all. There was a message, but I could barely make it out."

Dr. Mitchell and Dr. Gray leaned in, hanging on his every word.

“Coming,” Jonathan said, his voice dropping to almost a whisper. “Ours. Soon.”

The room fell into a stunned silence as Jonathan's words sank in. Dr. Mitchell was the first to break it.

"Coming, ours, soon?" she repeated, her voice trembling slightly. "Jon, are you saying…"

"Yes," Jonathan nodded, finally catching his breath. "I think we're about to have visitors. And soon."

Dr. Gray's face paled. "This changes everything. We need to alert the authorities, prepare defenses, we need to—"

Suddenly, the artifact in the center of the room pulsed to life, emitting a low, rhythmic hum. All eyes turned to it as patterns of light began to dance across its surface.

"It's responding," Dr. Mitchell whispered in awe.

Jonathan stepped towards the artifact, his earlier exhaustion forgotten. "No," he said, his voice filled with a strange certainty. "It's not responding. It's counting down."

As the three scientists gathered around the now-active artifact, the facility's alarms began to blare once more, while outside, unbeknownst to them, the night sky was changing, preparing for an arrival that would alter the course of human history forever.

The race to decipher the artifact's message and prepare for what was coming had begun, with Jonathan, Dr. Mitchell, and Dr. Gray standing at the forefront of humanity's first true contact with an alien civilization.

Jonathan looked up at Dr. Gray in disbelief. "Dr. Gray," he said, his voice barely above a whisper, "I know what this is. And it's bigger than anything we could have imagined."

He stood with his gaze locked on the artifact and continued, "Because this isn't just some alien technology."

"We need to assemble the team now," Jonathan said, a new determination in his voice. "There's work to be done, and we don't have much time."

Dr. Gray nodded, still looking shaken. "Time for what, Dr. Avery?"

Jonathan turned to him, his eyes blazing with purpose. "They aren't just calling out to the artifact. They're coming for it."

"Project B," Dr. Gray began, his voice heavy, "was initiated a decade ago, right after we received the artifact. We didn't make the connection; we simply sealed the artifact in a container and stored it. We worked on creating quantum links with distant stars, hoping to detect signs of advanced civilizations. What we didn't anticipate was the artifact's involvement. Now we're facing the consequences."

Jonathan's mind reeled. "This is a result of our own actions?"

Dr. Gray nodded grimly. "We inadvertently created a network, a cosmic web of consciousness, thus showing them where the artifact could be found."

Dr. Mitchell leaned forward, her eyes intense. "And how did you do that exactly?"

"We're not entirely sure," Dr. Gray admitted.

"So it found the artifact and called out to it? And now it's answering," Jonathan finished, the gravity of the situation sinking in. "Leading them to us?"

Suddenly, the facility shook violently. Alarms blared as they rushed back to the main lab. The star map was alight with activity, pulses of energy racing along the quantum pathways they'd created.

"We're running out of time," Dr. Gray said, his voice tense. "We need to alert the authorities, prepare a response team—"

"No," Jonathan interrupted, a look of determination settling on his face. "We can't risk anyone else interfering. Whatever's coming, it responded to me. I'm meant to be there when they arrive."

Dr. Mitchell grabbed his arm, her eyes wide with concern. "Jon, you can't be serious. It's too dangerous. We don't know what their intentions are!"

"Exactly," Jonathan replied, gently removing her hand. "We don't know. But if they wanted to harm us, why give us advance warning?"

Dr. Gray looked conflicted, but after a moment, he nodded. "As much as I hate to admit it, Dr. Avery might be right. His connection to the artifact, his ability to decipher the star's message. He might be our best chance at peaceful first contact."

Another tremor shook the building, more violent than the last. Alarms blared with renewed intensity, and the sound of approaching footsteps echoed from the hallway.

"Dr. Gray, I need you to create a diversion. Buy me enough time to get out of here. Dr. Mitchell," Jonathan said urgently. "I need you to trust me."

Just then a bright point of light began to form in the center of the lab, growing larger and more intense by the second. The air crackled with energy, and the smell of ozone filled the room.

"There’s no time! It's happening faster than we anticipated!" Jonathan shouted over the chaos. “Intelligence, whatever it is, it's using our own mistakes against us!"

A beam of light shot down, and within it materialized a figure that was unmistakably alien. Its form was both beautiful and terrifying, with features that seemed to shift and change as Jonathan tried to focus on them.

After staring at them for a while, the creature let out a sharp cough releasing a stream of green, foamy saliva from its mouth. Jonathan stepped back quickly as the spit created a foul-smelling puddle on the floor.

"What the hell?" Dr. Mitchell said, stepping further back.

With a casual shrug, the creature used its arm to wipe its mouth.

The alien's voice resonated in Jonathan's mind, bypassing his ears entirely. "Human," it said, the word filled with disdain. "We have come for what is ours. The item is not meant for your kind."

Jonathan swallowed hard, trying to keep his voice steady as he responded. "We've been studying it, trying to understand—"

The alien cut him off with a mental wave that felt like a slap. "Your understanding is irrelevant. The item is beyond your comprehension. It has a key to powers you cannot fathom. Surrender it to us now."

Feeling a surge of protectiveness for the artifact that had brought him to this moment, Jonathan stood his ground. "And if we refuse?"

The alien paused, a flicker of interest passing through its ever-changing form. "Speak quickly, human. Our patience wears thin."

Jonathan's mind raced as the ultimatum hung in the air. The thought of the billions of people on Earth, blissfully unaware that their fate was being decided at this very moment.

But mostly he thought of Sherry, who was patiently waiting at home for that occasional phone call that he was permitted to make.

The alien's form seemed to grow larger, more menacing. "Then we will take it by force. Your weapons are useless against us. Your cities will crumble. Your planet will burn. We will destroy everything, including your Earth, to reclaim what is ours."

Jonathan took a deep breath, knowing that his next words could determine the future of his entire species. He had to find a way to turn this confrontation into a dialogue.

As he prepared to state his case, Jonathan silently prayed that his understanding of the artifact, combined with his scientific knowledge and human intuition, would be enough to prevent a catastrophe and possibly forge a new path forward for both species.

"We need to get out of here!" Dr. Mitchell yelled.

But Jonathan caught her arm, his eyes fixed on the growing light. "Wait," he said, an inexplicable calm washing over him. "I don't think we can run now. We need to face it."

A voice resonated in their minds, vast and ancient: "We have waited for this moment. You have given us a bridge, and we have crossed it. Now, you will return what is ours."

Jonathan stepped forward, his heart pounding but his voice steady. "We welcome you. We have so many questions."

"As do we," the creature responded. "Your actions have irreversibly altered the cosmic order. The age of isolation is over. You will return to us what is ours!"

The being's form rippled, and images of distant worlds and advanced civilizations flashed through their minds as it communicated. "Now, it is time for you to listen, and us to speak."

As the tension reached its peak, a sudden movement caught Jonathan and Dr. Mitchell's attention. To their shock, Dr. Gray appeared seemingly out of nowhere, the artifact clutched in his hands. Jonathan's heart raced, fearing that Gray was about to surrender their most valuable asset.

"No, Dr. Gray!" Jonathan shouted, his voice filled with desperation. "You can't give it to them!"

Dr. Mitchell, overwhelmed by the sudden turn of events, felt tears welling up in her eyes. "Please, don't do this," she pleaded.

But as Dr. Gray approached the creature, a strange look of determination on his face, something unexpected happened. The alien's form shifted, radiating what could only be described as confusion and anger.

"This is not what we seek," the alien's voice boomed in their minds. "You dare to deceive us?"

Jonathan and Dr. Mitchell exchanged bewildered glances. If the artifact wasn't what the aliens wanted, then what were they after?

Dr. Gray, standing firm, addressed the alien. "We have hidden nothing from you. This is the artifact we discovered, the one that has been communicating with us."

The alien's form pulsed with fury. "Lies! Return what is ours immediately, or face the consequences!"

Suddenly, the artifact in Dr. Gray's hands began to glow, emitting a soft hum. Patterns of light danced across its surface, and it seemed to be communicating directly with the entity.

Jonathan, Dr. Mitchell, and Dr. Gray watched in awe as an incomprehensible exchange took place before them. The artifact's lights pulsed and shifted rapidly, while the alien's form rippled and changed in response.

"What's happening?" Dr. Mitchell whispered, her eyes wide.

Jonathan shook his head, frustration evident in his voice. "I don't know. It's like they're having a conversation, but I can't make out what they're saying."

As the silent dialogue continued, they stood helplessly by. Their fate hung in the balance, dependent on a conversation they couldn't decipher.

Dr. Gray turned to Jonathan and Dr. Mitchell, "This is clearly more complicated than we ever imagined."

As they watched the exchange between the artifact and the alien, Jonathan couldn't help but wonder: If the artifact wasn't what the aliens were after, what could be so important that they would threaten to destroy an entire planet to retrieve it? And more importantly, did they unknowingly possess this mysterious object without even realizing its significance?

The answers to these questions, it seemed, lay in the indecipherable conversation unfolding before them, a cosmic mystery that held the key to the future.

As the incomprehensible dialogue between the artifact and the alien continued, Jonathan, Dr. Mitchell, and Dr. Gray stood in tense silence, their minds racing to make sense of the situation.

Suddenly, the Aliens glow intensified, and a wave of energy pulsed outward. In one swift move, the creature was in front of the artifact with his arm raised back smashing the artifact out of Dr. Gray's hand, sending it across the room where it violently fell to the floor.

A loud piercing sound engulfed the room, and the artifact pulsed. Then something peculiar happened. The artifact began to levitate itself, moving and aligning itself with the light. A small flicker of flame appeared, swirling over its surface. Then a flash of intense fire jolted toward the creature.

"Move!" Dr. Mitchell yelled, covering her ears, "The damn thing is alive!"

Jonathan shoved Dr. Gray just as the fiery flame passed his body crashing into the wall and dissipating.

Scarcely daring to breathe, Jonathan watched the flame float over to the Alien where it stayed suspended in the air for a moment before changing its direction and floating slowly toward Jonathan. Instinctively, he dropped to his hands and knees. The flame halted, then floated back, absorbing itself within the artifact that floated, seemingly suspended in the air.

The alien's form shimmered, its anger seeming to subside slightly. When it spoke again, its mental voice carried a new tone - one of grudging respect mixed with frustration.

"It appears we have been misinformed," the alien communicated. "The artifact is not what we seek, yet it speaks of something else. Something hidden within your kind."

Jonathan stepped forward cautiously. "Within our kind? What do you mean?"

The alien's form shifted, focusing its attention on Jonathan. "You, human. The artifact speaks of you, and others like you. You carry the knowledge within you, though you know it not."

Dr. Mitchell gasped, her mind flashing back to their earlier conversations about Project B and genetic markers. "Dr. Gray," she whispered, "could this be related to what you mentioned earlier? About certain individuals being able to interface with alien technology?"

Dr. Gray nodded slowly, his face pale. "It's possible. We never fully understood the implications of those genetic markers."

The alien, growing impatient, interjected. "Enough discussion. You have little time to return what is ours!"

Jonathan's heart raced as he realized the implications. "And if I can’t?"

The alien's form darkened ominously. "Then we will take you by force, until we get what is ours, regardless of the consequences to your species. If we find it first we will destroy all things around it."

As the tension mounted once again, the artifact in Dr. Gray's hands suddenly levitated, positioning itself between Jonathan and the alien. Its glow pulsed rhythmically, and to everyone's surprise, a voice emanated from it - not in their minds, but audibly in the air around them.

"The choice is not yours to make," the artifact spoke, its voice a harmonic blend of tones. “The human needs more time.”

The alien recoiled, clearly taken aback by this development. "You overstep your bounds, Guardian. This matter does not concern you."

"On the contrary," the artifact - or Guardian - replied, "it is precisely my purpose to protect the conduit until such time.”

As this new standoff unfolded, Jonathan, Dr. Mitchell, and Dr. Gray exchanged looks of amazement and confusion. The situation had evolved far beyond their understanding, with cosmic forces now seemingly at odds over Joanthan's fate.

He felt a strange sensation building within him. It was as if something dormant was awakening, responding to the presence of the alien and the Guardian.

"Wait," Jonathan said, his voice surprisingly steady despite the fear coursing through him. "I understand what's happening."

All attention turned to him - the alien's shifting form, the Guardian's pulsing glow, and the anxious faces of Dr. Mitchell and Dr. Gray.

"You're looking for something within me," Jonathan continued, addressing the alien. "Information I carry but don't fully comprehend. And you," he turned to the Guardian, "you're protecting me until I do? But why?"

The Guardian's voice resonated once more. "You are a conduit, Dr. Jonathan Avery. A bridge between worlds, between times. What you carry is knowledge - ancient and powerful - but it is not yet complete."

The alien's form rippled with impatience. "What we seek belongs to us. We have come to reclaim what is rightfully ours."

Jonathan felt a surge of determination. "I won't let you take me or whatever it is by force," he said to the alien. "But perhaps there's another way. A way for us to work together, to uncover what I have that you seek."

The alien's form seemed to hesitate, considering Jonathan's words. For a tense moment, silence fell over the group. Then, slowly, the alien's form began to anger, taking on a more threatening appearance.

"Your proposal is denied, human!" the alien shouted.

With that, the creature's form began to fade, retreating back to the light hovering above. As it disappeared, the oppressive atmosphere lifted, leaving Jonathan, Dr. Mitchell, and Dr. Gray standing in awe of what had just transpired.

The Guardian, still hovering between them, spoke one last time. "You will discover the item they search for, but you must do it quickly. For the sake of your species and many others."

The artifact pulsed again. But this time no flame came to its surface. Instead, a blue hue of light emitted itself around the object. The color was unlike any Jonathan had seen before, a hypnotic deep blue that seemed to resonate with something inside him.

As the artifact's glow faded and it gently lowered itself back into Dr. Gray's hands.

"Well," Dr. Mitchell said, breaking the silence with a shaky laugh, "that was different."

"You're right Dr. Mitchell. I guess we better get busy. But first…" Jonathan said, "Let's get some fresh air."

They sat outside looking at the night sky. What once a canvas of wonder and mystery, now felt like a looming threat.

“We need to figure out what the item is," Jonathan said, breaking the tense silence.

Dr. Mitchell nodded, her analytical mind already at work. "We should start by reviewing all our data on the artifact and the star system. There might be clues we missed before."

"Agreed," Dr. Gray added, his voice grim. "But we need to be cautious. If word gets out about what just happened, panic would spread quickly."

“What’s that?” Dr. Mitchell said, pointing to the lights of several official-looking dark vans approaching.

"Looks like we're not the only ones who noticed our visitors," Jonathan muttered.

The peaceful night was shattered by the screech of the tires and the slamming of car doors. Before Jonathan, Dr. Mitchell, and Dr. Gray could react, soldiers burst from the doors.

Jonathan felt rough hands grabbing his arms, dragging him from his seat. He struggled, but the soldiers were too strong. In a blur of motion, he found himself thrown into the back of one of the vans, the metal floor cold against his skin.

Dr. Mitchell barely had time to scream before she was hauled into another one. The van's doors slammed shut behind her, plunging her into darkness.

Dr. Gray tried to reason with the soldier’s. His words fell on deaf ears as he was unceremoniously bundled into another waiting van. Dr. Gray's confusion was apparent as the van sped away.

Each van took a different route, weaving through the streets. Their destinations were unknown, but their purpose was clear: interrogation about their encounter with the alien that had turned their lives upside down.

As the vehicles disappeared into the night, the only evidence left was the echo of engines fading into the distance, leaving behind three coffee cups and a laboratory full of scientists blissfully unaware of the drama that had unfolded.

The vans sped through the night, each taking a different route but converging on the same destination.

After a tense 30-minute drive, they arrived at a government building on the outskirts of the city.

Jonathan, his heart racing, felt the van slow to a stop. The doors swung open, revealing a brutalist concrete structure before him. Rough hands yanked him out, his feet stumbling on the pavement. He straightened his rumpled jumpsuit as best he could, determined to face whatever lay ahead with dignity.

Dr. Mitchell's van pulled up moments later. She blinked in the lights, disoriented and afraid. As she was led from the vehicle, Jonathan caught a glimpse of her being escorted inside. Their eyes met briefly, a flash of shared fear and confusion passing between them.

Dr. Gray arrived last, his typically composed demeanor shaken. He squinted at the building, his scientific mind already analyzing their situation despite the circumstances.

Three separate teams of stern-faced agents guided them through different entrances. The building's interior was a maze of sterile hallways and locked doors.

As the doors closed behind them, Jonathan, Dr. Mitchell, and Dr. Gray found themselves isolated together at a conference table. The questioning about their alien encounter was about to begin, and none of them knew what to expect.

A man in a black suit stepped in and set up a video call on the massive screen in front of them.

Colonel Sultrier appeared on the screen. "Dr. Avery, Dr. Mitchell, Dr. Gray. We need a full debriefing on what just occurred."

The room behind the camera erupted into murmurs and heated discussions. Colonel Sultrier raised his hand for silence. "Dr. Avery, you have our full attention. Please, start from the beginning."

As Jonathan began recounting the events of the day, he felt the weight of every word. He described the alien encounter, the Guardian's intervention, and the cryptic warning about finding the mysterious item.

Dr. Mitchell interjected occasionally, providing scientific context, while Dr. Gray offered insights into the artifact's behavior. As they spoke, Jonathan observed the changing expressions on Colonel Sultrier's face -

from skepticism to concern, and finally to grim determination.

When they finished their account, Colonel Sultrier leaned forward, his voice low and serious.

"This is beyond anything we've prepared for. Dr. Avery, do you have any idea what this item might be?"

Jonathan shook his head. "No, sir. But the guardian seemed to think we'd be able to find it if we looked hard enough."

Colonel Sultrier nodded, then turned to address the room. "Ladies and gentlemen, as of this moment, finding this item becomes our top priority. All other projects are suspended. We'll be operating under the highest level of secrecy."

He turned back to Jonathan, Dr. Mitchell, and Dr. Gray. "You three will lead this investigation. Whatever resources you need, you'll have them. But understand this - the fate of our world may rest on your shoulders."

As the meeting adjourned and people behind him began to file out. Once they were alone, Colonel Sultrier's demeanor softened slightly. "Jonathan, I've read your file. Your insights, your intuition - they're unparalleled. If anyone can figure this out, it's you. But I need to know: are you prepared for what this might entail? The pressure, the risks?"

Jonathan met the Colonel's gaze steadily. "Colonel, with all due respect, I don't think any of us are truly prepared for what's coming. But I'm ready to do whatever it takes to protect our world."

Colonel Sultrier nodded, a hint of approval in his eyes. "Good. Because I have a feeling this is just the beginning of a much larger story. Get some rest, Dr. Avery. Tomorrow, we start our search in earnest."

After hours of intense questioning, Jonathan, Dr. Mitchell, and Dr. Gray were unexpectedly led to a waiting area in the government building. Their faces showed a mix of exhaustion and relief.

"Are you both okay?" Jonathan whispered, his voice hoarse from the interrogation.

Before either could respond, they were ushered outside where a single van waited. This time, they were placed in the vehicle together, a stark contrast to their earlier separate journeys.

As the van pulled away from the building, Dr. Mitchell leaned close to the others. "Where do you think they're taking us now?"

Dr. Gray's eyes narrowed behind his glasses. "Given the nature of what just happened, there is no telling."

The drive was longer this time, the urban landscape giving way to desert terrain. After what felt like an hour, they approached the heavily guarded Area 52 compound in the middle of the barren landscape.

Standing in his room, Jonathan's heart sank as he heard Sherry's voice, thick with emotion, on the other end of the line. The weight of everything that had happened in the past few hours suddenly collided with the realization of how much time had passed since he'd last spoken to her.

"Sherry," he said softly, his own voice cracking with emotion. "I'm so sorry. I had no idea it had been that long."

"A week, Jon," Sherry sobbed. "No calls, no messages. I've been worried sick. What's going on? Are you okay?"

Jonathan sank onto the edge of his bed, running a hand through his hair. The urge to tell her everything was overwhelming, but he knew he couldn't. Not over the phone, and not with the level of secrecy surrounding recent events.

"I'm okay, Sher," he assured her, trying to keep his voice steady. "Things have been intense here. More than I could have ever imagined. I lost track of time, and I'm so, so sorry for that."

Sherry's sobs quieted, but he could still hear the hurt in her voice. "What's happening, Jon? This isn't like you. I know you can't tell me everything, but please give me something."

Jonathan closed his eyes, weighing his words carefully. "Sherry, I've discovered something. Something big. It's going to change everything, and I'm right in the middle of it. I wish I could tell you more, but I can't. Not yet."

There was a pause on the other end of the line. When Sherry spoke again, her voice was calmer, but tinged with worry. "Are you in danger, Jon?"

He wanted to reassure her, to tell her everything was fine, but he couldn't bring himself to lie. "I don't know," he admitted. "But I'm doing important work here. Work that could make a difference for everyone."

Sherry sighed. "Just promise me you'll be careful. And please, don't disappear on me again. I can't bear it."

"I promise," Jonathan said, his voice filled with determination. "I'll call you soon, even if it's just for a minute. I love you, Sherry. More than anything."

"I love you too, Jon," Sherry replied, her voice softening. "Come back to me soon, okay?"

As they said their goodbyes, Jonathan felt a mix of guilt and resolve. He knew the path ahead would be challenging, but hearing Sherry's voice had grounded him, reminding him of what he was fighting for.

He lay back on his bed, staring at the ceiling, his mind racing with thoughts of alien encounters, mysterious artifacts, and hidden items of cosmic importance. But through it all, Sherry's voice echoed in his mind, a beacon of normalcy in a world that had suddenly become anything but normal.

The item they sought could be anywhere, could be anything. But Jonathan was determined to find it. Tomorrow will come soon enough. But for now, he allowed himself a moment of quiet reflection, gathering his strength.

Chapter Fourteen: Betrayal of the Light

By the next week, the city was abuzz with the news of the sighting of a second star. A religious leader, a Rabbi, had interpreted the event as a divine intervention, a sign from above that the world needed to come together in peace. He called for a global assembly to take place two weeks later, at the UN Headquarters in New York.

The announcement shook the city, and soon, the streets were filled with people from every corner of the globe. People of all faiths and nationalities, drawn by the promise of understanding and protection.

Back at the lab in Area 52, Jonathan was watching the news in the breakroom. The TV showed a replay of a reporter interviewing religious leaders expected to be at the assembly.

“Leaders from various religions gathered at UN Headquarters in New York on Friday to observe a moment of prayer for peace amid the world's terrible divisions.” The reporter said.

A rabbi said, "Peace is more important now than ever because war and conflict have driven tens of millions of people from their homes and unleashed terrible poverty and hunger."

The reporter continued. “Even peaceful nations are dealing with disparities and political division as the entire world struggles with climate chaos.”

Another religious leader stepped forward, “People of New York, I am the bringer of peace and prosperity!” the man declared, bold and unwavering. “For too long you have wandered in the shadows, divided by fear and strife. I am here to illuminate your path, to unite your hearts!”

A woman in the front row, trembling with hope, called out, “How will you bring us peace? The world is full of chaos!”

With a piercing gaze, he responded, “Fear not! I am here to guide you! Together, we shall forge a new dawn!”

His words were cold and calculated as he spoke of the new world order, one shaped by his own will. The man’s words carried on the wind, a toxic blend of scripture and science fiction.

“The ceremony took place in front of the famous Knotted Gun sculpture, which has come to represent the UN's dedication to world peace, on the Visitors' Plaza at the Secretariat.” The reporter said.

When the channel cut to a commercial, Jonathan turned to Dr. Mitchell, who was sitting beside him in the breakroom.

"Sarah," he said, his voice low and urgent, "doesn't that man remind you of someone?"

Dr. Mitchell looked at him quizzically. "What do you mean?"

"The way he speaks, the use of his voice, it's Lucien Bennett," Jonathan explained. “I would know him anywhere. But that doesn’t look like him…”

Dr. Mitchell's eyes widened as she considered Jonathan's words. "But that's impossible, right? Bennett is supposed to be in federal jail."

Intrigued by the possibility, Dr. Mitchell pulled out her phone and quickly typed in Bennett's name. As she scrolled through the search results, her expression changed from curiosity to shock.

"Jon," she said, her voice barely above a whisper, "according to this, Lucien Bennett has been released from federal custody."

Jonathan leaned in closer, his heart racing. "What? When? Why?"

Dr. Mitchell shook her head, frustration evident in her voice. "It doesn't say. The article just mentions that he was released, but there's no information about the reasons behind it. It's all very vague."

Jonathan sat back, his mind reeling. "This can't be a coincidence. A charismatic figure appears, preaching unity and a new world order, just as we're dealing with the aftermath of an alien encounter and searching for a mysterious item? And now we find out Bennett is free?"

Dr. Mitchell nodded, "It does seem too convenient to be a chance. But what does it mean? Is Bennett somehow involved in all of this?"

"I don't know," Jonathan replied, running a hand through his hair. "But I have a feeling we're missing something big here. We need to dig deeper into Bennett's release and this new religious leader. There has to be a connection."

As they sat there, the TV continuing to replay scenes from the mysterious man's speech, Jonathan couldn't help but wonder if the alien item, Bennett's release, and this new figure calling for global unity - were interconnected in ways they were only beginning to understand.

"We need to tell Colonel Sultrier about this," Jonathan said, standing up.

Dr. Mitchell nodded in agreement, already gathering her things. As they left the breakroom, the image of the robed figure lingered on the TV screen, his arms outstretched as if embracing the world - or perhaps reaching for something beyond it.

After ending the call with Colonel Sultrier, Jonathan and Dr. Mitchell exchanged worried glances. the Colonel's instruction to keep Dr. Gray in the dark was unexpected and troubling.

"Why wouldn't he want us to tell Dr. Gray?" Dr. Mitchell asked, her voice hushed despite the empty corridor they stood in.

Jonathan leaned against the wall, his mind racing. "I'm not sure, but it can't be good. Gray's been with us from the beginning. He knows as much about the artifact and the alien encounter as we do."

Dr. Mitchell nodded, her brow furrowed. "Do you think Colonel Sultrier suspects Gray of something? Or maybe he's trying to protect him?"

"Or protect us from him," Jonathan added grimly. "We can't rule out the possibility that Gray might be involved in something we're not aware of. Remember how he suddenly appeared with the artifact during the alien encounter? There's still a lot about that moment we don't understand."

Dr. Mitchell sighed, running a hand through her hair. "This is getting more complicated by the minute. First, the mysterious item we need to find, then Bennett's release, this new religious figure, and now secrecy within our own team."

Jonathan nodded, feeling the weight of their situation. "We need to be careful. Until Colonel Sultrier gets here and explains why we're keeping Dr. Gray out of the loop, we should act as normal as possible around him."

"Agreed," Dr. Mitchell said. "But Jon, what if Dr. Gray is innocent in all this? What if keeping him in the dark puts him in danger?"

Jonathan looked at her, his expression serious. "That's a risk we'll have to take for now. We don't have enough information to make a call. Let's just hope Colonel Sultrier has a good reason for this."

As they made their way back to the lab, both scientists felt the tension of their new secret.

The facility, once a place of exciting discovery, now felt like a maze of hidden agendas and potential threats. They knew that every interaction, every piece of information, could be crucial in unraveling the cosmic mystery they faced.

Jonathan couldn't help but wonder how many more secrets were lurking within the walls of Area 52, and how they all connected to the looming threat from beyond the stars. As they prepared to face Dr. Gray and continue their work, both he and Dr. Mitchell silently vowed to stay vigilant, knowing that the fate of humanity might depend on their ability to discern friend from foe in the days to come.

They both went to their separate workstations hoping that if they were not together then Dr. Gray would not interject himself.

Jonathan's mind raced with the thought that it could be Bennett was the item that the aliens were looking for when he mumbled, "Could it be Lucien Bennett? The so-called god?

Unable to shake the feeling that Bennett was connected to this somehow Jonathan couldn't concentrate. He found himself standing outside, the cool breeze flowing through his hair as he stared up at the heavens.

Jonathan's eyes were fixed on the star that hovered above, pulsating as a reminder that time was not on his side.

With the Assembly only two weeks away, Jonathan was running out of time and his patience had started to stretch thin. Frustrated, he looked up at the sky, unsure what he was even looking for. He began to pray.

As soon as the name Lucien Bennett fell from his lips, the star flared, a brilliant flash that illuminated the entire sky. The whispers grew in their intensity, filling his mind with images of Bennett and his speeches. As they played in his mind the picture became clear:

Lucien Bennett was the knowledge he held. He was the item. The realization shook him to his core.

Leaving everything behind, Jonathan raced down the hall and grabbed Dr. Mitchell.

“It’s Lucien Bennett!” Jonathan shouted. “He’s the item they want!”

"What do you mean, Jon?" Dr. Mitchell asked, her voice trembling slightly.

Jonathan paced the floor as he recounted his revelation. "When I prayed for guidance, the star responded. It showed me Bennett's face, his words echoing through my mind!"

Dr. Mitchell's eyes widened as she processed Jonathan's words. "If you're right, this changes everything. But how can we be sure?"

Jonathan ran his hand through his hair, his excitement mixed with a growing sense of urgency. "I don't know how to explain it, Dr. Mitchell, but I'm certain. The way the star reacted, the visions, it all fits. Bennett's sudden release, his reappearance as this religious figure. It can't be a coincidence."

Dr. Mitchell nodded, her analytical mind already racing. "Okay, let's think this through. If Bennett is the 'item' the aliens are after, what does that mean? Is he aware of it? And how does this connect to the knowledge you're supposed to be carrying?"

Before Jonathan could respond, they heard footsteps approaching. Dr. Gray rounded the corner, his face etched with concern.

"What's going on? I heard shouting," Gray said, looking between Jonathan and Dr. Mitchell suspiciously.

Jonathan and Dr. Mitchell exchanged a quick glance, silently agreeing to keep their discovery to themselves for now.

"Sorry, Dr. Gray," Jonathan said, forcing a smile. "We just had a breakthrough in our research. Got a bit excited."

Gray didn't seem entirely convinced but nodded slowly. "I see. Well, keep me informed of any significant developments. We're all in this together, after all."

As Gray walked away, Dr. Mitchell leaned in close to Jonathan. "We need to tell Colonel Sultrier about this immediately. If Bennett is what the aliens want, we might be the only ones who can stop whatever's coming."

Jonathan agreed, pulling out his secure phone to contact the Colonel. As he dialed, a thought struck him. "If they don't find Bennett before the aliens do, innocent people will suffer at the hands of the aliens who for whatever reason are seeking vengeance."

Dr. Mitchell's face paled at the implication. "We need to stop that assembly, Jon. But how? We can't exactly tell the world that a religious leader is the target of an alien invasion."

As the phone rang, Jonathan looked out the window at the pulsing star above. "I don't know, Sarah. But we're running out of time. Whatever we're going to do, we need to do it fast."

The line connected, and Colonel Sultrier's voice came through. "Dr. Avery? What's the situation?"

Jonathan took a deep breath, knowing that what he was about to say would set in motion events that could determine the fate of humanity. "Colonel, we've identified the item the aliens are after. It's not a what, it's a who. And we need to act now."

As Jonathan finished explaining their discovery to Colonel Sultrier, the line went silent for a moment. When he spoke again, his voice was grave.

"Dr. Avery, if what you're saying is true, we're facing a crisis of unprecedented proportions. I'm ordering a full lockdown of Area 52. No one goes in or out without my express permission. I'll be there within the hour."

After ending the call, Jonathan turned to Dr. Mitchell, his face etched with determination. "We need to gather all the evidence we can before Colonel Sultrier arrives. Every piece of data on Bennett, every scrap of information about the star and the artifact."

Dr. Mitchell nodded, already moving towards her workstation. "I'll start compiling everything we have. But Jon, what about Dr. Gray? If we're right about Bennett, we might need his expertise."

Jonathan hesitated, torn between following the Colonel's orders and trusting his instincts about Gray. "Let's wait until he gets here. We'll present what we have and let him make the call about Dr. Gray."

As they worked feverishly to gather their research, alarms began to blare throughout the facility. The lockdown was in effect. Scientists and security personnel rushed through the corridors.

Amidst the chaos, Jonathan's mind raced. If Bennett was indeed the item the aliens were after, what did that mean for the knowledge Jonathan himself carried? Were they connected somehow? And how did the artifact fit into all of this?

Suddenly, the lights flickered, and a low hum filled the air. Jonathan and Dr. Mitchell exchanged alarmed glances as they realized the sound was coming from the artifact chamber.

"We need to check it out," Jonathan said, already moving towards the door.

As they approached the artifact chamber, the hum grew louder. Inside, they found Dr. Gray standing before the artifact, which was pulsing with an intensity they'd never seen before.

"Dr. Gray?" Dr. Mitchell called out cautiously. "What's happening?"

Gray turned to them, his eyes carried a strange look of excitement. "It's responding to something. I've never seen readings like this before."

Jonathan stepped closer to the artifact, feeling a familiar pull. As he did, images began to flash through his mind: Bennett standing before a massive crowd, the pulsing star growing brighter, and a sense of impending doom.

"We need to stop him," Jonathan gasped, stumbling back. "Bennett. Whatever he's planning at that assembly, we have to prevent it."

Just then, Colonel Sultrier burst into the room, flanked by armed guards. His eyes darted from the pulsing artifact to the three scientists.

"Dr. Avery, report. What the hell is going on here?"

As Jonathan opened his mouth to explain, the artifact suddenly emitted a blinding flash of light. When it faded, a holographic image hung in the air before them: a map of New York City, with a pulsing point of light centered on the UN Headquarters.*

"My God," the Colonel whispered. "It's showing us where Bennett will be standing."

Jonathan nodded grimly. "And where the aliens will likely make their move. Colonel, we're out of time. We need to act now."

As the group stood there, staring at the holographic map, they all knew that the fate of humanity now rested on their next move. The countdown to the global assembly had begun, and with it, a race against time to prevent a cosmic catastrophe.

With no clear plan but a burning urgency, they decided to talk to the Rabbi. Jonathan had to stop the Assembly.

Colonel Sultrier quickly took charge of the situation. "We'll take a military transport plane to New York immediately. Dr. Avery, Dr. Mitchell, you're coming with me. Dr. Gray, I need you to stay here and monitor the artifact. Report any changes directly to me."

As they rushed to prepare for departure, Jonathan couldn't shake a nagging feeling.

“Colonel," he said, "I think we should bring the artifact with us. If it's connected to Bennett somehow, it might be crucial to have it on hand."

The Colonel hesitated, then nodded. "Agreed. Dr. Gray, secure the artifact for transport."

Within the hour, they were airborne, the artifact safely stored in a specially designed containment unit. As the transport flew towards New York, Jonathan briefed the team on his plan.

"We need to find this Rabbi," he explained. "He seems to be the key to reaching Bennett. If we can convince him of the truth, he might be able to shut down the assembly before the aliens arrive."

Dr. Mitchell frowned. "But how do we find him? And more importantly, how do we get him to believe us? Our story isn't exactly conventional."

Jonathan smiled grimly. "We'll have to be convincing. And fast."

As they neared New York, the city's skyline came into view, dominated by the UN Headquarters where Bennett's assembly speech was set to take place. The streets below were already filled with people from all over the world, drawn by the promise of unity and peace.

Landing at a secure military facility, the team wasted no time. They set out to find the Rabbi.

Their search led them through crowded streets, past makeshift shrines to the new "divine intervention," and through a sea of believers all eagerly awaiting Bennett's address. Finally, they found themselves outside a modest synagogue where the Rabbi was said to be staying.

As they approached the entrance, Jonathan felt a familiar sensation - a pull, similar to what he experienced with the artifact. He knew they were in the right place.

Jonathan's heart raced as he pushed open the heavy wooden door of the synagogue, the air thick with the scent of old prayers and flickering candles. He had to speak with the Rabbi and warn him of the dangers that lie ahead within Lucien Bennett and the Assembly.

"Rabbi!" Jonathan called out, urgency lacing his voice.

The Rabbi was seated at his desk, poring over a worn Torah scroll. He looked up from his as they entered, "Come in please, have a seat," he said, his voice calm as he gestured at the empty chairs in front of him. "What troubles you?"

"The assembly..." Jonathan breathed, stepping closer. "You have to cancel it."

The small room was dimly lit, shadows dancing along the walls as the Rabbi sat in silence, his hands clasped before him. The air was thick with tension as Dr. Mitchell and Jonathan exchanged glances, their voices barely above a whisper.

The Rabbi's eyes searched theirs, looking for the truth behind their words.

"The star, it's not what you think it is. It's a warning!" Dr. Mitchell added, her voice shaking with conviction.

The Rabbi leaned back in his chair, stroking his beard. "A warning? What is it that you are saying he will do, my friends?"

Jonathan took a deep breath and recounted his experience with the alien. "But I don't know what the plan ultimately is…" Jonathan said. "But it's bad… We need to find Bennett. We just can't take that kind of chance with so many lives."

The Rabbi listened intently, his expression unreadable. Then the Rabbi leaned back, contemplating. "You understand the weight of such a request?"

"I do, but I can't stand by while you put lives at risk. We can't wait until it's too late!" Jonathan's words were rushed.

The Rabbi took a moment to respond, his voice low and solemn. "What you say is troubling. But we must have faith. The star is a sign from above, a beacon of hope. And the assembly speaks of unity, of peace. How can you be sure that this is not the answer to our prayers?"

Jonathan's heart sank. They had hoped that the Rabbi would understand, that he would see the potential for the destruction. But instead, he seemed even more entranced by the idea.

"You must come to the Assembly and see for yourself," the Rabbi urged. "You will understand then. The world is changing, and we are part of something greater than we can comprehend. Trust in the wisdom of the heavens and the word of those who interpret it!"

They left the synagogue feeling defeated. The search for Bennett had led them to the Rabbi, but it seemed they had found only more obstacles.

The clock was ticking down to the Assembly with each passing hour. They had to find Bennett. They had to convince someone with the power to shut it down before it was too late.

Jonathan and Dr. Mitchell went from there to the local authorities to ask that they cancel the gathering. However, the information was met with more skepticism and dismissal. The star's significance had been co-opted by religious and political factions, eager to claim it for their own narratives.

It seemed that Bennett had infiltrated every level of the city's infrastructure, and his grip on power was stronger than Jonathan had initially imagined.

Now with less than 3 days until the Assembly, the situation grew more urgent. The more they tried to stop the assembly, the stronger Bennett seemed to become. His followers were everywhere, their eyes glinting with a fanatical fervor that was both mesmerizing and terrifying.

The streets were plastered with posters of Bennett's face, his words echoing through the city like a siren's call. But still, they couldn't locate him.

Everywhere they went was a hub of clandestine discussions about the upcoming assembly. They had gathered a small but devoted group of like-minded individuals, all of whom had seen or heard the same cryptic warnings that they had. But without knowing where Bennett was, it was hard to convince anyone of anything.

Talk of Bennett's impending address to the world was growing louder with each hour that ticked by. Then the first real information presented itself. They were sitting in a cafe when Jonathan heard a hushed conversation emanating from a nearby table, the words barely audible over the noise of the bustle in the cafe. Pressing closer, Jonathan's acute hearing, sharpened from countless nights spent stargazing in the quiet of the countryside, picked up snippets of their dialogue.

"It's a sign from the heavens," one of Bennett's devoted followers murmured to another.

"It's a chance to show the world the truth of his power," another responded.

Jonathan's heart raced. He gestured for Dr. Mitchell and Colonel Sultrier to lean in. They exchanged a knowing glance. This was it, the breadcrumb he had been searching for.

The conversation grew clearer, detailing an event that was set to occur during the assembly to prove his divine right to lead. The men talked in cautious whispers, hinting at a celestial event, and Bennett's desire for power. A plan that was as grand as it was sinister.

"We have to do something," Dr. Mitchell whispered, her voice heavy with concern. "We can't just let this happen."

Jonathan's mind raced, this was the first time they had concrete information.

The city streets became a treasure trove of information and resources, but they had to be discreet. They had to find Bennett but each step closer, the picture grew more alarming.

The next morning they were able to gain even more information. In the coffee shop there was a small group of people that were talking about Bennett and were against his plans. Jonathan listened as they spoke, quickly realizing they had reliable information, and for the right price, they were willing to share it.

The group identified themselves to be an underground network of rebels plotting to expose Bennett as a fraud.

"We don’t know where he is but we know where he'll be the day of the assembly," one of the rebels said, his eyes darting nervously around the bustling shop.

"Where?" Jonathan asked, his hand firmly grasping the edge of the table.

"The hotel right beside the UN Headquarters," the rebel whispered. "That's where he says the heavens will anoint him. He's going to do something there, something powerful."

"What is it?" Jonathan asked.

"Don't know but it isn't going to happen anyway," a rebel said smugly.

Jonathan felt the gravity of the situation weighing down on him. He knew the significance of the location. The UN Headquarters was one of the busiest sites in the world. And in less than two days, it was going to be the home to one of the largest gatherings in the world. A global assembly. Over one hundred of the nation's most prestigious officials from around the world would be brought together under one roof. If Bennett showed up, the consequences would be catastrophic.

Jonathan paid the men and thanked them for the information before quickly leaving.

"I just don't know," he told Dr. Mitchell. "I don't know how much they are willing to do to stop Bennett from being there."

The tension in the air grew thick as evidence of Lucien Bennett's lies were laid out before them. The fate of not just Jonathan, but potentially the entire world, hung in the balance.

Chapter Fifteen: A Cosmic Opening

The small hotel room they'd commandeered was cluttered with maps, documents, and hastily scrawled notes when Jonathan and Dr. Mitchell entered the room where Colonel Sultrier was waiting for them.

"Colonel," Jonathan said as they burst through the door, "we've got new information. Bennett's planning something at the hotel next to the UN Headquarters on the day of the assembly."

The Colonel's eyes narrowed. "What exactly is he planning?"

Dr. Mitchell shook her head. "We don't know the details, but our sources say it's going to be powerful. And there's more - there's an underground group of rebels planning to stop Bennett from even showing up."

"Rebels?" The Colonel's voice was sharp. "We can't have vigilantes interfering."

Jonathan paced the room, his mind racing. "We need to coordinate with local law enforcement, set up a perimeter around the hotel and the UN building. But we can't tip our hand too early - if Bennett suspects we're onto him, he might change his plans."

Dr. Mitchell added, "And we need to find a way to evacuate the area without causing panic. If Bennett really is the item the aliens are after, we can't risk civilian casualties if they decide to make their move."

The Colonel nodded grimly. "I'll make some calls, see if we can get some covert operatives in place. But we're walking a tightrope here. One wrong move and we could have an intergalactic incident on our hands."

As they discussed strategy, the artifact, which had been quiet since their arrival in New York, suddenly began to pulse with a soft light. Jonathan felt a familiar tug in his mind.

"Wait," he said, holding up a hand. He approached the artifact, placing his hand near its surface. Images flashed through his mind: Bennett standing atop the hotel, arms raised to the sky; the pulsing star growing brighter; and a sense of impending doom that made his blood run cold.

"We're running out of time," Jonathan said, his voice barely above a whisper. "Whatever Bennett's planning, it's going to happen soon. And I think it's going to open some kind of portal. A gateway for the aliens to come through."

Dr. Mitchell's eyes widened. "But why? Why would Bennett do that?"

Jonathan shook his head. "I don't know. Maybe he thinks he's bringing about some kind of cosmic enlightenment. Or maybe he's being controlled somehow. But one thing's for sure - we need to stop him."

The Colonel straightened, his face set with determination. "Alright, here's what we're going to do.

Dr. Avery, you and Dr. Mitchell will try to make contact with these rebels. See if you can get them to work with us instead of against us. I'll make the local authorities listen and set up our defensive measures."

As they prepared to put their plan into action, Jonathan had a feeling that they were missing something crucial. The pieces were all there - Bennett, the aliens, the artifact - but how did they all fit together?

With less than a day until the assembly, they knew they were in a race against time. The fate of the world hung in the balance, and they were the only ones who could tip the scales in humanity's favor.

"Let's move," Jonathan said, heading for the door.

As Jonathan and Dr. Mitchell left the hotel, the bustling streets of New York seemed oblivious to the cosmic drama unfolding in their midst. They made their way back to the coffee shop, hoping to reconnect with the rebel group.

"Do you think they'll trust us?" Dr. Mitchell asked, her voice low.

Jonathan shook his head. "I don't know, but we have to try. We need all the help we can get."

As they entered the coffee shop, they immediately noticed the tension in the air. The rebels were huddled in a corner, their eyes darting suspiciously towards the door. Jonathan approached slowly, his hands raised to show he meant no harm.

"We need to talk," he said quietly. "What you're planning is bigger than you realize."

The leader of the group, a wiry man with intense eyes, leaned forward. "Who are you really? And why should we trust you?"

Jonathan took a deep breath. "Because the truth is stranger than you can imagine. Bennett isn't just a fraud. He's part of something much bigger. Something that could endanger the entire planet."

For the next hour, Jonathan and Dr. Mitchell laid out their story - the alien encounter, the artifact, the cosmic knowledge hidden within Bennett. As they spoke, they could see the disbelief on the rebels' faces slowly give way to a mix of fear and awe.

"So what do you want from us?" the leader finally asked.

"We need your help," Dr. Mitchell replied. "We need to stop Bennett, but we can't do it alone. And we need to do it without causing panic or alerting the aliens."

As they discussed potential strategies, Jonathan's phone buzzed. It was a message from the Colonel: "Situation escalating. Bennett sighted near the UN. Get back here ASAP."

Jonathan's heart raced. "We have to go," he told the rebels. "But we'll be in touch. Please, don't do anything rash. We're all in this together now."

As they hurried back to their base, the sky seemed to darken ominously. The pulsing star that had been a constant presence since their arrival in New York was now visibly larger, its eerie light casting strange shadows across the city.

"Jon," Dr. Mitchell said, her voice trembling slightly, "I think it's starting."

They burst into the hotel room to find the Colonel poring over a map of the UN complex. He looked up as they entered, his face grim.

"Bennett's made his move," he said without preamble. "He's holed up in the hotel next to the UN, and he's calling for his followers to gather. We're running out of time."

Jonathan moved to the window, staring out at the growing crowd below. People from all walks of life were converging on the area, drawn by Bennett's call of unity and enlightenment.

"We need to get to him," Jonathan said, his voice filled with determination. "Before the aliens can make their move."

Dr. Mitchell joined him at the window. "How? The place will be crawling with his followers, not to mention whatever security he has."

Jonathan turned to face the Colonel and Dr. Mitchell, his mind racing with possibilities. "I have an idea," he said slowly. "But it's risky. And it involves using the one thing Bennett might not expect."

"What's that?" The Colonel asked.

Jonathan's eyes flickered to the pulsing artifact in the corner of the room. "Me," he said quietly. "We use the knowledge I carry. The same knowledge the aliens are after. If I can tap into it, maybe I can counteract whatever Bennett's planning."

The room fell silent as the weight of Jonathan's proposal sank in. They all knew the dangers involved, the unknown consequences of meddling with cosmic forces beyond their understanding.

But as the star pulsed ominously overhead and the crowd below grew larger by the minute, they also knew they were out of options. The final confrontation was at hand, and the fate of humanity hung in the balance.

"Alright," the Colonel said finally. "What's the plan?"

Jonathan took a deep breath, steeling himself for what was to come. "First, we need to get as close to Bennett as possible. And then we fight fire with fire. Cosmic knowledge against cosmic knowledge. It's time to see what he's really capable of."

Jonathan, Dr. Mitchell, and Colonel finalized their plan, the atmosphere in the city grew increasingly tense. The streets surrounding the UN Headquarters and the adjacent hotel were now packed with Bennett's followers, their faces a mix of hope and fervent anticipation.

"We need to move now," the Colonel said, checking his watch. "Our window of opportunity is closing fast."

Jonathan nodded, his hand resting on the containment unit housing the artifact. "Let's go."

They made their way through the crowded streets, using a series of pre-arranged security checkpoints to get closer to the hotel. As they approached, Jonathan could feel a strange energy in the air, a tingling sensation that seemed to resonate with something deep within him.

"Jon," Dr. Mitchell whispered, her eyes wide, "look at the sky."

The pulsing star had grown even brighter, its light now visible even in the daytime. Strange patterns danced across its surface, reminiscent of the symbols they had seen on the artifact.

As they reached the hotel's perimeter, they could hear Bennett's voice booming from speakers set up around the building. "My children," he called out, his voice filled with a hypnotic power, "the time of ascension is upon us! Together, we will open the gateway to a new era of cosmic enlightenment!"

Jonathan felt a surge of urgency. "We need to get inside. Now."

Using the credentials the Colonel had procured, they managed to slip past the security point and into the hotel. The lobby was chaos, filled with Bennett's inner circle and security personnel rushing about in preparation for whatever was about to unfold.

"The penthouse," Dr. Mitchell said, pointing to a private elevator. "That's where he'll be."

As they approached the elevator, a group of guards moved to intercept them. Jonathan felt a sudden warmth emanating from the artifact, and without thinking, he stepped forward.

"We're expected," he said, his voice carrying a strange, compelling quality that he didn't recognize. The guards hesitated, then stepped aside, their eyes glazed over.

"How did you do that?" Dr. Mitchell asked as they entered the elevator.

Jonathan shook his head, bewildered. "I don't know. It just happened."

As the elevator ascended, Jonathan could feel the knowledge within him stirring, responding to the proximity of Bennett and whatever cosmic forces were at play. He closed his eyes, trying to focus, to prepare himself for what was to come.

The elevator doors opened, revealing a luxurious penthouse suite. And there, standing on the balcony overlooking the gathered masses, was Lucien Bennett. He turned as they entered, his eyes locking onto Jonathan.

"Ah," Bennett said, a smile spreading across his face. "I've been expecting you, Dr. Avery. You're just in time for the grand finale."

Jonathan stepped forward, the artifact in his backpack began humming in its containment unit. "It's over, Bennett. Whatever you're planning, it stops now."

Bennett laughed, a sound that sent chills down Jonathan's spine. "Oh, my dear boy. It's far too late for that. The gateway is already opening. Our cosmic benefactors are on their way. And you..." his eyes gleamed with an otherworldly light, "you are the final piece of the puzzle."

Suddenly, the star in the sky flared blindingly bright. Bennett raised his arms, and a beam of energy shot from the star, enveloping him in a cocoon of light. Jonathan felt a tremendous pull, as if something was trying to tear the very essence of his being from his body.

Jon!" Dr. Mitchell cried out, reaching for him.

As the cosmic forces swirled around them, Jonathan knew that the final confrontation had begun. The fate of humanity hung in the balance, and he was the only one who could tip the scales. With a deep breath, he embraced the knowledge within him, preparing to face whatever cosmic horror Bennett had unleashed.

As the energy swirled around Bennett, Jonathan felt a surge of power within himself. The artifact in the containment unit began to pulse in sync with his heartbeat, its glow intensifying with each passing second.

"You don't understand what you're doing, Bennett!" Jonathan shouted over the roar of cosmic energies. "You're not bringing enlightenment, you're putting the people in danger! They are not joining you! They are coming for you!"

Bennett's eyes, now glowing with an unearthly light, fixed on Jonathan. "You're wrong, Avery. I'm fulfilling our destiny! Humanity will ascend, guided by our cosmic benefactors!"

Suddenly, the air between them seemed to tear, revealing a shimmering portal. Through it, Jonathan could see glimpses of impossible landscapes and beings that defied description. The aliens were running to the open portal.

Acting on instinct, Jonathan reached out with his mind, tapping into the knowledge that had lain dormant within him. He felt a connection forming between himself, the artifact, and the cosmic forces at play.

"Dr. Mitchell, Colonel, get back!" he yelled, as tendrils of energy began to emanate from his body.

Bennett's face contorted with rage. "No! You can't interfere!" He thrust his hands forward, sending a wave of energy towards Jonathan.

Jonathan raised his own hands, surprised to find he could deflect Bennett's attack. The two men stood locked in a battle of wills and cosmic power.

As they fought, Jonathan began to understand. The knowledge within him, the artifact, Bennett's power - they were all pieces of a larger cosmic puzzle. Humanity wasn't meant to coexist with the aliens yet; they were meant to be guardians, keeping the balance between worlds.

"Bennett," Jonathan called out, his voice resonating with newfound authority, "You don't understand! They have come to retrieve what they believe is theirs!"

For a moment, doubt flickered across Bennett's face. In that instant of hesitation, Jonathan pushed forward with all his might, channeling the power of the artifact and his own innate abilities.

The portal began to waver, its edges flickering. Bennett screamed in defiance, but Jonathan could feel the tide turning. With a final, monumental effort, he forced the cosmic energies back through the portal.

There was a blinding flash of light, and then silence.

As Jonathan's vision cleared, he saw Bennett crumpled on the floor, the unearthly glow fading from his eyes. The portal was gone, and the pulsing star in the sky had vanished.

Dr. Mitchell rushed to Jonathan's side, supporting him as he swayed on his feet. "Jon! Are you alright? What happened?"

Jonathan looked at his hands, still tingling with residual energy. "I closed the door. At least for now."

The Colonel approached Bennett's unconscious form cautiously. "Is it over?"

"No," Jonathan said, his voice heavy with the weight of his new understanding. "This was just the beginning. They will come again for him, and we need to be ready."

"What do we do with Bennett until then?" she asked, glancing at the unconscious figure on the floor.

"Take him into custody," Jonathan said. "Study him if you must, but be careful. He may still be dangerous, even without his powers."

The Colonel nodded reluctantly. "And the artifact?"

Jonathan's eyes widened as he realized his backpack no longer held the containment unit. He quickly stood up, looking around frantically. "I don't know."

"It has to be here somewhere," Jonathan muttered, a growing sense of dread building in his stomach. After an hour of intense searching, they regrouped, all wearing expressions of disbelief and worry.

"This doesn't make sense," Jonathan said, running a hand through his hair. "It couldn't have just vanished."

Dr. Mitchell suddenly spoke up. "What if the aliens took it?"

“But how?" Jonathan asked. "We would have noticed if they had somehow grabbed it."

Colonel Sultrier nodded slowly, his face grim. "Not necessarily. We've seen the kind of advanced technology they possess. It's possible they have ways of retrieving objects without being detected."

"It makes sense," Dr. Mitchell added. "The artifact was important to them. They wouldn't just give up after one failed attempt."

As the implications of this sank in, Jonathan felt a mix of fear and frustration. "If they have the artifact, what does that mean for us? For Earth?"

Colonel Sultrier's expression was grave. "It means we're potentially facing a significant threat. Without the artifact, our understanding of their technology and intentions is severely limited."

Dr. Mitchell spoke up. "But Jon, you said the knowledge is within you now. Doesn't that count for something?"

Jonathan nodded, feeling a glimmer of hope. "You're right. The artifact might be gone, but what it awakened in me is still here. We're not defenseless."

Dr. Mitchell stepped forward, her face set with determination. "We need to start preparing immediately. Jon, you need to learn how to harness and control this knowledge. And we need to set up a system to detect any further alien activity."

Colonel Sultrier agreed. "I'll mobilize our resources. We'll need to establish a new base of operations, something more secure than Area 52."

As sirens wailed in the distance and the confused murmur of the crowd below drifted up to them, Jonathan realized that his life, and the course of human history, had been irrevocably changed. The knowledge within him, once dormant, was now awake. Earth's first line of defense against cosmic threats was no longer a secret government project - it was him.

"What now?" Dr. Mitchell asked.

Jonathan looked out over the city. "Now," he said, "I'm going home."

Jonathan's words hung in the air, heavy with finality and unexpected simplicity. Dr. Mitchell and Colonel Sultrier exchanged surprised glances.

"Home?" Dr. Mitchell repeated. "Jon, after everything that's happened, is that really the best course of action?"

Jonathan turned to face them, his eyes reflecting a weariness that seemed to go beyond physical exhaustion. "It's exactly what I need to do. This cosmic knowledge, this power - it's overwhelming. I need time to process, to understand what I've become."

The Colonel stepped forward, his face etched with worry. "Dr. Avery, I understand your need for reflection, but we can't just leave things as they are. There are questions to be answered, preparations to be made. The threat isn't over."

"I know," Jonathan replied, his voice firm but gentle. "And I'm not running away from my responsibilities. But I can't be effective, I can't protect Earth, if I don't understand myself first. And for that, I need to go home. I need to see Sherry."

At the mention of Sherry's name, Dr. Mitchell's expression softened. She understood the pull of loved ones in times of crisis.

As they prepared to leave the penthouse, Jonathan took one last look at the New York skyline. The pulsing star was gone, the sky returned to its normal blue. But he knew the universe would never look the same to him again.

The trio hailed a taxi, giving the driver Jonathan’s home address. As the city streets flew by, Jonathan closed his eyes, focusing on the steady beat of his heart and the gentle hum of the road. He was going home, back to Sherry, back to a semblance of normalcy. But he knew that nothing would ever be truly normal again.

The taxi pulled up to his house, and Jonathan took a deep breath before stepping out. He walked up the familiar path to his front door, the weight of cosmic knowledge balanced against the simple desire to hold his wife again.

As he reached for the doorknob, Jonathan silently vowed to find a way to bridge these two worlds - the cosmic and the personal. But first, he needed to remember what he was fighting for. He needed to go inside.

As Jonathan turned the key in the lock, he could hear movement inside the house. The door swung open, revealing Sherry's surprised face.

"Jon?" she gasped, her eyes widening as she took in his disheveled appearance. Her gaze then shifted to the two figures standing behind him - Colonel Sultrier and Dr. Mitchell.

"Surprise," Jonathan said weakly, attempting a smile. "I'm home."

Sherry's expression cycled through a range of emotions - relief, joy, confusion, and concern. She stepped forward, enveloping Jonathan in a tight embrace. "Oh my God, Jon. I've been so worried. I've been trying for days, and I couldn't find you."

As she pulled back, her eyes locked onto the strangers behind him. "What's going on? Who are these people?"

Jonathan took a deep breath. "Sherry, this is Colonel Donald Sultrier and Dr. Sarah Mitchell. They're colleagues. And we have a lot to talk about."

Sherry's brow furrowed, but she nodded, stepping aside to let them in. "Of course, come in. I'll put on some coffee."

As they settled in the living room, the atmosphere was thick with unspoken tension. Sherry returned with a tray of coffee, her hands shaking slightly as she set it down.

"Alright," she said, taking a seat next to Jonathan. "I think it's time you told me what's really been going on."

Jonathan exchanged glances with Dr. Mitchell and Colonel before turning back to his wife. "Sherry, what I'm about to tell you is going to sound impossible. Crazy, even. But I need you to listen with an open mind."

He reached out, taking her hand in his. "It all started with a star, and an artifact that changed everything we knew about the universe."

As Jonathan began to recount the incredible events of the past weeks, Sherry listened with growing astonishment. Dr. Mitchell and the Colonel chimed in occasionally, filling in details and confirming the wild tale.

When Jonathan finally finished, the room fell into silence. Sherry sat there, her coffee long forgotten, as she tried to process the cosmic revelations.

"So," she said slowly, "my husband is now what? Earth's defender against alien threats?"

Jonathan nodded, his expression a mix of apology and determination. "I know it's a lot to take in. And I understand if you're angry or scared. But I needed to come home, to tell you everything. Because whatever happens next, whatever challenges we face, I want to face them with you by my side."

Sherry was quiet for a long moment, her eyes searching Jonathan's face. Finally, she squeezed his hand. "Jon, I married you for better or worse. I just never imagined that worse might include alien invasions."

A small smile tugged at the corners of her mouth, and Jonathan felt a wave of relief wash over him.

"So," Sherry continued, her voice stronger now, "what's our next move?"

Jonathan blinked, surprised by her quick acceptance and readiness. "Our next move?"

Sherry nodded, her eyes now alight with determination. "Yes, our next move. If my husband is going to be Earth's cosmic defender, then his wife better be prepared to help. Now, Colonel Sultrier, Dr. Mitchell, why don't you tell me more about this while I get us all some more coffee? I have a feeling we're going to need it."

As Sherry stood to refill their cups, Jonathan felt a surge of love and gratitude. He had come home seeking understanding and support, and he had found it in spades. Whatever cosmic challenges lay ahead, he knew he wouldn't face them alone.

The universe had thrust an impossible responsibility upon him, but with Sherry by his side and his newfound allies in Dr. Mitchell and the Colonel. Jonathan felt ready to take on whatever the cosmos might throw their way. The next chapter of their incredible journey was about to begin, right there in their living room.

Chapter Sixteen: The Secret Revealed

The warm summer breeze carried the aroma of grilled meat across Dr. Jonathan Avery's backyard. The sizzle of the barbecue and the clink of ice in glasses provided a stark contrast to the weighty conversation about to unfold.

Jonathan exchanged glances with Colonel Sultrier and Dr. Mitchell, his companions from that fateful encounter two years ago. His wife, Sherry, had just asked the question they'd all been avoiding: "So why were the aliens after Lucien Bennett?"

The trio fell silent, the weight of classified information and cosmic secrets hanging heavily in the air. Jonathan took a deep breath, realizing it was time to finally reveal the truth to Sherry.

"Honey," he began, setting down his drink, "it's complicated, but you deserve to know." He looked to his colleagues for support, and they nodded in agreement.

Dr. Mitchell leaned forward, her voice low despite the privacy of the backyard. "Sherry, what we're about to tell you is still highly classified. The government has kept this under wraps to prevent panic."

Colonel Sultrier cleared his throat. "Mrs. Avery, Lucien Bennett wasn't just a false prophet. He was a vessel."

Sherry's brow furrowed. "A vessel? For what?"

Jonathan took over, his astrophysicist's mind struggling to put the cosmic concept into words. "For knowledge, Sherry. Ancient, alien knowledge. The beings we encountered, they've been seeding Earth with information for millennia, hiding it within human DNA."

"Bennett," Dr. Mitchell continued, "was a culmination of this process. Generations of carefully guided evolution and genetic manipulation had made him a perfect repository for this cosmic database."

Sherry's eyes widened as she processed this information. "But why? Why go to all that trouble?"

Colonel Sultrier's face grew grim. "Insurance, Mrs. Avery. The aliens were using Earth as a backup drive for their civilization's knowledge. Bennett was meant to be the key to accessing it all."

Jonathan reached out and took Sherry's hand. "When we stopped Bennett from 'ascending,' we effectively locked away that knowledge. The aliens wanted him because he was their failsafe, their way of recovering eons of lost information."

Sherry sat back, her mind reeling. "So what does this mean now? Are they coming back?"

The three colleagues exchanged worried looks. Jonathan squeezed Sherry's hand, his voice a mix of determination and concern.

"We don't know, honey. But that's why we're still working with the government. We're Earth's first line of defense if they do return."

As the gravity of the situation settled over the backyard gathering, the distant chirping of birds and the continued sizzle of the barbecue served as a reminder of the normal life they were all fighting to protect. The truth was out.

Sherry took a moment to process the information, her eyes moving from Jonathan to Dr. Mitchell to Colonel Sultrier. Then, to everyone's surprise, she let out a small chuckle.

"You know," she said, shaking her head with a bemused smile, "two years ago, this would have sounded absolutely insane. But after everything that's happened, it actually makes a strange kind of sense."

Jonathan felt a wave of relief wash over him. He'd been worried about how Sherry would take the news, but her calm acceptance was reassuring.

"So," Sherry continued, reaching for her glass, "what's our next move? I assume we're not just sitting around waiting for the aliens to come back?"

Colonel Sultrier nodded approvingly. "Your wife's got a good head on her shoulders, Avery. And you're right, Mrs. Avery. We've been working on a few projects."

Dr. Mitchell leaned forward, her question hung in the air for a moment, casting a sudden pall over the relaxed atmosphere. She looked directly at Colonel Sultrier, her eyes searching for answers. "As long as we're sharing secrets," she said, her voice quiet but firm, "why did we leave Dr. Gray out? What did he do?"

The jovial mood at the barbecue shifted, and everyone's attention turned to Colonel Sultrier. He set down his drink and took a deep breath, his expression growing serious.

"I suppose you all deserve to know the truth," Colonel Sultrier began, his voice low and measured. "Dr. Gray's actions during the incident were problematic, to say the least."

Jonathan and Sherry leaned in, their curiosity piqued. Even Jonathan, who had worked closely with Gray, wasn't fully aware of what had transpired behind the scenes.

Colonel Sultrier continued, "As you both know, Dr. Gray attempted to give the artifact to the aliens. It was a severe breach of trust and a major government offense. His motivations were complex. He believed that by cooperating with the aliens, he could secure a position of power for himself in whatever new order they might establish."

Dr. Mitchell gasped softly, her hand covering her mouth. "I had no idea. He was just missing in action after the incident."

Jonathan shook his head in disbelief. "I never would have believed he'd do something like that."

"Unfortunately," Colonel Sultrier said, his tone grim, "that's exactly what happened. We managed to intercept him before the damage was done. He's currently being held in a high-security government facility."

Sherry, processing this new information, asked, "Is he being treated well? I mean, I understand the severity of what he did, but..."

Colonel Sultrier nodded, appreciating her concern. "He's being treated humanely, Mrs. Avery. But the nature of his actions means he'll likely remain in custody for a very long time. The information he has is simply too sensitive to risk him being out in the world."

A somber silence fell over the group as they contemplated the fate of their former colleague. It was a reminder of the high stakes involved in their work and the temptations that came with knowledge of cosmic proportions.

After a moment, Jonathan spoke up, his voice resolute. "Well, I guess that's all the more reason for us to stick together and trust each other. We're dealing with forces beyond our comprehension, and we can't afford to have any weak links."

Dr. Mitchell and Colonel Sultrier nodded in agreement, and Sherry reached out to squeeze Jonathan's hand supportively.

"You're right," Dr. Mitchell said. "We're in this together, and we need to have each other's backs."

As the conversation gradually shifted back to lighter topics, the revelation about Dr. Gray lingered in the background, a sobering reminder of the responsibilities and challenges they faced as Earth's defenders against cosmic threats.

Dr. Mitchell chimed in, "That's why we've been developing new detection systems, trying to create an early warning network for any potential alien activity. Jonathan's insights have been invaluable."

"And," Jonathan added, giving Sherry's hand a squeeze, "we've been studying the residual energy patterns from the artifact and Bennett. We're hoping to understand more about this cosmic knowledge and how it works."

Sherry nodded, taking it all in stride. "Is there anything I can do to help? I may not be an astrophysicist or a military strategist, but I want to contribute if I can."

The others looked at each other, pleasantly surprised by Sherry's offer. Colonel Sultrier was the first to speak up.

"Actually, Mrs. Avery, your background in public relations law could be incredibly useful. If we ever need to disclose any of this to the public, having someone who knows how to manage the message would be crucial."

Dr. Mitchell nodded enthusiastically. "Plus, your perspective as someone outside the scientific and military spheres could provide valuable insights we might overlook."

Jonathan felt a surge of pride and love for his wife. "What do you say, Sher? Ready to join Earth's cosmic defense team?"

Sherry raised her glass, a determined glint in her eye. "Count me in. Someone's got to keep you all grounded while you're exploring the cosmos."

They all laughed, clinking their glasses together in a toast to their expanded team. As the conversation shifted to more mundane topics and Jonathan returned to the grill to check on the food, there was a sense of unity and purpose in the air.

The backyard barbecue had transformed into something more – a gathering of Earth's unlikely defenders, bound together by shared secrets and a commitment to protecting their world from whatever the universe might throw at them next.

The conversation around the barbecue had begun to drift back towards lighter topics when Sherry suddenly sat up straighter, a mix of excitement and nervousness crossing her face.

"By the way," she said, her voice cutting through the chatter, "I was going to wait, but I can't hold it in any longer." She paused, looking at each of them in turn before her eyes settled on Jonathan. "We're going to have a new generation of Earth's defenders. I'm pregnant."

The announcement was met with a moment of stunned silence, followed by an eruption of joy and congratulations.

Jonathan's eyes widened in shock before a huge grin spread across his face. He pulled Sherry into a tight embrace, laughing and crying at the same time. "We're having a baby? Oh my God, Sherry, that's amazing!"

Dr. Mitchell was the next to react, jumping up to hug Sherry as soon as Jonathan released her. "Congratulations! Oh, this is wonderful news!"

Even the usually stoic Colonel Sultrier broke into a broad smile. "Well, I'll be damned," he chuckled, raising his glass in a toast. "To the newest member of Earth's defense team!"

As the initial excitement settled, Jonathan knelt beside Sherry's chair, taking her hand in his. "How long have you known? Why didn't you tell me sooner?"

Sherry smiled, squeezing his hand. "I found out a week ago, but I wanted to be sure before I said anything. And then, well, this seemed like the perfect moment."

Colonel Sultrier, ever the pragmatist, spoke up. "This is certainly cause for celebration, but it also means we need to think about the future in a new light. Another child will be born into a world that's more complicated than most people realize."

Jonathan nodded, his expression growing serious for a moment. "You're right, Colonel. But that's all the more reason for us to work hard to protect this world. Our child deserves to grow up in a safe universe."

Sherry placed a hand on her stomach, her eyes shining with determination. "And who knows? Maybe this little one will grow up to be the greatest defender Earth has ever seen."

The group raised their glasses once more, toasting to the future - both the immediate joy of a new life and the long-term hope for humanity's place in the cosmos. As the sun began to set, casting a warm glow over the backyard, they all felt a renewed sense of purpose. They weren't just protecting the Earth anymore; they were safeguarding it for the next generation.

The barbecue continued late into the evening, filled with laughter, plans for the future, and the unshakeable bond of a team that had faced the unknown together and come out stronger. And now, with a new life on the way, their mission felt more important than ever.

As the evening wound down and the excitement of Sherry's announcement settled into a warm glow of anticipation, Colonel Sultrier's phone buzzed. He excused himself to take the call, his expression growing serious as he listened to the person on the other end.

When he returned to the group, his face was grim. "I'm sorry to break up this celebration, but we've got a situation."

Jonathan, Dr. Mitchell, and Sherry all turned to him, their moods shifting instantly from joy to concern.

"What's happening, Colonel?" Jonathan asked, standing up.

The Colonel took a deep breath before explaining. "We've received intelligence about a new figure emerging in Europe. He's calling himself 'The Cosmic Shepherd' and claiming to have received visions from 'benevolent alien beings'."

Dr. Mitchell's eyes widened. "Another false prophet? So soon after Bennett?"

"Exactly," the Colonel nodded. "And given what happened last time, we can't afford to let this escalate."

Jonathan ran a hand through his hair, his mind racing. "What do we know about this 'Cosmic Shepherd'?"

"Not much yet," the Colonel replied. "But he's gaining followers rapidly. His message is similar to Bennett's - promises of cosmic enlightenment and a new age for humanity. We need to investigate and, if necessary, expose him before he can amass too much influence."

Sherry, who had been listening intently, spoke up. "Why is it so crucial to act quickly this time?"

Jonathan turned to his wife, his expression serious. "Because last time, we almost lost everything. If this new prophet is anything like Bennett, he could be a vessel for alien knowledge or worse, a willing collaborator with forces we don't fully understand."

Dr. Mitchell nodded in agreement. "And now that we know the aliens' interest in Earth, we can't risk another potential conduit for their plans."

The Colonel added, "Plus, the public is still recovering from the Bennett incident. If we can nip this in the bud, we might be able to prevent widespread panic and maintain stability."

Sherry stood up, her face set with determination. "Then we need to act fast. My PR experience could be crucial in managing this situation and crafting a narrative that discredits this 'Cosmic Shepherd' without causing panic."

Jonathan looked at his wife with a mix of pride and concern. "Are you sure about this, Sherry? In your condition?"

Sherry placed a hand on her stomach, her eyes filled with resolve. "More than ever, Jon. We're not just protecting Earth now; we're securing a future for our child. I want to do my part."

The Colonel nodded approvingly. "Alright, team. We leave for Europe in two hours. We need to gather intel, assess the threat, and formulate a plan to expose this false prophet before he can do any real damage."

As they quickly cleared the backyard and prepared for their mission, Jonathan couldn't help but feel a sense of deja vu mixed with newfound purpose. They had faced this kind of threat before, but now the stakes felt even higher.

With renewed determination, the group headed out, ready to confront this new challenge. As they drove towards the airport, Jonathan took Sherry's hand, both of them silently vowing to create a safer world for their unborn child - a world free from the manipulation of false prophets and the looming threat of cosmic interference.

As their plane touched down in Geneva, Switzerland, the team was already in full operational mode. Colonel Sultrier had briefed them on the latest intelligence during the flight, and now they were ready to hit the ground running.

"The Cosmic Shepherd is scheduled to give a public address in Plainpalais tomorrow," the Colonel informed them as they made their way through the airport. "We need to gather as much information as possible before then."

Dr. Mitchell, who had been analyzing data on her tablet, looked up. "I've been cross-referencing his supposed 'visions' with known astronomical phenomena. There are some troubling correlations that suggest he might have access to advanced knowledge."

Jonathan nodded grimly. "Just like Bennett. We need to find out if he's in contact with the aliens or if he's just a very well-informed charlatan."

As they reached their secure safehouse on the outskirts of the city, Sherry began setting up a makeshift command center. "I've been monitoring social media chatter," she reported. "His following is growing exponentially. We need to act fast to control the narrative."

The team worked through the night, gathering intelligence, analyzing patterns, and formulating a strategy. By dawn, they had a plan.

"Alright," Jonathan said, addressing the group. "Dr. Mitchell and I will attend the public address, posing as curious scientists. We'll use our equipment to scan for any unusual energy signatures or technology."

The Colonel nodded. "I'll coordinate with local authorities and keep our extraction team on standby, just in case things go south."

"And I'll be managing our media response," Sherry added. "I've prepared statements debunking his claims and emphasizing the importance of scientific skepticism. We'll release them strategically during and after his address."

As they prepared to leave for Plainpalais, Jonathan pulled Sherry aside. "Are you sure you're up for this?" he asked, his concern evident.

Sherry smiled, placing a hand on her stomach. "Absolutely. Our little cosmic defender here is giving me all the strength I need. Besides, someone needs to make sure you scientists don't get too caught up in the technical details and forget about the human element."

Jonathan chuckled, pulling her into a quick embrace. "What would we do without you?"

As they joined the others, ready to head out, there was an obvious sense of determination between them. They had faced false prophets before, and had seen the damage they could do. This time, they were prepared, united, and driven by more than just duty. They were fighting for the future, for a world where their children could look to the stars with wonder rather than fear.

The streets of Geneva were already buzzing with anticipation as they made their way to Plainpalais. Crowds were gathering, drawn by the promise of cosmic revelations. Little did they know that among them were Earth's true defenders, ready to expose the truth and protect humanity from manipulation, whether Earthly or cosmic in origin.

As they took their positions, Jonathan exchanged a determined look with Dr. Mitchell. "Let's do this," he said. "For Earth, for the future, for the truth."

The stage was set for a confrontation that would shape the course of Earth's relationship with the cosmos. The Cosmic Shepherd was about to face a reckoning he never saw coming.

As the crowd in Plainpalais grew denser, Jonathan and Dr. Mitchell carefully made their way towards the front, their specialized equipment disguised as ordinary tablets and smartphones. The air was thick with anticipation, and murmurs of excitement rippled through the gathering.

Suddenly, a hush fell over the crowd as a figure appeared on the makeshift stage. The Cosmic Shepherd, dressed in flowing robes adorned with celestial symbols, raised his arms dramatically.

"My children of the stars," his voice boomed through the speakers, "I bring you tidings from beyond the veil of our mundane existence!"

Jonathan and Dr. Mitchell exchanged glances, activating their scanning devices. As the Cosmic Shepherd began to describe his "visions," Dr. Mitchell's tablet began to pick up unusual readings.

"Jon," she whispered urgently, "I'm detecting low-level energy emissions. They're similar to what we saw with Bennett, but different somehow."

Jonathan nodded, his own device corroborating the data. "He's definitely using some kind of technology. But is he aware of it, or is he being manipulated like Bennett was?"

As they continued to gather data, the Cosmic Shepherd's speech took a concerning turn.

"The celestial beings have shown me the path to ascension," he proclaimed. "In three days' time, at the alignment of the stars, we shall all transcend our Earthly bonds and join our cosmic brethren!"

The crowd erupted in cheers, but Jonathan felt a chill run down his spine. This was escalating faster than they had anticipated.

Meanwhile, at their command center, Sherry was coordinating their media response. "Colonel," she said, "we need to act now. His claims are gaining traction online, and people are already talking about mass gatherings for this 'ascension' event."

The Colonel nodded grimly. "Agreed. Initiate our media protocol. We need to discredit him before this gets out of hand."

Back at Plainpalais, Jonathan and Dr. Mitchell had gathered enough data. As they prepared to leave, Jonathan's communicator buzzed with a message from Sherry: "Media campaign launched. Prepare for potential backlash."

Almost immediately, phones throughout the crowd began to chime with news alerts. The Cosmic Shepherd faltered mid-speech as he noticed the shift in the audience's attention.

"Do not be swayed by the doubters!" he cried, a note of desperation creeping into his voice. "They fear what they do not understand!"

But it was too late. Murmurs of doubt began to spread through the crowd as people read the scientifically backed rebuttals to the Shepherd's claims.

Suddenly, the energy readings on Dr. Mitchell's device spiked. "Jon, something's happening!"

The Cosmic Shepherd's robes began to glow faintly, and his eyes took on an unnatural sheen. "My masters," he whispered, though his mic still picked it up, "why have you forsaken me?"

At that moment, Jonathan realized the truth. "He's in control," he said to Dr. Mitchell.

As chaos erupted in the square, with confused followers clashing with skeptics, Jonathan knew they had to act fast. They had exposed the false prophet, but in doing so, they might have triggered something far more dangerous.

"Colonel," Jonathan called into his communicator, "we need extraction now. And prepare for potential alien interference. This isn't over yet."

As they moved through the panicking crowd, Jonathan couldn't help but think of Sherry and their unborn child.

Jonathan and Dr. Mitchell managed to get closer to the stage where the Cosmic Shepherd stood, looking increasingly panicked and confused. The glow from his robes had faded, and his eyes no longer held that unnatural sheen.

Colonel Sultrier's voice crackled over their communicators. "Team, we've got new intel. You're not going to believe this."

Jonathan and Dr. Mitchell exchanged glances as they listened to the Colonel's update.

"It turns out our Cosmic Shepherd is just a local street performer named Marcel Dubois," the Colonel explained. "He's got a history of elaborate hoaxes and publicity stunts. No alien connection, no advanced technology - just smoke and mirrors."

Dr. Mitchell's eyes widened in disbelief. "But the energy readings, the knowledge he seemed to have..."

As if on cue, a small drone buzzed overhead, projecting holographic images that had given the illusion of celestial phenomena during the Shepherd's speech. The glow from his robes had been nothing more than cleverly hidden LED lights.

Jonathan couldn't help but chuckle, despite the seriousness of the situation. "He fooled us all. Used our own expectations against us."

On stage, Marcel Dubois, now stripped of his Cosmic Shepherd persona, was being questioned by local authorities. He looked less like a prophet and more like a scared street performer who had gotten in way over his head.

Sherry's voice came over the comm. "Well, this certainly changes our PR strategy. From alien threat to elaborate hoax. The media's going to have a field day with this."

As the situation de-escalated, Jonathan, Dr. Mitchell, and the team regrouped at their safehouse. There was a mix of relief and embarrassment in the air.

"I can't believe we fell for it," Dr. Mitchell said, shaking her head.

The Colonel looked equally chagrined. "We were so focused on preventing another Bennett situation that we saw patterns where there were none."

Sherry, ever the voice of reason, spoke up. "Look at it this way - we proved that our response system works. We identified a potential threat, investigated it, and resolved the situation quickly. The fact that it turned out to be a hoax is actually the best possible outcome."

Jonathan nodded, putting an arm around his wife. "Sherry's right. We're prepared for the real thing when it comes. And in the meantime, we've shown that we can handle these situations without causing widespread panic."

As the team began to relax, Jonathan couldn't help but feel a sense of irony. They had come expecting to face another cosmic threat, only to find a very human, very mundane explanation. It was a reminder that not every mystery had an extraterrestrial answer, and sometimes, the simplest explanation was the correct one.

"Well," the Colonel said, a hint of a smile on his face, "I suppose we should be thankful. It's not every day we get to practice our world-saving skills on a street performer."

The room filled with laughter, the tension of the past few days finally breaking. As they prepared to head home, Jonathan held Sherry close, thankful that this time, the threat had been nothing more than an elaborate hoax. But they all knew that somewhere out there, the real challenges were waiting.

As the realization sank in that their cosmic threat was nothing more than an elaborate hoax, the mood in the safehouse shifted from tense relief to something lighter. Jonathan looked around at his team - Dr. Mitchell, Colonel Sultrier, and his wife Sherry - all of them a bit worn out but also somewhat amused by the turn of events.

Sherry was the first to break the silence. "You know," she said, a mischievous glint in her eye, "since we're already here in Geneva, it seems a shame to just pack up and go home right away."

Dr. Mitchell perked up at the suggestion. "That's not a bad idea. When was the last time any of us actually took a moment to enjoy a city we were in, rather than just chasing down potential alien threats?"

Even Colonel Sultrier, usually all business, seemed to consider the idea. "I suppose a day or two of local cultural sites wouldn't be entirely out of order. For morale purposes, of course."

Jonathan couldn't help but grin. "Are you suggesting we play tourist, Colonel?"

The Colonel tried to maintain his serious demeanor, but a small smile cracked through. "I'm suggesting we take advantage of an unexpected lull in our usual activities to broaden our horizons."

"Well, I'm all for it," Sherry said, rubbing her barely-visible baby bump. "This little one should get to experience Switzerland, even if it's from the inside."

And so, the Earth's cosmic defenders found themselves embarking on a very different kind of mission. They visited the Jet d'Eau, marveling at the massive water fountain in Lake Geneva. They strolled through the Old Town, admiring the architecture and history. Dr. Mitchell insisted on a visit to CERN, much to Jonathan's delight and the others' amusement.

As they sat in a quaint cafe, enjoying Swiss chocolates and watching the world go by, Jonathan felt a sense of peace he hadn't experienced in a long time. He looked at Sherry, her face glowing with happiness, and then at his friends - Dr. Mitchell engrossed in a guidebook, and even the Colonel looked relaxed for once.

"You know," Jonathan said, raising his cup of hot chocolate, "here's to false alarms and unexpected vacations. May we have just enough of them to keep us sane in between saving the world."

They all laughed and clinked their cups together. As they continued to plan out their impromptu Swiss adventure, Jonathan couldn't help but feel grateful. Yes, there were cosmic threats out there, and yes, they would have to face them eventually. But for now, at this moment, they were just friends and family, enjoying a beautiful day in a beautiful city. And somehow, that felt like the most important mission of all.

Chapter Seventeen: Connections in the Cosmos

As they stepped through the doorway of the quaint inn they were staying in, the group was immediately enveloped by the warmth and charm of the place. The old lady who owned the inn, Madame Elise, greeted them with a genuine smile that crinkled the corners of her eyes.

"Ah, mes chers," she called out in her melodious French accent, "you return! And just in time for dinner, no?"

The enticing aroma of home-cooked food wafted from the kitchen, causing their stomachs to growl in unison. They hadn't realized how hungry they were until that moment.

"Something smells wonderful, Madame Elise," Sherry said, inhaling deeply.

"Oui, it is my special Gruyère fondue tonight," Madame Elise replied, her eyes twinkling. "Perfect for a chilly evening, n'est-ce pas?"

Colonel Sultrier, usually so formal, couldn't help but smile. "It smells delicious. We'd love to join you for dinner if there's room."

"But of course!" Madame Elise exclaimed, ushering them towards the cozy dining room. "There is always room for friends at my table."

The dining room was warm and inviting, with wooden beams crossing the ceiling and a crackling fire in the hearth. They settled around a large, rustic table, the stresses of the day melting away in the comfortable atmosphere.

Dr. Mitchell leaned back in her chair, looking more relaxed than she had in days. "You know, I could get used to this. It's nice to just be normal for a change."

Jonathan nodded in agreement, his hand finding Sherry's under the table. "It's a good reminder of what we're fighting to protect."

As Madame Elise bustled about, setting the table and bringing out steaming pots of fondue, the conversation flowed easily. They shared stories and laughter, deliberately avoiding any talk of work or cosmic threats.

Sherry, her eyes bright with contentment, raised her glass of sparkling water. "To unexpected adventures and new friends," she toasted, nodding towards Madame Elise.

"And to taking time to enjoy the simple pleasures," Jonathan added.

As they dipped bread into the creamy, melted cheese, savoring every bite, there was a collective sense of gratitude. For this moment of peace, for the warmth of good company, and for the reminder that sometimes, the most extraordinary experiences could be found in the most ordinary of places.

The evening wore on, filled with good food, pleasant conversation, and the kind of comfort that only comes from being in exactly the right place at the right time. As they finally bid goodnight to Madame Elise and headed to their rooms, they all felt refreshed and rejuvenated, ready to face whatever challenges the future might hold.

In the quiet of their room, Jonathan pulled Sherry close. "Thank you," he whispered.

"For what?" she asked, looking up at him.

"For reminding us all to slow down and enjoy moments like these," he replied, placing a gentle hand on her stomach. "Our little one is lucky to have you as a mom."

As they drifted off to sleep, the inn settled into a peaceful quiet, the Swiss night wrapping around them like a comfortable blanket. Tomorrow would bring new adventures, but for now, all was well in their cozy corner of the world.

The next morning dawned with a gentle light that seeped through the curtains. The old woman woke them early, a sense of adventure in her voice. "Get dressed," she whispered. "It's a long way to show you something. We must leave before the city stirs."

They followed her through the quiet streets, their footsteps echoing off the ancient stones. The air was still cool, carrying with it the scent of rain-soaked Earth. The sky above was a clear, brilliant blue, the stars of their childhood dreams replaced by a new horizon filled with uncertainty of their destination.

The old woman led them to a library on the outskirts of the city, nestled in a small, peaceful village that had somehow remained untouched by the chaos that had ravaged the world beyond its borders. It was a modest building, surrounded by a lush garden that whispered secrets of a time before modernization had ever darkened their city. The scent of old books and the whispers of forgotten knowledge greeted them as they stepped inside.

Inside, the library felt like a fortress of knowledge. In the corner, rocking gently in a chair that had seen better days, was an ancient man with a long white beard. His eyes sparkled with an inner light that seemed to defy his years.

"This is Anslem," the old woman said. "The keeper of the library."

Anslem looked up, his gaze sharp and focused, despite the years etched into his face. "You are the ones who stopped the prophet," he murmured, his voice carrying the weight of a thousand stories. "You have done what many said was impossible."

The old woman nodded solemnly. "They have. And now, they need your help to see..."

Anslem held a hand up and studied them, his eyes piercing through the shadows of the library. "Your journey is far from over," he said, his voice a blend of wisdom and weariness. "The truth you seek is here, but it is not only found within the books, it's something else. It is a living, breathing thing that requires protection and nurturing."

The old woman spoke up, her voice filled with urgency. "Anslem, they need to know."

The old man looked past them as he began to explain the prophecy, the real intentions of the extraterrestrial force, and the battle they had just witnessed. He spoke of them reclaiming the Earth from the clutches of a false savior.

The men listened intently, their eyes never leaving the man's face. The words painted the picture of the story that had unfolded years ago. They had not shared that with anyone. Yet somehow the old man before them knew. Their trust in the man was as steadfast as the stars that had once filled Jonathan's young mind with wonder.

As the story unfolded, the color drained from Jonathan's face.

"But you will find allies within. Anything that you protect and nurture will be a strength to you." The old man said,

The old man was right. The rebel network that had provided them with information, a light that saved their lives, a warm place to stay, the artifact. They had all been allies, and together, they brought a light to the darkness.

Jonathan stood, his gaze sweeping over the rows of ancient books, each one a piece of knowledge that had been hidden for too long. He approached one, his hand hovering over it. It was bound in a material that looked like metal, but was lighter than air. He opened it carefully, his eyes scanning the pages. The symbols danced before his eyes, whispering secrets of the cosmos.

The book spoke of ancient civilizations that had harnessed the power of the stars, and the price they had paid for their excessive pride. It was a warning of what awaited those who sought to manipulate the universe for personal gain.

As he read, he felt a strange kinship with those long-dead scientists and philosophers. They too had looked to the heavens for answers, and in doing so, had unlocked the potential for unimaginable power. But they had also learned the lesson that power without wisdom was a destructive force.

He looked over at Sherry, who was deep in conversation with the old woman, discussing the logistics of their journey home. He knew they had to leave soon, but the allure of the library's secrets was too strong to resist.

Turning to another shelf, he found scrolls that spoke of prophecies and the signs that would herald the end of an era. His heart raced as he read about a time when the heavens would open and a great deception would befall the Earth. The words were eerily similar to the events they had already witnessed.

He couldn't help but feel a tremor of fear of the alien fleet that had retreated. What if they returned?

The old man, having noticed Jonathan's preoccupation with the scrolls, joined him. "These texts hold the key to understanding the true nature," he said, his voice hushed with reverence.

"But you must be careful. The knowledge within these walls is not for the faint of heart. It is a double-edged sword that can cut through ignorance, but also destroy those who wield it without respect."

Jonathan walked slowly down the aisles, his fingertips brushing over the spines of books that held the whispers of millennia. The air was thick with the scent of history, each page a silent witness to the trials and triumphs of those who had come before them.

He paused before a particularly ancient-looking book, its leather cover cracked and worn. As he opened it, the pages fluttered like the wings of a trapped butterfly, revealing intricate diagrams that danced with an otherworldly glow.

The diagrams depicted celestial bodies in various stages of transformation, the stars and planets twisting and merging in a cosmic ballet that seemed to speak of a power beyond human understanding. The symbols that adorned the pages were not unlike the ones he had seen etched into the sphere not so long ago, hinting at a shared origin or knowledge.

The old man watched him, his eyes gleaming with curiosity. Still holding the book in his hands, Jonathan pulled a worn book from the shelf. It was a Bible, its pages yellowed with age and worn by the touch of countless hands. The leather was cracked and the edges frayed, but there was a warmth to it that belied its antiquity.

"That book," he said softly, his eyes misting over with memory, "has been passed down from generation to generation. It belonged to my grandfather. He was a man of deep faith and great intellect who was a great scholar of the heavens."

Jonathan held the Bible with reverence, feeling the weight of its history. The pages were indeed worn, with the edges frayed and the leather cover showing signs of age. Yet, the book's presence in this place of ancient wisdom suggested a connection between the divine and the cosmic that he had never considered before.

Anslem hobbled over, leaning heavily on his walking stick. "You seek the truth, do you not?" he asked, his eyes piercing into Jonathan's soul. "The truth is, these books are the same. They are but vessels for the wisdom of the ages."

Jonathan looked up, his eyes searching the old man's face for clarity. "What do you mean?"

Anslem took the book from him, his gnarled fingers caressing the leather with a gentle touch. "The truth you seek is not in the stars or in the words of long-dead civilizations," he said, his eyes shining with an inner light. "The truth is within you, and in the hearts of all who seek it."

He opened the Bible to a random page, and a soft glow emanated from it, the same as from the ancient scrolls. The room grew quiet, and even the whispers of the wind outside seemed to hush. The old woman gasped, and Colonel Sultrier stepped closer, his curiosity piqued. "Do you see?" Anslem said, pointing at the text. "The same symbols that speak of cosmic power are also woven into the words of your faith."

Jonathan's eyes scanned the page, and he realized that the scripture was intertwined with the same symbols he had seen before. His heart raced.

"This is the convergence of knowledge and faith," Anslem explained, his voice resonating through the library. "For millennia, humanity has sought to understand the heavens. Some looked through the lens of science, others through the lens of religion. Yet, in their quest, they often forget that both paths lead to the same destination. The truth."

The revelation struck Jonathan like a meteor in the night sky, illuminating the vastness of understanding that lay before him. He had spent his life in pursuit of the cosmos, but now, in this sacred space of books and beliefs, he had proof that the stars and scriptures were two sides of the same celestial coin. He felt a profound connection to the seekers of old, whose wisdom was preserved in these very pages.

Anslem placed the ancient Bible back on the shelf with a knowing smile. "The books are indeed the same," he said. "For they are all written by the same hand—that of the universe itself. The stars whisper their secrets to those who dare to listen, and the words of the divine guide those who seek meaning in their lives."

Jonathan's mind raced as he digested this revelation. His lifelong pursuit of the cosmos had always been intertwined with his mother's stories of celestial guardians and divine intervention. Now, standing in this library where science and spirituality were one, he knew that his path was not a deviation but an extension of his heritage.

On the flight home Jonathan sat looking out the window. As their plane cruised at altitude, Sherry noticed his pensive expression. He had been unusually quiet since they left Geneva, his brow furrowed in deep thought. Finally, unable to contain her concern any longer, she gently placed her hand on his arm.

"Jon," she said softly, "is everything alright? You seem preoccupied."

Jonathan turned to her, his eyes refocusing as if coming back from a distant place. He smiled softly, appreciating her concern.

"I'm fine, Sher," he replied, placing his hand over hers. "I've just been thinking about something Anselm showed me at the library before we left."

Sherry tilted her head, curiosity piqued. "Anselm? You mean the old man?"

Jonathan nodded. "That's the one. He's quite the biblical scholar, you know. Before we left for Geneva, he showed me some books that, well, they've given me a lot to think about."

"What kind of books?" Sherry asked, settling in for what she sensed would be an interesting conversation.

"Books that suggest there might be a biblical explanation for everything we've been experiencing," Jonathan explained, his voice low. "The cosmic events, the knowledge hidden within certain individuals, even the potential for otherworldly beings visiting Earth. Anslem believes it's all there in the scriptures, if we just know how to look."

Sherry's eyebrows raised in surprise. "Really? That's quite a claim. What do you think about it?"

Jonathan sighed, running a hand through his hair. "I'm not sure, to be honest. As a scientist, my first instinct is skepticism. But some of the correlations Anslem pointed out are intriguing, to say the least."

"Like what?" Sherry prompted gently.

"Well, did you know there are links between spirituality and science?

“What are you talking about?” She asked, puzzled.

“Okay, so take that passage from Genesis, for example. It talks about the creation of the universe. Now think about the big bang theory.”

“They are two different things,” she retorted.

“No they’re not, at least not exactly. The idea of the universe starting from a single, infinitely dense point, and then expanding and cooling over time… it's all there, in Genesis!”

"Well, for instance, he talked about the 'sons of God' mentioned in Genesis, suggesting they might be interpreted as beings from other worlds. And the visions described by prophets like Ezekiel - some of them sound remarkably like what we might describe as advanced technology or even spacecraft."

Sherry nodded, listening intently. "That's fascinating, Jon. I never thought about it that way before."

"Neither had I," Jonathan admitted. "It's opened up a whole new perspective for me. I'm not saying I'm convinced, but it's certainly given me a lot to ponder."

Sherry squeezed his hand supportively. "Well, if there's one thing I know about you, it's that you'll approach this with an open mind and a critical eye. Maybe when we get back, we could visit Anselm together? I'd love to hear more about these theories."

Jonathan smiled, feeling a wave of gratitude for his wife's understanding and support. "I'd like that," he said. "Who knows? Maybe by combining our scientific knowledge with these biblical interpretations, we might gain new insights into the cosmic mysteries we've been facing."

As they settled back into their seats, the conversation drifting to other topics, Jonathan felt a sense of peace. The world was full of mysteries, some scientific, some spiritual, and he was grateful to have Sherry by his side as they explored them together.

The rest of the flight passed comfortably, with the couple discussing their plans for the nursery and speculating about their child's future. As they began their descent towards home, Jonathan felt reinvigorated, eager to delve deeper into this new avenue of exploration, balancing his scientific background with the possibility of ancient wisdom hidden in sacred texts.

As they talked further, Jonathan couldn't shake those unsettling parallels between these modern-day occurrences and the ancient biblical text of the Book of Ezekiel. The prophet's vivid descriptions of celestial beings and mysterious flying objects seemed to echo the reports of strange craft and enigmatic encounters that now filled the headlines.

The similarities were uncanny. Ezekiel's vision of wheels within wheels and the appearance of a man amidst the celestial beings bore an eerie resemblance to the accounts of advanced, intelligently controlled aerial vehicles that defied conventional understanding. Jonathan's mind raced, trying to reconcile the ancient and the contemporary, the sacred and the scientific.

As soon as they arrived home, he quickly set down their luggage in the entryway and made a beeline for the bookshelf in his study. Sherry watched with a mix of amusement and curiosity as he ran his finger along the spines of the books until he found what he was looking for – an old, leather-bound Bible that had belonged to his grandfather.

"Found it!" he exclaimed, carefully pulling the book from the shelf. The worn cover and slightly yellowed pages spoke of years of use and care.

Sherry leaned against the doorframe, a soft smile on her face. "I don't think I've ever seen you so eager to read that before."

Jonathan looked up, his eyes bright with enthusiasm. "I know, it's just after talking with Anslem and thinking about it on the flight, I can't help but wonder what I might have missed all these years."

He settled into his favorite armchair, the Bible open on his lap. Sherry approached, perching on the arm of the chair.

"Where are you going to start?" she asked, genuinely intrigued by her husband's newfound interest.

"I think I'll begin with Genesis," Jonathan replied, flipping to the first pages. "Anslem mentioned something about the 'sons of God' that I want to re-examine."

As he began to read, his brow furrowed in concentration. Sherry watched as his eyes darted back and forth across the pages, occasionally pausing to jot down notes on a nearby pad.

"You know," Sherry said after a while, "it's kind of exciting to think that answers to our cosmic questions might have been here all along, just waiting for the right interpretation."

Jonathan nodded, looking up from the book. "It's fascinating, really. The way ancient texts might hold clues to modern mysteries. Of course, we'll need to approach this critically, cross-referencing with our scientific knowledge."

Sherry couldn't help but chuckle. "Always the scientist, aren't you?"

"Well, yes," Jonathan admitted with a grin. "But maybe that's exactly what's needed – a bridge between ancient wisdom and modern understanding."

As the evening wore on, Jonathan continued his exploration of the Bible, occasionally sharing interesting passages with Sherry. She listened attentively, offering her own insights and questions.

The atmosphere in their home was one of peaceful curiosity, a far cry from the tension and urgency that often accompanied their work. This new avenue of exploration seemed to energize Jonathan, and Sherry was happy to see him so engaged.

As night fell, they finally decided to call it a day. Jonathan carefully marked his place in the Bible, already looking forward to continuing his study in the morning.

"Thank you for understanding," he said to Sherry as they prepared for bed. "I know this might seem a bit out of character for me."

Sherry smiled, kissing him softly. "Jon, your curiosity and openness to new ideas are part of why I love you. Who knows? Maybe this is the start of something big."

For weeks after Jonathan had immersed himself in the study of both the UAP reports and the ancient text, searching for clues that might shed light on this perplexing phenomenon. The more he read, the more convinced he became that there was a deeper connection, a hidden truth that had been obscured by the passage of time and the biases of human interpretation.

As he meticulously cross-referenced the biblical accounts with the latest data, a startling realization dawned upon him.

"The answers I've been seeking are not in the vastness of space, but within the pages of the Holy Bible," he murmured, his voice trembling with excitement.

Driven by this newfound conviction, he began to study the scriptures with a renewed fervor, searching for the hidden connections between the divine and the scientific. He found himself captivated by the intricate details and the profound insights that the Bible offered, seemingly in direct opposition to the prevailing scientific consensus.

Chapter Eighteen: Confessions of the Wrong

Two years had passed, bringing with it a whirlwind of changes. Sherry stood in the kitchen, gently feeding their baby girl, Sarandon, named in honor of Colonel Sultrier and Dr. Mitchell. The sound of cooing and the clinking of a spoon against a bowl filled the warm, sunlit room.

"Jon," Sherry called out, her voice carrying a mix of love and mild exasperation, "can you get the door? My hands are full."

Jonathan, who had been engrossed in his latest research combining biblical texts and astrophysics, looked up from his papers spread across the dining table. "Of course, honey," he replied, rising to his feet.

As he approached the front door, he heard a gentle knock. Opening it, he found himself face to face with a young woman he didn't recognize. She had an earnest expression, her eyes bright with determination.

"Hello," she said, her voice soft but clear. "My name is Rachel. I was hoping I could come in and talk to you. It's important."

Before Jonathan could respond, he noticed movement behind Rachel. To his surprise, he saw Colonel Sultrier and Dr. Mitchell walking up the steps, suitcases in hand, having just returned from their honeymoon.

"Colonel, Sarah!" Jonathan exclaimed, a broad smile spreading across his face. "Welcome back! How was the trip?"

The newlyweds approached, their faces glowing with happiness tinged with curiosity at the scene before them.

"It was wonderful, Jon," Dr. Mitchell replied, her eyes moving from Jonathan to the young woman standing at the door. "But who's this?"

Rachel turned, seeming a bit startled by the new arrivals. "Oh, I'm sorry, I didn't mean to intrude on a reunion. I can come back another time if…"

"Nonsense," Jonathan interjected kindly. "Why don't we all go inside? I'm sure Sherry would love to see you two," he added, nodding to Colonel Sultrier and Dr. Mitchell. "And Rachel, we can hear what brought you here."

As they all filed into the house, Jonathan couldn't help but feel a sense of anticipation. Something told him that Rachel's visit wasn't a coincidence, especially coming on the heels of the Colonel and Dr. Mitchell's return.

"Sherry," he called out as they entered, "we have some visitors. And I think we might be in for an interesting conversation."

"Coming," Sherry said, as she walked out holding Sarandon on her side exposing her very pregnant belly.

She sat the baby on the floor and rubbed her belly. “Little guy is getting too big to live here too much longer.”

The atmosphere in the house was charged with curiosity about their unexpected guest. As they gathered in the living room, Jonathan had a feeling that their lives were about to take another unexpected turn.

"I know what you did," she began, her voice trembling. "I know about the artifact, the UAP’s and Bennett."

They had not spoken openly about the UAPs since that fateful night. The secrets they held were too dangerous to share. But something about her spoke to them, a spark that resonated with the light they had brought to the city.

Jonathan studied her closely, his curiosity piqued. "How do you know about us?"

"I was there," she said, her voice low. "I saw the light. I felt the change. And now, I want to help."

The room grew quiet as they absorbed her words. Her name was Rachel, and her story was one of disillusionment and a search for truth. She had once followed Bennett, drawn in by his promises of salvation. But when she had witnessed the light during the battle, something within her had shifted.

Rachel had been part of Bennett's inner circle, and she had seen the dark underbelly of his power, the manipulation and fear that held his followers in thrall.

She had been tasked with spreading his message of fear, but now she wanted to help spread theirs—the message of love and hope.

They listened as she spoke, her words painting a picture of a world that was still broken, still desperate for guidance. She had seen the power structures that remained, the remnants of Bennett's control that threatened to rise again.

The city was a tapestry of rebuilding, the scars of the past slowly being mended. They moved through the streets with purpose, their hearts heavy but their spirits high.

Jonathan turned to the Colonel, his gaze serious. "We need to go to the UN," he said. "We need to understand how Bennett managed to infiltrate their ranks, how he became their president."

"What are we looking for?" The Colonel asked, his mind racing with questions.

"Anything," Jonathan replied. "Evidence, connections, a way to prevent this from happening again."

They had been to the UN headquarters before, but they had felt out of place. On this day they knew that the light was with them, that the love they carried was stronger than any weapon. And as they stood before the gleaming façade of the new UN headquarters, they took a collective deep breath.

They were ready to take the fight to the enemy's doorstep. Ready to bring the truth to the very heart of the beast. The doors to the headquarters swung open, and they stepped inside. They walked the halls with a purpose.

The new command center was now a place where information flowed freely and the voices of the people were heard. Their victory had reached the corners of the globe, and the once-mighty institution was now a symbol of hope, a beacon for those seeking the truth.

The world had changed, and with it, so had the organization's goals. No longer would it be a tool of fear and control, but a bastion of peace and understanding.

Jonathan and the Colonel approached the new UN President, Mr. Castillo, with a mix of caution and hope. The man behind the desk looked up from his paperwork, his expression one of curiosity as he regarded the unannounced visitors.

"Mr. Castillo," Jonathan began, his voice steady, "We need to know how Lucien Bennett managed to ascend to this office. We must understand the mechanisms of his rise to power to prevent a repeat of his tyranny."

The President leaned back in his chair. "I have been expecting you. Mr. Bennett's election was unconventional," he admitted. "He played upon the fears and divisions of our time, promising peace and unity through his supposed divine mandate."

"But how did he convince you of this?" The Colonel pressed. "How did he manipulate the system to get here?"

Castillo sighed heavily, his gaze drifting to the window behind him, where the cityscape of New York was bustling back to life. "He had allies," he said finally. "In high places. People who believed in his cause, or were swayed by the power he seemed to wield."

The room was quiet for a moment, the weight of the revelation settling on them like a heavy cloak.

"We need to find out who these people are," Colonel Sultrier said, his voice firm. "We need to dismantle the network that allowed him to rise to power."

Castillo nodded gravely. "We have already done that. There was a long history of humanity's quest for power in play here. But he has no allies here anymore."

As they spoke they found evidence of bribery, blackmail, and manipulation that had paved the way for his presidency. The sphere had indeed played a part, whispering in the ears of those who were desperate for change, promising power and security.

They thanked him, feeling the gravity of their visit lifted off their shoulders. As they left the building the corridors of the UN headquarters felt colder, the echoes of past deals and deceits seemingly trapped within the very walls themselves.

As Jonathan and the Colonel pulled up to the house, they noticed an unusual flurry of activity. The front door was wide open, and they could hear excited voices from inside

"What do you think is going on?" The Colonel asked, his brow furrowed with concern.

Jonathan shook his head, a mix of confusion and anticipation on his face. "I'm not sure, but let's find out."

They rushed into the house to find Dr. Mitchell and Rachel helping Sherry, who was clearly in labor. Sherry's face was flushed, and she was breathing heavily, one hand on her swollen belly.

"Jon!" Sherry exclaimed, relief flooding her features as she saw her husband. "The baby's coming. We need to get to the hospital now!"

Jonathan's eyes widened in surprise and excitement. "Now? But it's early! Are you sure?"

Dr. Mitchell, ever the calm presence, stepped in. "We're sure, Jon. Her water broke about twenty minutes ago, and the contractions are getting closer together."

Rachel, who had been gathering Sherry's hospital bag, added, "We've been timing them. It's definitely time to go."

The Colonel, always ready for action, immediately took charge. "Right, let's move. I'll bring the car around. Jonathan, help Sherry to the door. Dr. Mitchell, Rachel, can you grab the bags and anything else we might need?"

As they all sprang into action, Jonathan couldn't help but marvel at the timing. Just moments ago, he and

The Colonel had been deep in discussion about Bennett and the mysteries surrounding his election to the UN. Now, all of that seemed far away as the imminent arrival of his son took center stage.

"Are you okay?" Jonathan asked Sherry softly as he supported her towards the door.

Sherry nodded, squeezing his hand tightly as another contraction hit. "I'm fine. Just ready to meet our little boy."

As they made their way to the car, Jonathan's mind raced with thoughts of the future. The UN investigation, the lingering questions about Bennett, the cosmic mysteries they'd encountered - all of it paled in comparison to the miracle that was about to happen.

The Colonel pulled up in the car, and they carefully helped Sherry into the backseat. As Jonathan slid in next to her, with Dr. Mitchell and Rachel following in Rachel's car, he couldn't help but feel a sense of awe at how quickly life could change.

"Ready?" he asked Sherry, giving her hand a reassuring squeeze.

She nodded, determination etched on her face. "Ready. Let's go meet our son."

As they drove off towards the hospital, Jonathan knew that whatever challenges lay ahead - be they cosmic, political, or personal - they would face them together, as a family. And soon, very soon, that family would grow by one more.

The atmosphere in the car was overwhelmed with nervous energy. Sherry's contractions were coming more frequently now, and Jonathan found himself torn between concern for his wife and anticipation of meeting his son.

The Colonel navigated the streets with practiced efficiency, occasionally glancing in the rearview mirror. "How are you holding up back there, Sherry?" he asked, his usually stoic voice tinged with worry.

"I'm okay," Sherry managed between controlled breaths. "Focus on getting us there quickly, please."

Jonathan held her hand, offering what comfort he could. "You're doing great, honey. We're almost there."

As they pulled into the hospital parking lot, Dr. Mitchell and Rachel arrived right behind them. The group moved with coordinated precision, helping Sherry out of the car and into a wheelchair that a nurse had brought out to meet them.

"We've got a woman in active labor here," Dr. Mitchell informed the nurse, her medical training kicking in. "Contractions are about three minutes apart."

The nurse nodded, quickly assessing the situation. "Right this way. We've got a room prepared."

As they rushed through the hospital corridors, Jonathan thought that it seemed like only yesterday they were here for the birth of Sarandon, and now they were about to welcome their son.

Once in the delivery room, things moved quickly. The doctor arrived, nurses bustled about, and Jonathan found himself by Sherry's side, coaching her through her breathing as they had practiced.

"You've got this, Sher," he encouraged, wiping her brow. "Our boy's almost here."

Hours passed in a blur of activity. Dr. Mitchell, Rachel, and the Colonel took turns waiting outside, each offering support in their own way. Dr. Mitchell took care of Sarandon and provided medical insights, Rachel offered words of encouragement, and the Colonel, ever the pragmatist, made sure everything outside the delivery room was taken care of.

Finally, after what seemed like an eternity, the room filled with the unmistakable cry of a newborn baby.

"Congratulations," the doctor announced, holding up a squirming, red-faced infant. "You have a healthy baby boy."

As the nurses cleaned and wrapped the baby, Jonathan felt overwhelmed with emotion. He looked at Sherry, her face glowing despite her exhaustion, and felt a surge of love for both her and their new son.

"Would you like to hold him?" a nurse asked, offering the bundled baby to Jonathan.

With trembling hands, Jonathan took his son into his arms for the first time. Looking down at the tiny face, he felt a profound sense of wonder and responsibility.

"Hello, little one," he whispered. "Welcome to the world."

As he placed the baby in Sherry's arms, Jonathan was struck by the perfection of the moment. All the cosmic mysteries, all the global threats they had faced – none of it seemed to matter in the face of this small miracle.

"What should we name him?" Sherry asked softly, her eyes never leaving their son's face.

Jonathan smiled. "How about Elijah Donald? It means 'Yahweh is God' in Hebrew. Given everything we've been through, it seems fitting."

Sherry nodded, a tired but happy smile on her face. "Elijah. It's perfect."

As the new family shared their first moments together, Jonathan knew that whatever challenges lay ahead, they would face them with renewed purpose and strength. The universe might be full of mysteries, but right here, in this hospital room, he held the greatest mystery of all – the miracle of new life.

As the first few hours of Elijah's life passed, the delivery room became a hub of quiet celebration. Dr. Mitchell, Rachel, and the Colonel were allowed in to meet the newest member of their extended family.

"He's beautiful," Dr. Mitchell whispered, gently stroking Elijah's tiny hand. Her eyes met Jonathan's, a silent understanding passing between them about the weight of bringing a child into their complex world.

Rachel couldn't stop smiling as she looked at the baby. "He has your eyes, Jonathan," she observed, her voice filled with wonder.

The Colonel, typically reserved, found himself unexpectedly moved. He placed a hand on Jonathan's shoulder. "Congratulations, old friend. He's going to change everything, you know."

Jonathan nodded, a mix of joy and determination in his eyes. "I know. And we'll be ready for whatever comes."

As the visitors took turns holding Elijah, Sherry rested, her face glowing with motherly pride. Jonathan sat beside her, holding her hand and marveling at how their lives had transformed in just a few short hours.

Suddenly, the Colonel's phone buzzed. He stepped out of the room to take the call, returning a few minutes later with a serious expression.

"Jon," he said quietly, "I hate to do this now, but we've got a situation. The UN just called an emergency session. Something's happening."

Jonathan felt torn, looking from the Colonel to Sherry and Elijah. Sherry, sensing his conflict, squeezed his hand. "Go," she said softly. "We'll be fine here. The world still needs you."

After a moment's hesitation, Jonathan nodded. He kissed Sherry and gently touched Elijah's cheek. "I'll be back as soon as I can," he promised.

As Jonathan and the Colonel prepared to leave, Dr. Mitchell approached them. "I'll stay here with Sherry and the baby," she assured them. "Rachel and I will make sure they have everything they need."

Jonathan thanked her, grateful for their support system. As he and the Colonel headed out, he cast one last look at his growing family. The sight of Sherry holding Elijah, surrounded by friends, filled him with a renewed sense of purpose.

In the car, the Colonel briefed Jonathan on the situation. "We don't have all the details yet, but there's been some kind of cosmic event. Multiple countries reported strange phenomena in the sky."

Jonathan's mind raced, thinking of the research he'd been doing, the biblical connections he'd been exploring.

The Colonel shrugged, his face grim. "I don't know what's going on, but I have a feeling we're about to find out."

As they sped towards the UN headquarters, Jonathan found himself in a familiar position, torn between the personal and the cosmic, the miracle of new life and the mysteries of the universe. But now, more than ever, he felt driven to uncover the truth and protect the world his son had just been born into.

The city lights blurred past them, and Jonathan steeled himself for whatever lay ahead. Whether it was otherworldly visitors, cosmic phenomena, or political intrigue, he was ready to face it. For Sherry, for Elijah, for the future of humanity - he would confront these challenges head-on.

As Jonathan and the Colonel approached the United Nations Headquarters, they could see an increased security presence. NYPD officers and UN security personnel were stationed at every entrance, their faces tense and alert.

"Looks like they're taking the threats seriously," Jonathan observed, noting the barricades and checkpoints that had been set up around the perimeter.

The Colonel nodded grimly. "Can't be too careful, especially given recent events. The uptick in political violence has everyone on edge."

They made their way through the security checkpoints, their high-level clearance allowing them expedited access. Inside the building, Diplomats and officials from various countries hurried through the corridors, engaged in hushed conversations.

As they entered the main assembly hall, Jonathan was struck by the sight of world leaders filing in, their faces grave. The recent cosmic event seemed to have overshadowed the usual political posturing.

"Dr. Avery, Colonel Sultrier," a voice called out. They turned to see a harried-looking UN official approaching. "Thank you for coming so quickly. The Secretary-General is about to address the assembly, but she wants to speak with you first."

They followed the official to a side room where the Secretary-General was waiting. Her usual composure was slightly shaken, a testament to the seriousness of the situation.

"Gentlemen," she greeted them, "I'm glad you're here. We're dealing with an unprecedented situation. The cosmic event has caused widespread panic, and we're receiving reports of increased political unrest in several member states."

Jonathan leaned forward, his scientific curiosity piqued despite the gravity of the situation. "What exactly did people see? Are we dealing with another appearance like the binary star system?"

The Secretary-General shook her head. "It's different this time. Multiple countries reported what appeared to be tears in the sky. Brief glimpses of something else. Another world, perhaps."

The Colonel's brow furrowed. "And the connection to political violence?"

"We're not sure yet," she admitted. "But the timing is too coincidental to ignore. We need your expertise, Dr. Avery. Your unique understanding of both the scientific and, shall we say, cosmic aspects of these events is crucial."

Jonathan nodded, his mind already racing with possibilities. The biblical research he'd been doing, the lingering questions about Bennett, the strange phenomena - it all seemed to be converging.

"I'll do whatever I can to help," he assured her. "But I have to ask - has there been any activity from Bennett or his followers?"

The Secretary-General's expression darkened. "Nothing overt, but we've detected chatter. They're mobilizing, Dr. Avery. Whatever's happening, they seem to think it's what they've been waiting for."

As they prepared to enter the main assembly, Jonathan felt the weight of responsibility settle on his shoulders. He thought of Sherry and the kids, safe in the hospital, and of the world they would inherit. Whatever was coming, he was determined to face it head-on.

"Let's get to work," he said, straightening his shoulders.

With that, they stepped into the assembly hall, ready to confront whatever cosmic or Earthly challenges lay ahead. The fate of nations hung in the balance.

Jonathan and the Colonel entered the main assembly hall, the room fell into a hushed silence. World leaders and diplomats turned to look at them. The Secretary-General took her place at the podium, her voice steady as she addressed the gathered representatives.

"Distinguished delegates, we face an unprecedented crisis," she began. "The cosmic event we've witnessed is beyond our current understanding, but we must remain united in our response."

As she continued her speech, outlining the known facts and calling for calm, Jonathan's mind raced. He scanned the room, noting the reactions of various leaders. Some seemed skeptical, others frightened, and a few were intrigued.

Suddenly, a commotion erupted near the back of the hall. A man stood up, his face contorted with a mix of fear and excitement. "It's happening!" he shouted. "Bennett's prophecy is coming true!"

Security personnel moved quickly to remove the man, but his outburst had sent ripples of unease through the assembly. Jonathan exchanged a meaningful glance with the Colonel. The mention of Bennett's name in this context was troubling.

As the Secretary-General tried to regain control of the room, Jonathan felt a tap on his shoulder. He turned to see a familiar face – Dr. Elena Petrova, a respected astrophysicist he had worked with in the past.

"Jonathan," she whispered urgently, "I need to show you something. It's about the 'tears' in the sky. We've managed to capture some data, you need to see this for yourself."

With a nod to the Colonel, Jonathan followed Dr. Petrova out of the main hall and into a makeshift command center nearby. Screens displayed various data readouts and satellite imagery.

"Look at this," Elena said, pulling up a series of spectral analyses. "The energy signatures from these 'tears' – they're unlike anything we've ever seen. But there's something familiar about the pattern. It's almost as if..."

"As if what?" Jonathan prompted, leaning in to study the data.

Elena hesitated, then said, "As if they're trying to communicate. These aren't random occurrences, Jonathan. There's a pattern, a rhythm to them. It's like a cosmic morse code."

Jonathan's eyes widened as he processed this information. The biblical texts he'd been studying, the strange phenomena, past cryptic warnings – it all seemed to be converging into a single, mind-bending possibility.

"We need to decode this message," he said, his voice filled with determination. "And we need to do it fast. Whatever's trying to communicate with us, I have a feeling it's not going to wait much longer."

As they dove into the data, Jonathan couldn't help but think of Sherry and the kids. He was doing this for them, for the future they deserved. Whatever cosmic force was reaching out to Earth, he was determined to understand it, to protect humanity from any potential threat.

The UN building buzzed with activity around them, but in that small room, Jonathan and Elena worked feverishly, racing against time to decipher a message from beyond the stars. Little did they know that their discoveries in the next few hours would change the course of human history forever.

Chapter Nineteen: Answering a Cosmic Calling

As Jonathan and Elena worked tirelessly to decipher the cosmic message, the world outside the UN building continued to churn with uncertainty and fear. News outlets across the globe were reporting on the strange phenomena, with amateur videos of the "sky tears" going viral on social media platforms.

Meanwhile, in a small hospital room across town, Sherry cradled newborn Elijah, her eyes fixed on the television mounted on the wall. The breaking news banner scrolled across the bottom of the screen, detailing the ongoing crisis at the UN and the global response to the cosmic event.

Dr. Mitchell sat beside her, alternating between playing with Sarandon and checking her phone for updates from the Colonel. Rachel paced near the window, her face a mask of concern as she watched the New York skyline, half-expecting to see one of the mysterious tears appear at any moment.

"I can't believe this is happening now, of all times," Sherry said softly, her voice tinged with a mix of worry and exhaustion. "Jon should be here with us, not..."

"Saving the world?" Dr. Mitchell finished with a small smile. "I know it's not ideal, Sherry, but if anyone can figure this out, it's Jonathan."

Rachel nodded in agreement. "He's been preparing for something like this, in a way. All that research he's been doing, combining scientific knowledge with biblical interpretations – maybe it's all been leading to this moment."

"You're right," Sherry said, her resolve strengthening. "And when Jon figures this out, he'll come back to us. We just need to be patient and strong for him – and for the kids."

Suddenly, Dr. Mitchell's phone buzzed with an incoming call from the Colonel. She answered quickly, putting it on speaker so they could all hear.

"Sarah? Are you with Sherry and Rachel?" The Colonel's voice came through, tension evident in his tone.

"Yes, we're all here. What's happening?" Dr. Mitchell replied.

"Listen carefully," he said. "Jonathan and Dr. Petrova think they're close to decoding the message. But there's something else – we've detected unusual activity near the prophets last known location. We think his followers might be planning something big."

The women exchanged worried glances as the Colonel continued, "I need you to stay alert. If anything unusual happens, anything at all, I want you to contact me immediately. We're sending additional security to the hospital, just in case."

As the call ended, the room fell into a tense silence, broken only by Elijah's soft breathing. Sherry held her son closer, a fierce protectiveness washing over her.

"I don't know what's coming," she said, her voice steady and determined, "but we'll face it together. For Jonathan, for the kids, for all of us."

Dr. Mitchell and Rachel nodded in agreement, each taking up positions near the door and window, ready to face whatever challenges the cosmos – or Bennett's followers – might throw their way.7

Outside, the New York sky remained calm for now. In a hospital room and a UN building, two groups connected by love, duty, and cosmic mystery prepared for what might be the most important moment in human history.

As the hours ticked by, the tension in the hospital room grew. Sherry, Dr. Mitchell, and Rachel took turns watching the news, caring for Elijah, and keeping a vigilant eye on their surroundings. The additional security the Colonel had promised arrived, taking up positions in the hallway outside their room.

Meanwhile, at the UN, Jonathan and Elena's breakthrough came suddenly and dramatically. As they pored over the data, a pattern emerged that seemed to transcend both scientific and religious understanding.

"My God," Jonathan breathed, his eyes wide with realization. "It's not just a message, Elena. It's an invitation."

Before Elena could respond, alarms began blaring throughout the building. The Colonel burst into the room, his face grim. "We've got a situation. The prophets' followers have mobilized. They're converging on multiple locations across the city, including..."

"The hospital," Jonathan finished, his heart racing. "Sherry and kids."

The sky outside the UN building shimmered, a massive tear opening up to reveal a breathtaking vista of stars and swirling cosmic energies. The sight was both terrifying and awe-inspiring.

Back at the hospital, Sherry was the first to notice the change. The room suddenly filled with an otherworldly light streaming through the window. "Sarah! Rachel, look!" she gasped, clutching Elijah protectively.

They rushed to the window, watching in amazement as the sky seemed to split open. But their wonder quickly turned to alarm as they spotted a group of robed figures approaching the hospital entrance.

"We need to move, now," Dr. Mitchell said decisively, her training kicking in. "Rachel, help Sherry with the kids. I'll coordinate with security."

As they prepared to evacuate, Sherry's phone buzzed with a message from Jonathan: Stay safe. I'm on my way. Whatever happens, remember – it's an invitation, not a threat. Love you."

Sherry felt a surge of hope and determination. Whatever this cosmic invitation meant, whatever the prophet and his followers were planning, she knew that Jonathan was working to understand and protect them all.

The security team ushered them out of the room and towards a secure exit. As they moved through the corridors, they could hear commotion from the floors below – The prophets' followers had entered the building.

Outside, the tear in the sky had grown larger, bathing the city in an ethereal glow. People on the streets stood frozen in awe, their faces upturned to the cosmic display.

As Sherry, Dr. Mitchell, holding Sarandon, and Rachel emerged from the hospital with Elijah, they found themselves at a crossroads of cosmic and Earthly drama.

The rioters were closing in from one direction, while the shimmering tear in reality beckoned from above.

In that moment, cradling her newborn son and flanked by her friends, Sherry made a decision. They wouldn't run. They would stand their ground and face whatever was coming – be it human zealots or cosmic entities.

"Jonathan will find us," she said with quiet certainty. "And when he does, we'll face this together – as a family."

As if in response to her words, the tear in the sky pulsed with energy, and a figure began to emerge from its depths. The cosmic invitation was about to be delivered in person.

As the figure emerged from the cosmic tear, time seemed to slow down. Rachel, Dr. Mitchell, now holding Sarandon tighter, stood transfixed, Elijah cradled protectively in Sherry's arms. The security team formed a protective circle around them, their weapons drawn but held as they faced a situation far beyond their training.

The being that descended from the tear was unlike anything they had ever seen. It had a form that seemed to shift and change, sometimes appearing humanoid, other times taking on more abstract, geometric shapes. Light emanated from within it, pulsing in a rhythm that felt strangely familiar.

At the same time, the prophets' followers had reached the hospital entrance. Led by the Bennett lookalike, they stopped short at the sight of the cosmic being. Their faces showed a mix of awe, fear, and fanatical excitement.

Suddenly, a car screeched to a halt nearby. Jonathan leaped out, followed closely by the Colonel and Elena. His eyes widened as he took in the scene – his family, the cosmic being, and the prophets cult all converging in this one moment.

"Sherry!" he called out, rushing towards them.

As Jonathan reached his family, the cosmic being spoke. Its voice seemed to bypass their ears, resonating directly in their minds.

"Children of Earth," it communicated, "we have watched your progress for eons. The time has come for you to join the cosmic community."

The Bennett lookalike stepped forward, his arms raised in supplication. "We are ready, great one! We have prepared for this moment!"

But the being's attention was focused on Jonathan and his family. "You," it addressed Jonathan, "have begun to understand. The knowledge within you, the connections you've made between your science and ancient wisdom – this is why we chose to make contact now."

Jonathan stood protectively in front of Sherry and his children, his mind racing. "The invitation," he said, "it's for all of humanity, isn't it? Not just a select few?"

The being's form shimmered in what seemed like approval. "Correct. But the choice must be made freely, and with full understanding. We offer knowledge, advancement, and a place among the stars. But it comes with great responsibility."

As the cosmic being spoke, more tears began to open in the sky above New York. Similar scenes were playing out across the globe, as humanity faced its greatest moment of choice.

The followers, realizing that their leader's promises of exclusive ascension were false, began to argue among themselves. Some fell to their knees in reverence, while others turned away in disillusionment.

Sherry stepped forward, Elijah in her arms. "And our children?" she asked, her voice steady. "What future do you offer them?"

The being's form softened, tendrils of light reaching out to gently touch Elijah's forehead. "A future of wonder, discovery, and infinite possibilities. But also one of great challenges and responsibilities. The choice you make today will shape their destiny."

Jonathan looked at Sherry, then at Dr. Mitchell, Rachel, and the Colonel. In their eyes, he saw the same mix of fear, hope, and determination that he felt. This was a decision that would alter the course of human history forever.

"We need time," Jonathan said to the being. "Time to discuss, to understand, to prepare our people for such a monumental change."

The being's form pulsed in what seemed like agreement. "Time you shall have. We will return when the first cycle of your planet is complete. Use this time wisely, children of Earth. The stars await your decision."

With that, the being began to ascend back towards the cosmic tear. As it retreated, the tears in the sky slowly began to close, leaving behind a world forever changed by the encounter.

As the last of the tears sealed shut, Jonathan embraced Sherry and his children tightly. "Well," he said, a hint of his old humor returning, "That's only ten years. I guess we have our work cut out for us."

Sherry nodded, looking down at their son. "Ten years to prepare humanity for the biggest decision in our history. No pressure, right?"

As they stood there, surrounded by friends and the remnants of the prophets' confused followers, they knew that the real work was just beginning. The next year would be filled with challenges, debates, and preparations as humanity grappled with its cosmic invitation.

But for now, at this moment, Jonathan was simply grateful to hold his family close.

The night after it happened, they gathered in Jonathan and Sherry's living room. The kids were asleep, both exhausted from a day of regular childhood concerns that now seemed impossibly quaint.

"They'll know something's wrong," Sherry said, curled into the corner of the couch, her PR instincts warring with maternal protection. "Sarandon already asked why you came home so late from work." She looked at Jonathan, who hadn't stopped pacing since Sarah and the Colonel arrived.

"Kids are perceptive," Sarah added softly, her hand finding the Colonel's in the dim light. "Especially at their age. They'll notice the changes in us, the nightmares, the..." She gestured vaguely, still struggling to describe what they'd witnessed in the park.

The Colonel sat ramrod straight in the armchair, decades of military bearing holding him together. "If we tell them, we make them targets. Every intelligence agency, every government entity that wants to understand what happened - they'll watch the children, thinking they might know something."

Jonathan stopped his pacing, looking down the darkened hallway where his children slept their last innocent sleep. "Elijah is too young to remember any of this," he said quietly. "But Sarandon is three, she might…." His voice cracked.

"We can't lie to them forever," Sherry whispered, her lawyer's mind already constructing arguments against her own position.

"We're not lying," the Colonel said firmly. "We're protecting them. Giving them the chance to grow up without knowing that everything they're learning in school, everything they think they understand about the universe..." He trailed off, his grip tightening on Sarah's hand.

"Is a children's picture book compared to what's really out there," Sarah finished.

Jonathan moved to sit beside his wife, feeling the weight of the decision settling around them. "So we say nothing. We lock it away. Let them believe in a world that makes sense, at least for a little while longer."

"We give them normal," Sherry said, understanding dawning in her voice. "We give them college applications and first dates and scientific certainty. We let them trust gravity and physics and the rules of reality."

"Even though we know those rules are more like... suggestions," Sarah added with a bitter laugh.

The Colonel stood, moving to the window where the night sky suddenly held too many possibilities. "We shield them from this knowledge," he said quietly. "Not forever. But long enough for them to become who they're meant to be without the weight of knowing."

They sat in silence then, four people who had seen too much, choosing to carry that burden alone to protect the sleeping children down the hall. Outside, the stars wheeled overhead, holding secrets that would wait another decade to be revealed.

"When the time comes," Jonathan said finally, "when they need to know - we'll tell them together. All of us."

None of them said what they were really thinking: that the universe might not wait for them to choose the right moment. That the truth they'd witnessed might not stay hidden behind their wall of protective silence.

That sometimes, knowledge finds its way out, like light leaking through the cracks of a carefully constructed shelter, illuminating everything they'd tried to keep in shadow.

Down the hall, Sarandon and Elijah slept on, dreaming normal dreams in a world that their parents now knew was anything but normal.

In the days following the cosmic encounter, the world was in a state of unprecedented upheaval and excitement. News outlets ran round-the-clock coverage of the event, with experts from various fields offering their interpretations and speculations. Social media was ablaze with discussions, theories, and personal accounts of the phenomenon.

Jonathan, Sherry, and their inner circle found themselves at the center of a global storm. As one of the few people who had directly communicated with the cosmic being, Jonathan was in high demand for interviews, consultations, and briefings.

A week after the event, Jonathan and Sherry's home had become an unofficial headquarters for their efforts. Sarandon played quietly while Elijah slept peacefully in a nearby bassinet, both blissfully unaware of the cosmic weight on their parents' shoulders.

"The UN wants to establish a global task force," the Colonel reported, looking up from his tablet.

"They're requesting your involvement, Jon, as a key advisor."

Jonathan nodded, running a hand through his hair. "I expected as much. We need to ensure that this task force represents a diverse range of perspectives – scientific, cultural, religious. This decision affects all of humanity."

Dr. Mitchell, who had been poring over medical journals, chimed in. "The scientific community is in overdrive. There's talk of accelerating our space programs, enhancing our communication technologies. They want to be ready for whatever comes next."

"And what about the public?" Sherry asked, her PR law instincts kicking in. "How are people processing all of this?"

Dr. Mitchell, who had been monitoring social media trends, sighed. "It's a mixed bag. There's a lot of excitement and hope, but also fear and skepticism. And Bennett's followers, while diminished, are still out there, spreading their own interpretation of events."

Jonathan stood up and walked to the window, looking out at the sky that had, just a week ago, torn open to reveal the cosmos. "Not just in preparing technologically or scientifically, but in helping humanity come to terms with its place in the universe," he said quietly. "This isn't just about whether we're ready for advanced knowledge or technology. It's about the responsibility that comes with it."

Sherry joined him at the window, slipping her hand into his. "We'll face it together, Jon. All of us. And we'll make sure that when the time comes to make the decision, humanity does so with open eyes and united hearts."

As if on cue, Elijah stirred in his bassinet, letting out a small cry. Sherry went to pick him up, cradling him gently.

"You know," Jonathan said, watching his wife with a tender smile, "in a way, the kids represent what we're fighting for. The future. A future where our children might grow up knowing they're part of something greater than just our planet. But also a future where they're grounded in what makes us human."

The group nodded in agreement, each feeling the weight and the wonder of the task before them.

"So," the Colonel said, breaking the contemplative silence, "where do we start?"

Jonathan turned back to the room, his eyes alight with determination. "We start by bringing people together. Scientists, philosophers, religious leaders, artists – everyone who can help us understand and prepare for this new reality. We have to get humanity ready for the biggest decision in our history. Let's make every day count."

As they began to plan their next steps, the room buzzed with a purpose. Outside, the world continued to grapple with the aftermath of the cosmic visitation. But in this room, a small group of dedicated individuals was already looking to the future, ready to guide humanity towards its date with destiny among the stars.

As the months turned into years, Jonathan and his team found themselves at the forefront of a global initiative unlike anything in human history. The United Nations established the Cosmic Preparedness Task Force (CPTF), with Jonathan serving as its chief scientific advisor.

Scientific progress began to accelerate, but with a focus on solving pressing terrestrial issues. Breakthroughs in sustainable energy, climate restoration, and medical technologies came in rapid succession. Space exploration continued, but with an emphasis on self-reliance and the colonization of our own solar system.

As the tenth year since the cosmic invitation dawned, the world's attention turned to a highly anticipated press conference. The venue, a state-of-the-art auditorium in Geneva, was packed with journalists from every corner of the globe. Screens worldwide prepared to broadcast the event live.

"Good morning," he began, his voice steady and resolute. "Ten years ago, we were extended an invitation that challenged everything we thought we knew about our place in the universe. Today, after careful consideration and extensive global consultation, I stand before you to announce our response."

He paused, allowing the weight of the moment to settle. "It is the conclusion of the Cosmic Preparedness Task Force, with the support of the United Nations, that it is not in humanity's best interest to join forces with the cosmic civilization at this time."

A collective gasp rippled through the audience, followed by a flurry of whispers and the rapid clicking of cameras.

"This decision was not made lightly. We have spent these years not only advancing our understanding of the cosmos but also deeply examining our own species – our strengths, our flaws, and our potential."

He continued, his tone measured and thoughtful. "While we are immensely grateful for the invitation and the knowledge it has brought us, we believe that humanity must continue on its own path of development and self-discovery. We are not rejecting the possibility of future cooperation, but rather asserting our need to continue our research."

Jonathan's expression softened slightly. "However, this decision does not mean we will cease our efforts to understand the universe around us. On the contrary, we will redouble our research initiatives. We will continue to explore our solar system, advance our technologies, and prepare ourselves for a future where we might engage with other civilizations as equals, not as novices."

He concluded with a note of optimism. "This is not an endpoint, but a new beginning. We face the future not in isolation, but with a renewed commitment to our own potential. The stars remain our inspiration, and the cosmic invitation a reminder of the wonders that await us when we are truly ready."

As Jonathan stepped back from the podium, the room erupted into a cacophony of questions and exclamations. The decision had been made, setting humanity on a course of independent development while keeping an eye on the vast cosmic frontier that had once seemed so close, and now felt both more distant and more achievable on their own terms.

Over the next ten years Earth underwent a profound transformation, but not in the way many had initially expected. The decision not to join the alien civilization immediately sparked a period of intense introspection and focused development.

Education systems worldwide were overhauled to emphasize critical thinking, ethical reasoning, and a deep understanding of Earth's ecosystems and cultures. A new generation grew up with a strong sense of global citizenship and responsibility.

Socially and politically, the world saw a gradual shift towards greater cooperation, driven by the shared goal of proving humanity's capacity for self-governance and problem-solving. International tensions decreased as countries recognized the need for unity in the face of potential cosmic challenges.

Environmental efforts took center stage as humanity recognized the need to preserve and restore Earth as its primary home. Significant strides were made in reversing climate change and protecting biodiversity.

Philosophical and religious dialogues flourished, focusing on humanity's unique place in the cosmos and the value of charting our own course. New ethical frameworks emerged, blending traditional wisdom with the challenges of a potential multi-species universe.

Art and culture experienced a renaissance, celebrating human creativity and diversity. The "Terrestrial Renaissance" movement gained global traction, influencing everything from literature to urban planning.

Some groups still argued for reconsidering the invitation, fearing isolation in the cosmos. Economic systems struggled to adapt to rapidly changing priorities. Debates raged about the balance between progress and preservation of human traditions.

Jonathan Avery, now a globally recognized figure, worked tirelessly to maintain humanity's resolve. He became not just a scientist, but a visionary leader, helping to shape Earth's independent future.

Chapter Twenty: Invitations to the Shadows

As the tenth year drew to a close, Earth was a changed world. More united, more resilient, yet still firmly committed to its decision not to join the alien civilization. The approaching deadline for their final answer loomed, and humanity stood ready to reaffirm its choice, looking to the stars not as a destination, but as a reminder of the vastness they would face on their own terms.

The question remained: Had they made the right decision? The answer would soon be tested, as Earth prepared to formally decline the cosmic invitation and chart its own course among the stars.

They gathered in a high-tech conference room at the UN headquarters, preparing for a worldwide broadcast. The room was a hive of activity, with technicians making last-minute adjustments and diplomats from various nations conferring in hushed tones.

Sherry, the CPTF's head of public relations, was going over talking points with Jonathan.

"Remember," Sherry said, straightening Jonathan's tie, "we need to strike a balance between excitement and caution. People need to understand the magnitude of this decision without feeling overwhelmed."

Jonathan nodded, his eyes reflecting a mix of determination and fatigue. The past months had been grueling, filled with endless meetings, research, and public appearances. "I know. It's a delicate line to walk."

The Colonel entered the room, his face serious. "We're live in five minutes. The Secretary-General will introduce you, then it's all you, Jon."

As they took their positions, Jonathan couldn't help but marvel at how far they'd come. The initial chaos following the visitation had gradually given way to a sense of purpose.

Scientists around the world were making breakthrough after breakthrough, spurred on by the promise of cosmic knowledge. Philosophers and religious leaders were engaged in deep discussions about the nature of humanity and its place in the universe.

But challenges remained. There were still those who feared change, who saw the cosmic invitation as a threat rather than an opportunity. The remnants of Bennett's followers had evolved into a vocal opposition movement, warning against what they called "cosmic colonization."

The red light on the camera blinked on, and the Secretary-General began her introduction. As Jonathan listened, he felt the weight of the moment settle on his shoulders. In a few moments, he would address not just a nation, but the entire world.

"...and now, to provide an update on our cosmic preparedness efforts, I present Dr. Jonathan Avery, chief scientific advisor to the CPTF."

Taking a deep breath, Jonathan stepped up to the podium. He looked directly into the camera, imagining he was speaking not to billions, but to each person individually.

"My fellow citizens of Earth," he began, his voice steady and clear, "ten years ago, our understanding of the universe and our place in it changed forever. We were offered an invitation – a chance to join a cosmic community beyond our wildest dreams. But with this invitation comes a profound responsibility."

As Jonathan spoke, outlining the progress made and the challenges ahead, he could feel the energy in the room. This wasn't just a status update; it was a call to action, a reminder to every person on Earth that they had a stake in this decision.

"In another month," he continued, "we will face a choice that will define not just our future, but the future of generations to come. It is a choice we must make together, with clear minds and open hearts. The road ahead will not be easy, but I believe that together, we can rise to this cosmic challenge."

As he concluded his speech, Jonathan glanced over at Sherry.. In that moment, he was struck by the enormity of what they were undertaking. They weren't just preparing for a decision; they were laying the groundwork for a new chapter in human history.

The broadcast ended, but Jonathan knew their work was far from over. As congratulations and questions poured in from around the world, he steeled himself for the challenges that lay ahead. The next six months would be crucial, and he was determined to ensure that when the cosmic beings returned, humanity would be ready to embrace its destiny among the stars.

Recognizing the need to address the spiritual and philosophical implications of the cosmic invitation alongside scientific and technological aspects, the CPT organized a series of global dialogues.

Jonathan led a diverse team of religious leaders, philosophers, and scientists in these discussions, aiming to bridge gaps between worldviews in light of the new cosmic reality.

On a warm evening, Jonathan stood before a mixed audience in a grand Roman auditorium. Scientists, religious leaders, and members of the public filled the seats. The Vatican had co-sponsored this event, acknowledging the importance of open dialogue.

"Friends," Jonathan began, his voice carrying a new depth of understanding, "we stand at a crossroads not just of human history, but of human belief. The cosmic invitation challenges us to expand our understanding of creation, of our place in the universe, and of the nature of divinity itself."

He went on to discuss how his own journey through biblical texts had led him to see connections between ancient wisdom and the new cosmic reality.

"The Bible speaks of many mansions in the divine realm," he explained. "However, despite these connections and the incredible opportunity before us, I believe Earth is not yet ready to join these cosmic beings."

Jonathan paused, his gaze sweeping across the attentive audience. He took a deep breath before continuing. "Our history is rife with conflict, prejudice, and a tendency to exploit rather than steward our resources. We've made great strides, but we still struggle with global issues like poverty, inequality, and environmental degradation. These are challenges we must overcome before we can responsibly engage with a broader cosmic community."

A murmur rippled through the crowd. Jonathan held up his hand, asking for patience.

He paced slowly across the stage, his words measured and thoughtful. "Moreover, our technological advancement, while impressive, is still in its infancy compared to what we might encounter out there. We need to ensure we can approach this invitation from a position of strength and wisdom, not vulnerability and naivety."

Jonathan's voice grew more passionate. "But perhaps most importantly, we need to achieve a greater unity as a species. Our divisions - political, religious, cultural - could be exploited or misunderstood by more advanced civilizations. We need to present a united front, a global consensus on our readiness to join this cosmic dialogue."

He paused, allowing his words to sink in. "This invitation is not just a test of our scientific capabilities, but of our moral and spiritual maturity. Are we ready to be responsible custodians of cosmic knowledge? Can we be trusted to use advanced technologies wisely? These are questions we must answer honestly before we can accept this cosmic invitation."

Jonathan's expression softened, filled with hope and determination. "This doesn't mean we should abandon the opportunity. Rather, we should see it as a challenge to better ourselves, to heal our divisions, to solve our global problems. Let this invitation be the catalyst that unites humanity in a common purpose - to become worthy of joining this cosmic community."

As he spoke, Jonathan could see the impact of his words. Scientists nodded thoughtfully, considering the value of ancient texts in this new context. Religious leaders leaned forward, intrigued by the idea of a broader, cosmic interpretation of their teachings.

After the talk, a Buddhist monk approached Jonathan. "Your words give us much to contemplate," he said. "In our tradition, we speak of interconnectedness."

Later that week, Jonathan found himself in Jerusalem, participating in a roundtable discussion with Jewish, Muslim, and Christian leaders. The conversation was intense but respectful, each faith tradition grappling with how to interpret their sacred texts in light of the cosmic invitation.

"The Quran speaks of signs in the heavens," an imam noted. "Perhaps this visitation is one such sign, calling us to a greater understanding of Allah's creation."

A rabbi added, "In our mystical traditions, we've long spoken of other worlds. This could be the fulfillment of ancient prophecies, but in a way we never expected."

Throughout these dialogues, Jonathan was careful not to push for any one interpretation or belief system. Instead, he encouraged open-minded exploration and respectful exchange of ideas.

In a private moment, Sherry found Jonathan poring over his Bible, making notes. "What are you working on?" she asked.

Jonathan looked up, his eyes alight with purpose. "I'm trying to create a framework," he explained. "A way to help people see that this cosmic invitation doesn't negate their faith. But there's more to consider beyond our own readiness. We must also question whether accepting this invitation is in humanity's best interest at all."

Jonathan's expression grew more serious as he continued, his voice carrying a note of concern. Sherry smiled, placing a hand on his shoulder. "You're not just preparing humanity for this decision," she observed. "You're trying to prepare our souls."

Jonathan nodded. "This decision isn't just about whether we're ready for advanced technology or knowledge. It's about whether we're spiritually and philosophically prepared to be part of something greater than ourselves. And that preparation needs to honor and include all the diverse beliefs of our world."

As the final days before the cosmic beings' return ticked away, Jonathan continued his work, bringing together minds and hearts from across the spiritual and scientific spectrum. He knew that when the time came for humanity to make its choice, it needed to do so not just with technological readiness, but with a deep, unified spiritual understanding of its place in the cosmic order.

In seeking to understand the cosmic invitation, humanity was also learning to better understand itself and its myriad beliefs. Whatever the final decision would be, this journey was already transforming the world in profound and unexpected ways.

As the day before the cosmic beings' return approached, Jonathan found himself at the epicenter of a global spiritual and scientific renaissance. The dialogues he had initiated had sparked a worldwide movement of interfaith and interdisciplinary cooperation.

The morning before the return, Jonathan stood before a diverse gathering at the newly established Cosmic Unity Center in New York. The audicnce included scientists, religious leaders, philosophers, and ordinary citizens from all walks of life.

"Throughout history, when technologically advanced civilizations have encountered less developed ones, the results have often been catastrophic for the latter. We need only look at our own past - colonialism, exploitation, and the decimation of indigenous cultures - to see the potential dangers."

He paused, letting the weight of his words sink in. "What guarantee do we have that these cosmic beings have our best interests at heart? Their motivations, their ethics, their very concept of existence might be utterly alien to us. We could be walking into a situation we're not equipped to handle or even fully comprehend."

Jonathan's voice grew more impassioned. "Furthermore, by accepting this invitation, we risk losing our autonomy as a species. Our development, our choices, our future would inevitably be influenced - perhaps even controlled - by these far more advanced beings. Are we prepared to potentially sacrifice our independence, our unique path of evolution and progress?"

He shook his head solemnly. "I fear that in our excitement and curiosity, we may be overlooking the profound risks involved. We could be opening Pandora's box, unleashing forces beyond our control or understanding."

"Therefore," Jonathan concluded, his voice resolute, "I propose that we respectfully decline this cosmic invitation. Instead, let us focus our energies on solving our own problems, advancing our own technologies, and uniting our own species. Let us approach the cosmos on our own terms, when we are truly ready, rather than rushing into an uncertain future at the behest of unknown entities."

As Jonathan finished, a tense silence filled the auditorium. His words had challenged the prevailing excitement about the cosmic invitation, presenting a perspective that many had not considered. The path forward suddenly seemed far less clear, fraught with ethical and existential dilemmas that would not be easily resolved.

A quantum physicist in the audience raised her hand. "Dr. Avery, how do you reconcile the scientific method with these spiritual interpretations?"

Jonathan smiled, appreciating the question. "Science and faith aren't opposites," he explained. "They're complementary ways of understanding reality. Science tells us the 'how' of the universe, while faith and philosophy often tackle the 'why'. This time, we need both more than ever."

It fell from somewhere above them, dropping through the Christmas Day sky from a tear in reality. Colonel Sultrier saw it first—a mass of writhing flesh and impossible angles that seemed to fold and unfold as it descended, leaving trails of something that might have been either light or liquid suspended in the air behind it.

"Jonathan," he said quietly, grabbing his friend's arm. "Look."

The thing hit the pavement with a wet sound that shouldn't have been audible from their position, but somehow echoed in their skulls rather than their ears. It landed in a heap that couldn't decide if it was solid or fluid, its surface rippling like oil on water but with suggestions of muscle and bone beneath.

As it tried to right itself, limbs sprouted and retracted seemingly at random—too many joints bending in directions that made the mind recoil. Its flesh was translucent in places, showing organs that pulsed in patterns that had nothing to do with any earthly circulation. What might have been a face emerged, then multiplied, then merged again, featuring too many eyes that blinked in sequence like binary code.

"Dear God," Jonathan whispered, though he wasn't sure God had anything to do with this thing.

The creature's skin seemed to shift between states of matter, sometimes glossy like wet plastic, sometimes mottled like diseased flesh, sometimes crystalline like dirty ice. When it moved, it left iridescent trails on the pavement that seemed to write themselves into symbols before evaporating.

It tried to form itself into something approximating a humanoid shape, but kept getting the proportions wrong—arms too long, torso segmented like an insect, neck bending in impossible curves. What might have been its mouth opened in multiple places at once, revealing geometries that shouldn't exist in three-dimensional space.

The worst part was the sound—not quite organic, not quite mechanical—a wet sliding punctuated by clicks and pops as its framework rearranged itself. It reminded Jonathan of breaking bones underwater, or of computers trying to process corrupted data.

The thing was looking at them, its multiple eyes focusing and unfocusing like camera lenses searching for the right depth of field. Its skin rippled with patterns that made Jonathan's vision blur and his stomach turn.

"Don't move," the Colonel ordered. "Don't even breathe."

It began to flow in their direction, leaving a trail of smoke when it touched the ground. Its attempt at walking looked like a video played backwards and forwards simultaneously, each step a violation of physics and anatomy.

Then it spoke, its mouth opened in multiple places at once. "You bring humanity's answer?" The words bypassed their ears entirely, forming directly in their minds with an oily sensation that made Jonathan want to scratch his brain.

"We do," Jonathan managed, forcing himself to look at the creature. Its skin was translucent in places, showing shadows of organs that pulsed in no rhythm he could recognize. The being's form rippled with what might have been anger. The others behind it began to shift and flow together, their shapes melding and separating in a display that sent Jonathan's mind screaming into primitive fight-or-flight responses.

“After careful consideration," Jonathan began, his voice steady despite the stench that always accompanied their visitors, "Earth has decided to decline your invitation to join the cosmic collective."

"This is not an invitation to decline," the being's thoughts slithered into their consciousness. "This is inevitable. All worlds join. All species merge. All flesh becomes one."

The Colonel stepped forward, his military bearing unchanged by the supernatural display before him. "With respect," he said, "Earth's major religions have raised significant concerns about the nature of your... collective."

"You speak of myths!" The beings shifted, their formation creating a crown of light above their assembled forms. "Your religions," the word carried a note of disdain, "are primitive attempts to understand what we have mastered."

"I speak of truth," Jonathan interrupted. "The same truth written in the patterns you leave in the air. The same truth hidden in the temperature drops that follow you. You're not gods. You're not even teachers. You're refugees."

"You have made a grave error," the lead entity said as its formation shifted again, more urgently now. "We will return. But you will not know the hour. And when the signs begin—when your world grows cold—you will remember this choice."

The beings' forms became agitated, their flesh rippling faster, features blurring between states of matter that shouldn't exist. The lead creature's limbs began to multiply and retract, its attempt at humanoid form slipping in its distress.

"You understand nothing," it projected, but there was fear in the thought now. "We offer ascension. Transformation. Power beyond—"

The cosmic decision was made on Christmas Day, not in the grand chambers of the United Nations as planned, but in the bitter cold of the UN Plaza where Dr. Jonathan Avery and Colonel Donald Sultrier faced the true form of our would-be "benefactors."

When humanity said no they showed the beings true nature. Their threats of return carried a hollow desperation, not the confidence of superior beings. Now humanity waited, watching the skies for signs of what would come next.

The End... and The Beginning.

ABOUT THE AUTHOR

Richard Taylor is a debut author embarking on a captivating series. He brings a level of authenticity to his storytelling that's both rare and compelling. His series, "The Ultimate Truth," is a gripping tale of the rising tension, unexpected twists, and high stakes of not believing in the Lord and Savior, Jesus Christ.

When Richard is not climbing the corporate ladder, or writing something, you can find him lounging in the backyard with his wife, Cheri and his dog, a Yorkie named Daisy.

Made in the USA
Columbia, SC
29 December 2024

50836214R00215